Praise for

"Cruelty and power go hand in hand throughout this darkly engaging novel. *The Girls with Games of Blood* is a must-read for this Halloween season."
—*The Davis Enterprise*

"Bledsoe weaves another dark, sexy, and breathtaking tale full of mesmerizing atmosphere and quiet escalating horror. You won't be able to put the book down until you've read to the end. Just because a monster's heart awakens, doesn't make it any less of a monster."
—Adrian Phoenix, author of *Beneath the Skin,* on *The Girls with Games of Blood*

"An intoxicating brew of mystery, humor, and horror. This edgy, enthralling, entertaining tale is recommended for all fantasy collections."
—*Library Journal* on *Blood Groove*

"I love vampire stories, and when one's as new and fresh as *Blood Groove*, it's just plain delicious. One very sweet read." —Whitley Strieber

"*Blood Groove* is a guilty pleasure, like rubbernecking at a terrible car wreck which 'sinks its teeth in' and doesn't let go. . . . If you're looking for a vampire romance like *Twilight,* this is not the story for you. No, this is a dark, wet, sticky, ugly, gritty visit to the anti-*Twilight*." —*SF Site*

"Hot and sticky and tangy as a slab of Memphis ribs. A trippy vamp-noir seventies feed-fest, complete with the requisite sex, drugs, and vintage rock."
—E. E. Knight, bestselling author of the Vampire Earth series, on *Blood Groove*

"An edgy, visceral page-turner that had me laughing one moment and shivering the next. Alex Bledsoe is a writer to watch!" —Jeri Smith-Ready, award-winning author of *Wicked Game*, on *Blood Groove*

"An action-packed, full-blooded thriller that will get your pulse pounding and then drain you dry. Alex Bledsoe delivers, with a bite." —Scott Nicholson, author of *They Hunger*, on *Blood Groove*

"*Dracula* meets *The Lost Boys* in this gritty tale of vampires in 1970s Memphis. Bledsoe deftly weaves dark humor and drama in a compelling tale that'll keep you turning the pages." —Adrian Phoenix on *Blood Groove*

TOR BOOKS BY ALEX BLEDSOE

The Sword-Edged Blonde
Burn Me Deadly
Dark Jenny
Wake of the Bloody Angel

Blood Groove
The Girls with Games of Blood

The Hum and the Shiver

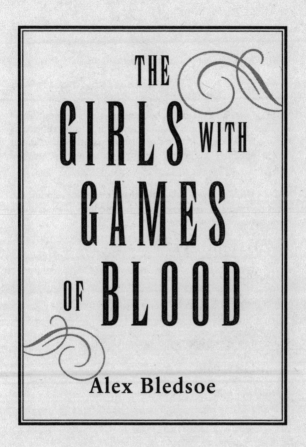

THE GIRLS WITH GAMES OF BLOOD

Alex Bledsoe

TOR®

A Tom Doherty Associates Book • New York

NOTE: If you purchased this book without a cover, you should be aware that this book is stolen property. It was reported as "unsold and destroyed" to the publisher, and neither the author nor the publisher has received any payment for this "stripped book."

This is a work of fiction. All of the characters, organizations, and events portrayed in this novel are either products of the author's imagination or are used fictitiously.

THE GIRLS WITH GAMES OF BLOOD

Copyright © 2010 by Alex Bledsoe

All rights reserved.

A Tor Book
Published by Tom Doherty Associates, LLC
175 Fifth Avenue
New York, NY 10010

www.tor-forge.com

Tor® is a registered trademark of Tom Doherty Associates, LLC.

ISBN 978-0-7653-6356-5

First Edition: July 2010
First Mass Market Edition: August 2012

Printed in the United States of America

0 9 8 7 6 5 4 3 2 1

To the memory of
Laura Nyro (1947–1997).
Without her, this novel would have no Patience.

SPECIAL THANKS

Teresa R. Simpson

Marlene Stringer

Paul Stevens

Dr. Elizabeth Miller

Amy, Roy, and the rest of the staff at Oliva's

Caroline Aumann

Valette, Jake, and Charlie

And in memory of Barbara Bova

Everybody's got a little light under the sun.
—"Flashlight," Parliament

THE GIRLS WITH
GAMES OF BLOOD

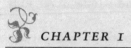

CHAPTER 1

Memphis, Tennessee
Late summer 1975

"Shit," the man said as he leaned his chin on his hand. He looked at the girl behind the bar and said doubtfully, "Are you *sure* you're old enough to be serving alcohol?"

She smiled as she dried a beer mug and placed it on the shelf in line with the others. Her canine teeth protruded ever so slightly over her lower lip. "Oh, I'm a lot older than I look, I promise."

"Ah, these days, *everyone* looks young to me," he said sadly. He wore his long hair feathered back in the current style, and a wide-lapelled, powder-blue jacket. He was about ten years too old for the look, though, and it seemed more like a costume on him than real clothes. He radiated weary discomfort with his very skin. "I feel positively ancient."

"I know the feeling," the girl agreed as she tossed the rag into the sink. In the empty, almost silent bar the *plop* echoed off the wood paneling. The girl's shiny metal name tag read FAUVETTE; soft, shoulder-length brown hair framed a face unlined and untroubled. Only her eyes convinced the man that she was indeed over the legal age of twenty-one. They had the haunted air of someone who'd seen awful things and would never fully forget them.

The man fluttered the front of his paisley-spotted polyester shirt. "This heat's murder, too. I guess a summer drought is normal around here, but you wouldn't think it'd be so humid without actually raining."

"There's the big river right down the road," she pointed out. "And it *is* the South."

"Yes," he said dourly. "The cradle of soul, and rock and roll. And if my luck is any indication, also their grave."

"So what do you do for a living that's got you so morbid this afternoon?" she said.

"I'm in the record business. I travel the country to find new talent, then sign them to contracts that suck the life right out of them. Can you believe that?"

"You don't sound like you enjoy it very much."

"That's because I never find what I'm looking for. The song. The face. The voice."

"Always a new one, eh?"

"Oh, no. I found it once, eight years ago, out in

California. Heard the song, saw the face, felt the voice. But I let it slip away." He paused for a sip of his drink. "I know people always dump on bartenders, sweetheart. But beauty like yours deserves deference, don't you think? So I'll shut up if you want."

She made a face. "I think I heard a compliment in there somewhere. Thanks." She looked around the otherwise empty bar. It was too late for the lunch crowd, too early for dinner, and she had nothing better to do. Besides, since taking this job she'd found that she enjoyed hearing people's stories. It gave her a sense of being connected to the world again. "And you can tell me anything. Just don't think I'm rude if we get another customer and I have to step away."

"I admire your work ethic," he said. "Well, this was in San Francisco, back during the days of Haight-Ashbury and the Summer of Love. Does that mean anything to you?"

"I've heard of San Francisco."

He laughed. Pretty girls with wry senses of humor were always his weakness. "The whole world felt like it was changing . . ."

. . . and if there was an epicenter, it was there. I had contacts everywhere, in all the clubs and bars and radio stations. I was always on the lookout for the Next Big Thing. But I only truly found it once. It started with a Polaroid snapshot that I held so the marquee's neon light fell on it. "I don't know," I said skeptically. "She looks like a chunky Morticia Addams."

"Oh, be nice," Andre said. As manager for the city's top underground radio station, he had tipped me off to some fairly successful acts in the past: the Thermodynamic Kiwis and Todd Slaughter's Band of Otters were our most recent signees. My reputation at the label, though, would not survive a spectacular blunder made just on Andre's say-so. Besides, as the ranking hippie-in-residence, I knew my job depended on judging not just what was hot now, but what the kids would be listening to in six months' time over their bonfires of draft cards and brassieres.

"It's nothing personal, I'm just kind of burned out on sensitive folksingers," I said. "If I hear one more Joan Baez sermon, I'll jump off a bridge. Besides, I think the trend is fading. I heard Dylan's even playing an electric guitar."

"But this girl is *incredible,*" Andre said earnestly. "I've never heard anything like her. She may not look like much in that photo, but she's the grooviest thing in the world onstage."

I looked at the picture again. The girl was in her early twenties, with long black hair parted in the middle. She had heavy eyebrows and wore dark lipstick. Her face was pleasantly round, and her black sleeveless dress showed pudgy upper arms. There was an appealing black-and-white starkness to her, in direct contrast to the multicolored psychedelia around us.

I checked my watch. The girl's first set began in fifteen minutes inside the Human Bean, the city's trendiest coffeehouse, which is why Andre dragged me down here. I sighed. "Okay, Andre, you win. I'll check her out. But she *better* be the grooviest thing in the world, or you owe me a nickel bag and a date with that receptionist of yours."

It was a time when everything seemed alive, and not just because of all the acid we were taking. The very air rippled with possibility, laced with an energy to which we all contributed, and from which we all partook. And on that night, the streets were even more filled than usual with tie-dyed shirts, bell-bottoms, dilated pupils, and the sense of impending destiny. So what happened shouldn't have been that surprising.

The Human Bean—a tiny room packed with round tables and wooden chairs, a mahogany bar across one wall, and a shallow stage along the opposite one—smelled of java and grass. Multicolored shirts glowed in the black lights, and strobes flickered in the corners. The face of Jimi Hendrix, as big as a Volkswagen, watched beneficently from a wall mural behind the bar. In front of the small stage, several kids sat cross-legged and swayed to music only they heard, or that was contained in the joints they passed around.

Someone handed one to me as we settled in at our table, and I took a sociable toke. Andre did likewise, and I ordered a beer and a bag of chips to offset the munchies I always got if I even looked sideways at marijuana. As the waitress returned with our order, the room grew dark and the stage lights came up.

The crowd applauded as the performer walked to the straight-backed chair placed at center stage. Just as in the Polaroid, she wore a short black sleeveless dress, black boots, and big earrings. She dramatically tossed her long hair behind her shoulders, arranged a capo on her guitar, and finally looked out at the audience with a mischievous little grin.

"They call me Patience," she said seriously as she settled into the chair. Her voice was deep and full, with an unmistakable Southern twang. "Do you know why? Because I've got a lot of it. But be careful." Then she smiled, and something seemed to radiate from her directly into me, like an electrical cord plugged into an outlet. "That's a lot of patience to *lose.*"

The crowd woozily cheered. Then she strummed her guitar and began to sing.

The songs she performed weren't important. The essential thing was that this slightly overweight dark-eyed chick had me, and the whole audience, riveted. In all my years as a passable musician, then as a much better talent scout, I had never experienced anything like it. Not Elvis, not the Stones, not even the Beatles commanded attention to this degree. On an emotional level the performance left me and everyone else drained.

But despite this, I noticed two things about Patience.

One was that after her initial comments she

hardly spoke to the audience or even acknowledged it. She stayed superfocused on her music.

The other was that despite the cramped, overheated, and underventilated club, she did not sweat.

🦎 Fauvette's eyebrows rose. "She didn't *sweat*? How close were you sitting?"

He smiled with the wistfulness of recalled youth. "Ah, you should get out more. The best music is always found in places without air-conditioning, where the heat makes you want to undress and the music makes you want to dance."

"I guess I'm sheltered," she said with a wry grin. "But you could really tell she wasn't sweating?"

"Yeah. It was strange enough I still remember it. Anyway, after the show . . ."

🦎 . . . I knocked on the dressing-room door. I was so exhausted I could barely walk, but since I depended on commissions and signing bonuses, I also had a serious work ethic. "Hello?" I said, stifling a yawn, and pushed the door open without waiting for an answer.

I stopped in the doorway. Patience, naked except for a black towel wrapped around hair still wet from the shower, sat with her feet propped on an upside-down trash can. The only light came from scented candles. The dressing room was so tiny her toes almost touched my shins, but like most kids of that time and place, she wasn't the least bit self-conscious about her nudity. It was provocative only in the sense that it challenged the mores of the square world.

She blew a smoke ring from a Mexican cigarillo and regarded me coolly. "Hello," she said in the same throaty drawl.

"Would you like me to close the door?" I asked.

She shrugged. "If it makes you feel less . . . vulnerable." Then she smiled, cold amusement twinkling in her eyes.

I managed to shut the door behind me, then handed her a business card. "Hi. I caught your show tonight and—" Another yawn struck me. "Sorry, for some reason I'm just *beat*. Anyway, I really dug it, I thought you were outstanding. Do you have a manager?"

She turned the card over in her fingers. Her nails were painted a shade of dark magenta. "I don't have much to manage. What there is, I can handle." She took another drag on the cigarillo. I was fairly used to being around naked girls—that's why I originally got into music, after all—so I kept my eyes on her strictly from her neck up. Finally she said, "So you want to make me a star, is that it?"

Despite her apparent youth, she had the demeanor of someone older and much shrewder. I mentally shifted from my usual "naïve young chick" spiel to the one I used on other professionals. "No, only the public can do that. But I think I can make you *and* me some money, and would love to get you into a studio as soon as possible. Do you have demos of any of your songs?"

She stubbed out the cigarillo in an ashtray on the floor, put her feet down, and sat forward until her breasts touched her knees. "I'm not completely sure what I do can be captured on vinyl."

"It can with the right producer," I said, and yawned again. "You could be the next Joan Baez, or even the next Dylan." And I yawned *again*.

She smiled. "Tired?"

"Very. Your show just sucked all the life out of me. In a good way, of course," I added with a laugh.

She slowly shook her head. "I'm sorry, but I'm really not interested. Music is just sort of a minor obsession for me right now. A kind of experiment." She lightly rested her fingers on the strings of her guitar, propped next to the chair. "But I'll tell you a secret. The first time I saw myself in the mirror holding a guitar was the first time I was able to stand what I saw there in a *very* long time." She looked back up at me and smiled. "No amount of money or success can really compete with that feeling. Can it?"

Oh, God, I thought, an *artiste*. If I hadn't been so tired I might have been more persuasive, pointing out that even Arlo Guthrie and Pete Seeger had to eat, but I wasn't up to it at that moment. "Will you keep my card, then? In case you change your mind?"

She nodded. "Yes. But I won't."

I turned to leave, and stopped in the doorway.

"Miss . . . Patience, I just want to say in all sincerity, I think you are a phenomenal performer. I attend concerts for a living, and yours was the best, most intense one I've ever seen. Even if you don't sign with me, I'll still be a fan."

She looked at me oddly, as if this had unaccountably moved her. "Thank you. That's the nicest thing anyone's ever said to me."

"My pleasure," I said. And I meant it.

Two days later I sat in an exclusive French restaurant, the only guy in the place with hair past my ears, and examined the folder of information that the record label's private detective dug up on Miss high-and-mighty Patience. There wasn't much, and it didn't take long to look it over.

According to the lease on her house, her full name was Patience Bolade. A year earlier, she'd taken some poetry classes at the local university, and worked in an off-campus bookstore. The most amazing thing was that she started performing music in public within two weeks of purchasing her guitar, only *four months* ago. Wow.

And that was all. He found no information on her family, or where she went to high school, or anything. She simply appeared out of nowhere.

The only other bit was that, in the "emergency contact" blank on her lease, she had written the name *Prudence Bolade,* but provided no phone number. He said that coincidentally, there was an old country song about two sisters with the very same names, who both died for the love of a scoundrel.

I found the song he mentioned, an old standard recorded in 1957 by Slack Whitside, the Singing Switchman. The album cover showed him seated on a train's cowcatcher with a guitar and a phony gap-toothed smile. Apparently he was as much a comedian as a singer, but he performed the song in question completely straight.

> *"There was two girls by the name of Bolade*
> *No prettier sisters God never made*
> *One dark like midnight, one bright like the sun*
> *But between them a hate to make Satan hisself*
> *   run . . ."*

The rest of the song, based on a true story from his native Tennessee, told how Patience Bolade killed herself when she found her lover in her sister's arms. Then Patience's ghost returned, to drive Prudence to suicide. But their restless spirits still haunted the night, and the song concluded with a warning:

> *"Listen to what I tell you, son, every word is*
> *   true*
> *The sisters haunt the night, and might fight over*
> *   you*
> *Nothing can steal your soul and stamp it in the*
> *   mud*
> *Like being the new play-pretty for the girls with*
> *   games of blood."*

· · ·

Fauvette said, "I've heard that song. Something about 'She put a bullet through her broken heart'?"

He nodded. "'She put a bullet through her broken heart, to spite the ones betraying her/But her soul, seeking the Pearly Gates, found her hatred was delaying her.'"

"My mama used to sing me that," she said, looking down at a spot on the bar. She grabbed a cloth and polished it clean. "I hadn't thought about it in a long time."

"I take it your mama's not around anymore?" he said sympathetically.

She shook her head, then smiled. "Ah, but that's a dull story. Yours is fascinating. So what did you do?"

"I found out that Patience only played the Human Bean one night a week . . ."

. . . and no one at the club had any idea what she did with the rest of her time. She also had no listed phone number. So late that afternoon I drove down her street, parked my car at the derelict church next door, and sneaked through the weed-infested cemetery to get a better look at her house.

I saw no sign of life, or even recent habitation. I scotch-taped a Xerox reproduction of the song lyrics to the front door, along with the admonition to meet me at the Human Bean that night.

I waited at the coffeehouse, breathed its pot-saturated air, and ate five packs of Twinkies, two bags of chips, and all the peanuts the waitress could find. And at sunset, just as the college crowd began to drift in, I looked up and saw Patience Bolade next to me.

"Hi," I said, and stood. She watched me with a neutral expression. "Sorry, if I don't stand when a lady approaches my table, my mother turns in her grave. Would you like to sit down?"

She wore almost the same outfit, a simple black sleeveless dress and big dangly earrings that looked like Christmas tree ornaments. She sat in the offered chair, back straight, hands in her lap.

I lit a cigarette—a regular one—and offered the pack to her, but she shook her head. "I never smoke . . . cigarettes," she said, and after a moment added, "So how did you find out about me?"

"Well, to be honest, I used a private detective."

She nodded. "I see." She closed her eyes and her shoulders sagged a little. "I guess I should be relieved. I knew it couldn't last, that if I did it long enough, someone would notice. Still, I hate to see it end."

"See what end?"

She gestured at the coffeehouse. "This. This . . . sanctuary. In the time I've been playing here, no one has had to *die*. If I write the songs well enough, and perform them with enough honesty, I can live off the energy of the crowd. It's such a relief not to have to be"—and she shuddered at the thought—"bloodthirsty. You have no idea."

"Apparently not," I agreed. "Just what are you talking about?"

She stared at me. "I . . . what are *you* talking about?"

"*I'm* talking about signing you to my label."

She sat very still for a long moment. "Wait . . . what do *you* think that song means? 'The Girls with Games of Blood'?"

I shrugged. "Hell, honey, I don't think it means a thing. You want to name yourself after a dead girl, dress in black, and sing songs about how miserable you are, that's great. It might even start a trend. All I know is, your effect on a crowd is amazing, and I think you, and me, and my company can all make an awful lot of money."

She leaned close to me, and her full lips turned up with just the hint of a smile. "You're serious, aren't you? That's all you're interested in."

"It's my job."

Now she really grinned. "Yes. It surely is. But I'm afraid my previous answer has to stand. What I do can't be broken down into vinyl grooves or magnetic tape strips." She stood and offered her hand. "Thank you for your kind words. I wish you luck."

I took her hand. It was ice-cold. Then she left, swallowed by the hazy night. And neither I nor anyone else ever saw Patience Bolade again.

The story finished, he watched Fauvette for a reaction. The girl's face was impassive, but neither amused nor doubtful. He'd expected to be gently mocked, as he was every other time he told the story. "So," he said after a moment, "what do you think?"

"I think you were probably well shed of her," Fauvette said.

He looked at his watch, sighed, and put some bills on the counter. "The Next Big Thing waits for no man. Thanks for listing to me . . . Foovette?"

"FAW-vette," she corrected.

"Fauvette. Hope to see you again soon."

He stood and walked out of the empty bar. When he opened the door, afternoon sunlight blasted in, overcoming the air-conditioning with no effort. Fauvette instinctively winced and looked away, even though she knew by now that sunlight was nothing to fear. Old habits died hard, and hers were older than most.

She bent to retrieve a fallen stack of napkins, which took several moments after she dropped them a second time. When she stood the door opened again and a woman carrying a guitar case was silhouetted against the sun, her long hair swaying as she looked around.

"You're letting out the air-conditioning," Fauvette called.

"Oh. Sorry," the woman said, and stepped inside. She walked to the bar, propped the guitar case against it, and climbed onto a stool. "Is the manager in?"

Fauvette started to answer, then stopped. The woman appeared to be in her early twenties, with long black hair parted in the middle. She had heavy eyebrows and wore dark lipstick. Her face was pleasantly round, and a low-cut peasant blouse showed white cleavage and pudgy upper arms. And despite the heat outside, she showed no signs of sweat.

The woman frowned uneasily at the scrutiny. "Is something wrong?"

"Did you see the man who just left? In the baby-blue leisure suit?"

"No. Why?"

Fauvette bit her lip thoughtfully before speaking. "This is a weird question, but is your name by any chance . . . Patience?"

"Yes," the woman said guardedly. "Do we know each other?"

Fauvette leaned her elbows on the bar and rested her chin on her hands. For a long moment the two women looked at each other. What they saw went beyond their mutual gender, and into the realm of unmistakable recognition that comes when one vampire recognizes another.

"Do you believe," Fauvette said at last, "in absolutely out-of-this-world, mind-boggling coincidence?"

CHAPTER 2

At the moment Fauvette met Patience, two other vampires drove an old Ford pickup with a camper shell along a county road to the east of Memphis. The vehicle's worn shocks transmitted each pothole and asphalt irregularity, and the scalding summer heat made the road shimmer ahead of them. Cornfields filled with rows of drought-stunted plants rippled past.

The vampire in the passenger seat looked like a typical urban black teenager. He wore a Memphis State tank top, faded denim jeans, and Converse high-top sneakers. He carried a pick comb tucked into the back of his Afro. But his eyes were cold, distant, and ancient, the only visible sign that Leonardo Jones had been the walking dead for over half a century.

At the moment Leonardo's attention was entirely focused on the vampire behind the steering wheel. This one wore a black shirt buttoned to the wrist and neck, crisp new jeans, and black leather boots. His long dark hair was tied back in a ponytail. He appeared to be around thirty years old, slender, and physically rather small. Yet like Leonardo, his true nature shone in his dark eyes.

Finally Leonardo spoke. He almost had to shout above the engine and the wind through the open windows. "C'mon, man, 'fess up. You killed Mark, didn't you?"

Rudolfo Vladimir Zginski shooed a fly from his face. The hot, sticky wind reminded him of a long-ago trip through Spain. "No," he said simply, "I did not."

"But you wanted to."

"Why do you question my honor in this matter?" Zginski's lilting middle-European accent had faded somewhat, but his archaic speech patterns remained.

"Come on. I seen the way you look at Fauvette. You and Mark both all broke out in monkey bites over her."

"I did *not* kill him."

"Oh, so he just conveniently left so you could be the only rooster in the henhouse? Awful nice of him. And he left you his wheels, too. Man knows how to treat his enemies, I'd say."

"Mr. Luminesca left the keys to the truck in the warehouse," Zginski said patiently. "I took them, but made no secret of it. If he wishes them returned, I will do so."

"And in the meantime you get a sweet ride out of both things, right?"

Zginski glanced at him in annoyance, then looked back at the road. He had only been driving for a few weeks, and had yet to relax into it. His latest long-term victim had taught him in her newer, better automobile, and he could easily have used that vehicle instead of the decrepit truck. But someone might recognize it, and he did not want to risk being connected to her publicly.

"I do not know why Mark left," he said. "I was not his confidant. If he told Fauvette, she has not mentioned it. But he was, and is, certainly free to go his own solitary way. Most of us do. The fact that we three remain companions is, in my experience, unique."

Even as he spoke, the meaning of his own words struck him anew. The uniqueness could be due to the fact that he'd shared his blood with Fauvette, Leonardo, and the now-vanished Mark in order to save them from destruction. It had been an impulsive thing in the heat of a crisis, and he'd waited for the ramifications to appear ever since. Perhaps his growing tolerance of Leonardo, whose Negro blood and peasant's attitude should have infuriated him, was the first real sign.

"And you had a lot of experience being a vampire, right?" Leonardo said. "All that time over in Europe, running around like Count Dracula?" He laughed and shook his head. "Shit, man. Sometimes I think you just tell us stuff to see what you can make us believe."

"You are free to think so."

Leonardo tapped his fingers on the side-view mirror. The wind blew down his arm and inside his tank top, causing it to ripple against his skin. After a moment he said, "So when you going to tell me how to do that wolf trick?"

"What makes you think it is a trick?"

" 'Cause, ain't no way a man can turn into a wolf. So I figure you know how to make folks *think* they seeing a wolf. Is that right?"

Zginski smiled. "You are free to think so."

As Leonardo laughed, Zginski watched the trees flash by, the summer sun cutting through the branches in stripes of debilitating heat. When Zginski first met these vampires, they had been convinced the sun would destroy them, just as the movies and television shows depicted. They lived in an abandoned warehouse and still slept in coffins, with grave dirt for mattresses. They acted, in fact, more like parasites than predators, roaming the Memphis shadows and lurking like cockroaches just beyond the light.

He had traded his understanding of their true nature for their knowledge of this era. He had spent sixty years in limbo, from the time a golden stake pierced his heart in 1915 to the time it was removed in 1975; in addition to driving, which now fascinated him the way electricity once had, he had learned much about this new time. Most ironically, he had discovered people were just as greedy, cowardly, and pathetic as they had always been, despite the great leaps in technology. He would fit into this world just fine once he mastered its devices.

Leonardo looked at the directions written on the back of an old envelope. "Okay, that's the third time up and down this stretch of road. We lost."

Zginski slowed the truck. There was no traffic in either direction. He took the envelope from Leonardo and perused it. "We traveled the correct highway into Appleville, and made the proper turn onto this county road. If there is an error, it is not in our diligence."

"You gonna ask directions?"

"Certainly. What sensible man would not?" He did an awkward U-turn and drove back to the one mail box they'd passed. The name on it was incomplete: only the letters BOL remained. It marked a driveway that disappeared into a thick stand of pine trees.

They emerged at one end of a long, unkempt lawn that was browned by the drought. At the far end rose a two-story house that, like the landscaping, looked sun-battered and dried up.

Zginski stopped the truck. He reached out with his vampiric senses, but in their daylight-weakened state he could not tell if anyone occupied the house. It certainly looked neglected, if not fully abandoned.

The house was built in a mixture of Greek and Colonial Revival styles, with columns around the front door and a carriage entrance on the building's left end. A tree shadowed part of the roof, the branches just touching the shingles. The brickwork was intact but gaps in the mortar indicated incipient weaknesses. The shrubbery grew tall and unwieldy, blocking most of the lower windows. Yet someone had recently painted the columns to a height of about ten feet. Was this a restoration in progress, or one abandoned?

As if sensing his uncertainty, Leonardo said, "I saw mail in the mailbox. Somebody must live here."

"Go and ask if they know where the Crabtree family lives."

"Me? Why me?"

"Because you are less threatening than I am."

"You really ain't learned shit about the South, have you?" But Leonardo opened the door and dutifully trudged down the driveway toward the house, muttering to himself about Zginski's racial cluelessness.

The four big columns rose to a level with the second-story roof, sheltering the porch and front door. Hornets and dirt daubers had long ago claimed it, and buzzed warnings that Leonardo ignored. Footprints showed in the dust and detritus, although none were as recent as Leonardo's own. He sensed no life inside, but thanks to Zginski he knew the sun weakened his powers.

He knocked firmly on the door, then stepped back. A short distance away, hidden behind a row of thick untended shrubs, he saw the black fence around a private cemetery. A lone mausoleum rose among the few tombstones. The lords of this decrepit manor would rest inside it, and their families and children in the ground around it. He knew that if any black people were buried on this land, their graves would be untended and likely unmarked.

After a long moment he heard the door lock click open. He put his hands in his pockets and lowered his head, a submissive stance that would, he hoped, prevent any trouble with the white folks.

The door opened no more than six inches and an elderly female voice said, "Yes? Oh, good Lord, a colored boy. What do you want?"

"Ma'am, I'm looking for the Crabtree farm. Am I anywhere near it?"

He glanced up at the source of the voice. He could make out the general silhouette of a small-framed, stooped woman in a floor-length dress long out of style, but could see no detail.

"Dark Willows?" she repeated. "You're looking for Dark Willows?"

"Yes, ma'am. My boss is supposed to pick up a car there, but we can't seem to find the turnoff."

She peered past him to the distant truck. Zginski stood beside it, plainly Caucasian even at this distance. The old woman seemed to take that as a comfort. She said, "Tell your employer to go past the four-way intersection and look for the sign on the right. Their driveway is considered its own street by the state."

"*Past* the intersection," Leonardo repeated. "That's what we did wrong. Thank you, ma'am."

"You're welcome. Now you run along." She closed the door, but he knew she'd peek out to make sure he did as he was told.

As he walked back to the truck, he shook his head at the sheer predictable madness of it. Even when a man dies, the color of his skin still puts him in his place. Of course, to be fair, most black folks who died didn't keep walking around. So perhaps his experience wasn't really typical.

"Did you get the information?" Zginski asked.

"We go past that four-way stop. It's on the right."

"Ah. Thank you."

"Don't mention it," Leonardo mumbled as he got back in the truck.

They followed the old woman's instructions and found the state-issued green sign proclaiming DARK WILLOWS ROAD. Below it was a yellow diamond-shaped marker that said DEAD END. One corner was ragged from a close-range shotgun blast. The name on the mailbox confirmed the location: CRABTREE.

Dark Willows Road was no more than two gravel ruts with a grass strip in the middle, so narrow there was no room for two vehicles to pass. The house was hidden from the highway by thick stands of trees, but once it came into view Zginski stopped the truck and leaned forward to stare through the windshield.

Like the other house they'd just visited, this one

stood two stories high at one end of a large, neglected lawn. But it was a considerably larger structure. The porch went along the entire front of the building and around either end, with columns braced by arches holding up the awning roof. The windows beneath it were tall and narrow, and when opened allowed those inside to directly exit onto the porch. The place carried the unmistakable aura of wealth and grandeur, of a home built to the specifications of a man used to getting his way.

Then Zginski blinked back to the moment. The house was in terrible disrepair: sections of shingles were missing, shutters were lost or broken, and one column stood at an angle so that the end of the porch sagged. Many of the windows were glassless and boarded up. For fifty feet around the house the yard was mostly dirt, with three old tractors parked in it. The sun-baked weeds protruding through the engines and empty tire rims said they had not moved in months.

"That is a shame," Zginski murmured to himself. "I had no idea that houses of such scale existed outside the city."

Leonardo, still annoyed by the old lady, snapped, "It's a goddam plantation house, you know that, right? A hundred years ago I'd have been worth no more than them busted-down tractors." He pointed to a row of roofs visible in the overgrown field to one side of the house. "See those? Slave quarters. Dog houses, except people like me were the dogs."

Zginski scowled at him. "That was some time ago. The world has changed since then, as you so often inform me."

Leonardo started to snap back, but Zginski was right: Leonardo had pointed out the other man's inherent racism many times, and always with the admonition that times were different. He couldn't very well claim now that they were the same, could he? Even though he had no trouble accepting the contradiction himself.

Zginski drove slowly up the driveway. To one side of the house was a low barn, the kind used to house other farm equipment. It, too, was in bad shape, crumbling and filled with rusted devices whose purpose Zginski could not fathom.

He stopped in the space between the barn and the house. For a moment he worried that the place might be deserted. Certainly there was no sign of recent tending: the yard was worn down to bare dirt, dried to a clinging, clay-based dust by the drought.

Then a beagle bounded down the porch steps, barking loud enough to be heard over the truck's engine. In a moment an unmistakably female form emerged from the house and stood in the shadows against one of the porch columns. She seemed in no hurry to welcome them.

Zginski opened the door just as the low, floppy-eared dog reached the truck. The animal skidded to a halt and stared at him. Then it gave one last growl and scampered away, yelping.

Leonardo did not immediately climb out. The place recalled things he never wanted to remember, with a vividness only possible to a vampire. He had not been a slave, but the life he was born into had been little different, and the old people around him all bore the scars of whips, branding irons, and manacles. He'd seen the world change in amazing ways since then, but this brought back all those old resentments and fears. *What good is being a vampire,* he thought, *if you still have to ride in the back of the hearse?*

Finally the woman on the porch said, "Y'all scared my dog."

"I merely looked at him," Zginski said calmly.

She stood with her back against one of the columns, her legs straight out and crossed at the ankles. She held a cigarette in one hand. "Only time I ever seen him run like that was when he started up a bobcat over in the barn. So what you want?"

"I am here about the automobile," Zginski said.

"Oh! You must be that Russian fella Daddy's waiting for." Her tone now verged on excitement. "Hold on, I'll go get him."

She disappeared back into the house. The dog ran from wherever it had hidden and rushed to follow.

Leonardo opened the door and got out. "You gonna have to do something about that accent pretty soon, you know."

"This is America, a land of foreigners and immigrants," Zginski said dismissively.

"Uh-huh. And this is Tennessee, the land of carpetbaggers and the Klan. They hate foreigners and immigrants as much as they do niggers."

Zginski grinned. His teeth were very even, his fangs not visible. It was a minor trick he'd mastered, a way of sliding his lower jaw slightly forward to hide the tips of his elongated canines. Not even the great spiritualist Sir Francis Colby had detected them on that fateful night in Wales. "Then between the two of us, we shall confuse them as to which to fear the most."

In a moment the girl returned, followed by a larger figure whose steps resonated on the wooden porch. They emerged into the sunlight together.

The man was wide, potbellied, clad in khaki shorts and a T-shirt. His hair was matted with sweat and sleep, and salt-and-pepper stubble covered his chin. To Zginski he said, "You the Russkie who called about the car?"

"I am," Zginski said, and turned to Leonardo. "And this is—"

"Your nigger boy can just wait here," the man said. "You can follow me." As he turned he glared at his companion. "Girl, I done told you about that smoking."

She made a dismissive wave with her hand. She was tall, with bright red hair and freckles, clad only in denim shorts and a red tube top too small for her burgeoning bust. Her hair was pulled back in a ponytail. Faint swimsuit lines were visible on her broad, smooth shoulders. She looked about sixteen.

Her father sighed and led Zginski toward the dilapidated barn. "I tell you, I can't keep her from smoking, drinking, or fooling around with boys. Look at her, half-naked and smoking like a chimney in front of that buck nigger. I swanney, if you ain't got no kids, don't have none . . ."

When they were out of sight, the girl turned to Leonardo. "Getting an eyeful?" she said disdainfully.

He shrugged. He knew that, to her, they appeared roughly the same age. "You showing it. I'm just appreciating it."

She smiled very slightly. "My daddy heard you say that, he'd drag you all the way to Covington behind his car."

Leonardo started to fire back another sarcastic reply, but there was something in the girl's tone that stopped him. He realized she was attracted to him, in a way that had nothing to do with a vampire's ability to sexually fascinate a victim. He said, "He didn't hear me say it. Just you did."

She took a drag off the cigarette and pulled it from her lips with a pop. Some sort of light pink lip gloss circled the filter. She pulled the smoke up into her nose, then let it slowly out. Her exposed skin now gleamed with sweat in the hot sun. "What's your name, boy?"

He gritted his teeth against the term "boy." "Leonardo. You can call me Leo."

"I don't call colored boys by their names unless I'm wanting 'em to do something," she said, her smile growing.

He stepped closer. This wasn't the first white girl he'd encountered intrigued by dark skin. "So is there something you want me to do, Miss Crabtree? I's just dyin' to be of service."

Now she fully smiled. It made her look very young, in direct contradiction to the paraded ripeness of her body. "I'm sorry, I was just teasing you. I ain't got nothing against colored folks. When I was little, that's all I had to play with besides the dogs." The girl extended her hand. "My name's Clora."

He took it lightly. "Nice to meet you."

Her eyes opened wide in surprise and she snatched back her hand. "Lordy, your fingers are like icicles."

"I was drinking a Co-Cola on the way here."

She nodded, then looked up and shielded her eyes. "Man alive, wish I had a cold Co-Cola. Come on, let's get up in the shade. I don't want my shoulders peeling for two weeks again." She turned and went up the steps.

Leo didn't move. "Are colored folks allowed inside through the front door?"

She stopped and turned, the movement both gracefully feminine and clumsily teen. "Course not. But Daddy won't mind if you're on the porch."

CHAPTER 3

Jeb Crabtree struggled to open the barn door, which hung by one rust-seized hinge. As he dragged its edge across the ground, a swarm of disturbed yellow jackets boiled up and around him. "God dang it!" he said, swatting and waddling back a few steps.

Zginski stepped forward, easily lifted the door, and pushed it flat against the wall. The insects did not approach him.

Crabtree finished slapping away the wasps, verified none had actually stung him, and said, "Thank you, son. Any of 'em get you?"

"No," Zginski said.

"That's good. Saw a fella who was allergic get swarmed once. Swole up like a beach ball. Died that afternoon."

Crabtree led the way into the barn. Sunlight filtered through spaces between the wallboards and gaps in the tin roof, illuminating dry air heavy with dust. Junked farm machinery filled the building like the skeletons of great monsters. In the center was an automobile covered by a water-stained tarpaulin. "This-here's your baby. Just like the ad said, less than two thousand miles and not a scratch on her."

"I believe the term is 'cherry,' is it not?" Zginski said.

"That's true enough. She ain't been up over sixty on the highway, so her cherry's still there for you." Crabtree waved in the air until his fingers found the light string. "So where you from again, boy?"

"Eastern Europe," Zginski said deferentially. "Near Rumania."

"A *Commie*," the man said in wonder, as if he'd seen some rare animal at the zoo. "A real Commie, here in my barn. How'd you end up in the U.S. of A., anyway?"

"I am a political refugee."

"Did you go over the Berlin Wall?"

"No, I hid myself in a cargo container." It was close to the truth: while locked in an iron coffin, a golden dagger impaled in his lifeless heart, his corpse had been shipped from England to the United States.

Crabtree whistled. "Have to admire that, for sure. Lots of Americans take freedom for granted these days. I served two years in Korea, and believe me, I appreciate what we got here." He took hold of the tarpaulin. "Well, welcome to the Land of the Free, then!"

With a flourish he whipped the cover aside. "Tada!" he said with a grin, then spit tobacco juice at the ground. "Ain't she a beaut? A 1973 Mach 1 Ford Mustang."

The vehicle was indeed in pristine shape, chrome gleaming and glass spotless. Zginski touched the shiny yellow hood with reverent fingertips, careful not to smear the waxed shine. He knew that under it waited an eight-cylinder 351 Windsor engine designed for no other purpose than speed. He could barely contain himself. "Eleanor," he whispered reverently.

"'Scuse me?" Crabtree said as he stuffed the cover between two bales of hay.

"Nothing."

"Oh, right, this is the car from that movie, ain't it? Where the fella steals all them other cars."

"*Gone in 60 Seconds*," Zginski said. He had decided, after viewing *Vanishing Point, Death Race 2000,* and *The Seven-Ups,* that cinema existed for no other reason than to showcase the automobile.

"They show American movies over in Russia?" Crabtree asked in surprise.

"No, I saw it here." He knelt and examined the tires, running his fingers along their road surfaces. The tread was deep and sharp-edged, and the little rubber whiskers had not yet worn away. He had no experience evaluating cars, but had pored over stacks of automotive magazines with the glee of a virginal young caliph on his first night in the harem. He sensed that Crabtree thought this one a jewel, and saw nothing to contradict that.

Zginski stood, brushed his hands on his jeans, and said, "You must tell me how you acquired this."

"I don't reckon that's any of your business, son," Crabtree said coolly. "She ain't stole, if that's what you're worried about. I got all the paperwork on her."

Zginski reached out with his vampiric influence. It was weak, but so was Crabtree's peasant resolve. "I wish," Zginski said firmly, "to know the provenance of this automobile."

Crabtree shrugged as if it now meant nothing. "A cousin of mine needed a fast car for his work, if you know what I mean." He mimed drinking from a bottle. "He gave me the money and had me buy it under my name, 'cause he knew the Feds were watching him. Then, before he could pick it up, he got killed in a wreck over across the line in Mississippi. So here she sits, collecting dust instead of road film."

"And why do you wish to part with it?"

He laughed. "I got no use for it out here. Every teenage boy in the county wants to take either it or my daughter for a ride, and at least I can lock her up in the house to keep an eye on her. I figure this'll just end up stole if I don't sell it, so . . ." He trailed off and spit more tobacco at the dirt floor.

Zginski opened the door and looked inside. Wood-grain inlays offset the mechanical chrome, and the high-backed bucket seats felt firm and inviting. A tiny spider had somehow gotten inside and spun its web between the rearview mirror and the steering wheel. Zginski pinched it between two fingers. "It would indeed be a crime to waste such a jewel," he said.

Crabtree laughed. "Ain't that the truth." Then he turned serious. "So let's talk money. I know you Commies are all about sharing the wealth, but that ain't the way it works here. And I sure ain't a bank, I don't finance over time. It's cash on the barrelhead. No pinks 'til I see the greens."

Zginski held up a folded sheaf of bills as he straightened. "That's exactly the way I want it."

🐾 Clora Crabtree again leaned against the column with the weariness of a small-town girl longing for new horizons. The position highlighted her long, freckled legs. She lit another cigarette from the butt of the first and said, "So, Leo. How come you running around with a Russkie?"

Leonardo laughed and stuck his hands in his jeans pockets. "That's a long story."

"He pay you?"

"Naw. I'm just learning stuff I couldn't find out about anywhere else."

"Like what?"

"Technical stuff." Until Zginski came along,

Leonardo had been certain exposure to sunlight would destroy him. It certainly weakened him, but having the day back after decades in the dark was worth a little weakness. "Pretty boring."

"What's he get out of it?"

He shrugged. "Somebody to talk to."

"Some days I'd pay for that, too," she said wistfully, and offered him a cigarette. He shook his head. Softly she added, "I got half a joint upstairs. Want me to go get it?"

"Your daddy might not like that."

She smiled out of the side of her mouth and said, "Daddy wouldn't like most of the things I do, if he knew about 'em. He just sees what he wants."

Her eyes were big, green, and somehow sad. Leonardo gazed into them, careful to mask his powers. He sensed that, with this girl, he might not need them.

They both jumped at the sound of "La Cucaracha" played on a car horn. A big featureless Buick with one fender the distinctive color of Bondo pulled into the driveway and stopped, blocking in the pickup. The driver revved the engine several times.

"Shit," Clora said, and tossed her cigarette aside. "*Byron.*"

"Who's Byron?" Leonardo asked, but Clora had already hopped off the porch and trotted toward the barn.

When Leonardo turned back, the biggest man he'd ever seen stood on the steps. Backlit by the sun, he looked like some enormous avenging angel, and there was certainly no kindness in his voice when he said, "Boy, what you doing on Mistah Crabtree's front porch?"

"Nothin', suh, jus' talking to Miss Clora." It was the way his family had talked decades ago, and the way many blacks still did when faced with white belligerence. *The trick is to blend in,* Zginski often told him, *not stand out,* and he knew this countrified deference was what the big white man expected.

The man snorted with cold humor. "That a fact."

Even with his vampire reflexes, Leonardo almost didn't see the blow coming in time to roll with it. The big man slapped him hard enough to stun a normal person, and Leonardo let the impact toss him off the porch into the grass. If he'd resisted, the man might've broken his hand, and that certainly would've gotten unwanted attention.

"Don't lie to me, boy," the big man said, not even bothering to look directly at Leonardo. "I'll kick your nigra ass from here to the Alabama line. Now where is Mr. Crabtree?"

"I think he in the barn, sir," Leonardo said, and got his first look at this "Byron." The big man had sandy hair cut long in the current fashion, thick sideburns, and a shirt with a wide collar. His face had once been handsome, but was now skewed, the chin uneven and one side of his jaw caved slightly inward. Scar tissue told the story of some terrible injury that had, apparently, done little to humble the man.

"Thank you, boy," he said, then headed to the barn. He walked with the swagger of a man who loved to provoke violence, and hardly ever lost a fight.

Leonardo stood, brushed off his jeans, then sat on the porch steps. Even sun-weakened, Leo knew he could snap this giant bully in half, but the man seemed inexplicably familiar, and until he could place him, it was best to lay low literally and figuratively.

🐾 Crabtree put the neat pile of cash into his pocket and shook Zginski's hand. If he noticed it was considerably colder than normal, he didn't mention it. He handed him a ring with three keys on it: two for the ignition, one for the trunk. "Reckon we got ourselves a deal, Mr. Zigeeinski."

Zginski did not correct the pronunciation as he tucked the title into his shirt pocket. "Indeed."

"Daddy!" Clora said urgently from the door. "You got more company."

A new voice called, "Jebediah Crabtree, what you doing out here? It's a day to be inside with the A.C. running."

Crabtree and Zginski turned. The big man stood beside Clora, one huge arm across her bare shoulders. The gesture was both parental and possessive, and Clora quickly squirmed out from under it. "I'll be back at the house," she said, giving the big man a disgusted look.

The man shrugged and strode into the barn, ducking to avoid the roof beams. He offered one enormous hand to Crabtree, who shook it with clear reluctance. "Howdy, Sheriff Cocker," he said demurely.

The big man laughed. "I ain't the sheriff no more, Jeb, I'm just a lowly civilian now." He turned to Zginski. "Don't believe we've met. I'm Byron Cocker."

Zginski had to look up to meet his gaze, as Cocker was a good foot taller and probably eighty pounds heavier. He noted the signs of facial surgery that almost, but not quite, made him look normal. He wondered how the man had originally been injured. "I am Rudy Zginski," he said, using the diminutive form of his first name. It seemed to make people less suspicious.

But not Cocker. Like a dog bred for fighting he considered direct eye contact a challenge, and frowned at the way Zginski met his gaze. "You a foreigner?"

"He's a refugee," Crabtree interjected. "He used to be a Red, but now he's seen the light and wants to be an American."

Cocker tightened his grip on Zginski's hand, and waited for the strain to show. Zginski simply smiled and let the man squeeze. Finally he said, "Your American handshakes last so long, I am reminded of the way lovers hold hands in *my* country."

Cocker quickly pulled his hand away, and fury

sparked in his eyes. Then he smiled and said, "Aw, we just like to be sure we're among friends, that's all. Ain't that right, Jeb?"

"That's a fact, Mr. Cocker. How's things in Appleville?"

Cocker ignored the question and turned to the car. "Jeb, I'm here to see about buying this little beauty from you. I still got my old state car, but it ain't good for much more than running to the Woolworth's and back, and I tore up the fender when I went sliding off a curve over on Mullins Road. I know your cousin got run over down in Mississippi, and when I seen the ad in the paper, I thought, 'I believe I'll do ol' Jeb a favor.' I'll give you fifteen hundred for it, hard cash, right now."

Crabtree swallowed hard, looking from Zginski to Cocker. "Ah . . ."

"I have already purchased the vehicle," Zginski said. "For the asking price of four thousand dollars."

Cocker's gaze hardened, but his smile grew wider. He put one huge hand on Crabtree's shoulder. "That a fact? Well, I know you ain't had time to sign over the title, Jeb, so why don't you just give this fella back his money and we'll do our own little deal." He turned to Zginski. "See, in America deals 'tween friends stack up higher than deals with strangers."

Zginski smiled as well. "I can appreciate that, Mr. . . . ?"

Cocker's face darkened, as if the idea someone

might forget his name was the worst insult imaginable. "Cocker. Byron Cocker."

"Mr. Cocker was our county sheriff," Crabtree said quickly. "He ran out the bootleggers and the whoremongers. They made a movie about him, too: *Swinging Hard*. You seen it?"

"I'm afraid not," Zginski said, never taking his eyes from Cocker's. "And it is immaterial. I have paid for the car before you, I have paid more than you offered, and Mr. Crabtree has given me the ownership documents. It is mine. That is the rule of commerce."

The air tingled with Cocker's repressed rage. At last, chest thrust out, he stepped so close Zginski had to look almost straight up to see his face. "I may not be the sheriff anymore," Cocker said quietly, "but it don't mean I can't pull strings. Now, I mean to have this car, for the price I named. Either go along with us, or you might find it real hard getting out of the county."

Zginski's eyes narrowed. The thought that he might have to kill everyone here did not bother him, although it meant he would have to give up the automobile. He chose instead to say, "Mr. Cocker, the decision is not mine. It is Mr. Crabtree's. He has my money in his pocket."

They both turned to the sweating man. Weakened by the sun, Zginski could not fully control him, but influencing Crabtree's feeble will would not require much energy.

Crabtree started to speak, then frowned as if a

new, completely unexpected thought had occurred to him. He looked at the car, then at Zginski, and finally at Cocker. "Sheriff, I know how long a reach you got, and how big a stick you carry. But I got to tell you, my cousin Gerry would purely turn over in his grave if he found out that I sold his car to an officer of the law. He never thought too highly of lawmen in general, and you in particular. That's just how he saw it. So I'm gonna have to keep my word, pass on your offer, and accept this man's money. That's just the way it is."

Now Zginski looked up at Cocker with a benign shrug. "The man has made his choice."

Cocker's face turned red, highlighting the scar tissue. His big fists clenched, but he merely said, "If that's the way you want it, Jeb. I'll be sure to see you around." He turned without a word and strode from the barn.

Crabtree was drenched with sweat, and as soon as Cocker disappeared he leaned against the car's fender and almost sobbed. "What in the hell did I just do? I won't be able to drive to the store now without getting pulled over by one of his pals."

Zginski said nothing; Crabtree's ultimate fate did not concern him. But he gazed through the open barn door at the house, its decrepitude only partially hiding its former magnificence. "Mr. Crabtree," he said quietly, "have you considered selling this place and relocating?"

Crabtree shook his head. "No, Dark Willows has been in the Crabtree family since before the Civil War. The carpetbaggers didn't get her, and nobody else will, either, long as a Crabtree's alive somewhere." He took a deep breath and used his shirttail to wipe the sweat from his face. "Jesus, I need a beer." He walked away without a backward glance.

Zginski looked at the house again. He smiled normally, allowing his fangs to show. Then he turned back to his new car.

CHAPTER 4

Cocker strode from the barn with a fury he hadn't known in years. The closest he could recall was the agony after waking up in the hospital and learning moonshiners had raped and murdered his wife after leaving him for dead. That had felt like a similar attack on his basic masculinity, a symbolic castration that left him with an unbearable need to reassert himself. He'd done it then by walking into the little country store that fronted for the bootleggers and killing three of them with his bare hands.

He was no longer a sheriff, though, and could not hide behind his badge. But he was still an American, a former Marine who would be God *damned* if some Red Communist foreigner would cheat him out of something he wanted. Yeah, that was it: it was not just an affront against him, it was a middle finger to the whole U.S. of A. And *that* could not stand.

He spotted the black boy again, now talking to Crabtree's nubile daughter. She'd certainly filled out over the last year, her curves now suggesting the supple figure of a grown woman instead of a lanky girl. Her clothes barely maintained her modesty. She was a dead ringer for her late mother, one of the few girls who'd turned Cocker down in high school. Cocker felt a stir of desire for her, but his fury quickly overrode it.

He gave the black teen the same high-intensity glare he'd used on die-hard murderers and said, "What you lookin' at, boy? I ought to take a two-by-four to that uppity head of yours."

There was the expected flicker of resentment, then the dark eyes looked down at the ground. "I ain't lookin' at nothin', sir," he mumbled.

"You best keep it that way, or I'll give you a case of road rash you won't ever forget. And Clora? You get on in the house. Don't be talking to this nigger trash, you hear me?"

"I hear you, Sheriff," she drawled.

Cocker returned to his car. He started the engine, then revved it repeatedly just to hear the great rumbling sound. He also wrote down the license number of the pickup truck that the Russkie must have driven. Then he put the car in gear, backed out hard and fast enough to stir a cloud of dust, then floored it once he hit blacktop, headed for Inman's Store, just across the city limit line from bone-dry Appleville.

He could almost taste the cold beer on his tongue when he remembered he still had Mama Prudence's groceries in the trunk.

Clora took another drag on her cigarette. "'I ain't lookin' at nothin', sir,'" she said, imitating Leonardo. "I thought you city boys were all tough. Black Power and all that."

"Tough ain't the same as stupid," Leonardo said. "That man's bigger than a tractor. And he's the sheriff, too."

"*Ex*-sheriff, and held together by pins and scars these days," Clora said. "Wonder what your friend did to get him all pissed-off?"

"How do you know it wasn't your daddy?"

She snorted, a little puff of smoke burping from her lips. "My daddy wouldn't no more stand up to Byron Cocker than he'd fly to the moon. Nobody around here would. Just because he ain't sheriff no more don't mean he still don't have fingers in every pie."

Leonardo and Clora turned as an exhausted-looking Jeb Crabtree, followed by a typically smug Zginski, emerged from the barn. Crabtree muttered, "Put some clothes on, I said," as he went indoors. He was clearly upset, and Clora's face creased in concern. She quickly masked it as Zginski joined them.

"Get your car squared away?" Leonardo asked.

"Of course." He turned to Clora. "Is your house as badly maintained as it appears to be?"

Clora's eyes narrowed in anger. "I beg your pardon? You ain't buying our house, mister, so just keep your snotty comments to yourself. I think you already upset my daddy enough for one day."

Zginski was out of patience with Philistine presumption and reached out with his power. Like her father, Clora's will was essentially weak. When the overwhelming sexual desire struck, she could only stand with her mouth open, staring at him. She whimpered slightly, and licked her suddenly dry lips.

Leonardo sighed and shook his head.

Zginski stepped close and gently brushed a stray hair from her face. She moaned at the fleeting contact and leaned her cheek toward his hand. "Now," he said gently, "tell me about the condition of the house."

Clora was so aroused she could barely breathe, and she lost all sense of her surroundings. This dark-eyed gorgeous foreigner made her legs so wobbly she had to cling to the column beside her. "I'm sorry, I . . . I didn't mean to be rude," she said, her voice a ragged whisper.

"It is of no concern," Zginski purred and stroked her face. "Tell me what the house is like."

"We only use the downstairs," she said, eyes closed. "Except for my room in the attic. The place is a mess, but Daddy always says the framework is too solid to ever fall down." She swallowed hard and said shakily, "Would you like to see my room?"

Zginski trailed a finger down the side of her

sweaty neck, stopping just at the edge of her tube top. Through her skin, he felt the hot blood pulsing in her carotid artery. "You will not remember that you and I spoke," he said, then released her from his influence.

She blinked back to the moment. Her body remained excited, but now she had no idea of the source. She stared at Leonardo and decided it must be a response to him. She'd been intrigued by him before, but *now* . . .

"We're going," Leonardo said to her. Why did he look so annoyed? she wondered. Had she done something?

"The new vehicle is filled with fuel and ready to be taken," Zginski said to Leonardo as he handed over the truck keys. "I will drive it. You follow."

"Okay," Leonardo said, "but just don't get flashy."

"He's got the right idea," Clora said, still inexplicably breathless. "You might not want to come back to this county for a long time."

"I do not let overbearing, swaggering coxcombs dictate my travels," Zginski said. "I will go where I wish." He nodded to her and said, "Thank you, my dear," then walked back to the barn.

Leonardo scowled at Clora's confused expression. She pressed one hand against her stomach, trying to calm the butterflies still fluttering there. "He's like that," he said gently. "Don't pay him no mind."

"I . . . I won't," she stammered, unable to think of anything to get him to stay.

Leonardo smiled. "Good girl. See you around."

"Promise?" she pleaded softly. Her gaze followed him as he went to the truck and drove away.

Byron Cocker was still steaming when he turned up the gravel drive to Mama Prudence's house. Unlike the Crabtrees' run-down residence, he could imagine how this place looked back in its glory days, when the South had both civilization and dignity. Since then, with the advent of civil rights, the end of the military draft, and the rise in drugs brought from the big cities, everything that gave the South its special grandeur and pride had seemed to decay, much like the Crabtree mansion. At least the Bolade place retained a hint of its majesty.

When he parked in the gravel space before the house, his eye as always was drawn to the small family graveyard. The lone mausoleum, unusual in both its size and placement, stood in the sun like a small marble work shed. He'd never gone over to see who was buried in it, and never remembered to ask Mama Prudence about it. One day he'd do both, but today the heat and his own simmering rage made him hurry to get the groceries inside. He opened the trunk, picked up the bags, and carried them to the porch.

With his arms full, he had to ring the doorbell with his elbow, and he knew it would take Mama Prudence forever to get there. But almost at once the door opened, so quickly it startled him. He jumped back, nearly tripping over his own feet. "Lord Amighty, Mama Prudence, you must've been peeking out watching for me."

The old woman laughed. "No, I happened to be standing right by the door," she said, her voice a dry rasp. "You scared the pee-diddle out of me, too. Come on in out of the heat, Sheriff."

He did as she asked. She had long gray hair in two braids, and wore a shapeless housedress beneath a tattered apron. Big rings glittered on her long, bony fingers. Her face seemed not so much wrinkled as *sunken,* like she was drying out instead of aging.

As always, once she closed the heavy front door the house was almost totally dark, the only light sifting in around the heavy curtains. It smelled like a museum, all musty and stale, but with a weird fruity tang that Byron could never identify. He'd finally decided that rather than clean, Mama Prudence simply sprayed air freshener everywhere on the days she knew he was coming.

"How about this drought we're having?" Byron said as he waited for his eyes to adjust. He doubted any of the lamps even had working bulbs anymore. The surprising thing was that all the flat surfaces seemed to be free of dust. Did the old woman spend all her waking hours wandering the house with a chamois cloth and a can of Pledge?

"A drought's just a sign the world's out of kilter," Mama Prudence said as she moved delicately across the foyer. Her steps made no sound on the hardwood floor. "Something isn't how it's supposed to be, and the world is just going to wait until it rights itself. Then we'll get the rain back."

"Never heard that one before," Byron said. She moved at a snail's pace; he could've crossed the room in three strides.

"Oh, us old folks have great stores of wisdom about things you youngsters have forgotten," she said in her genteel Southern lilt. "You do yourselves a disservice by shutting us away in homes for the elderly. You think that when our bodies go, we have nothing left to contribute."

"You're taking care of yourself pretty well," he observed.

"I do all right. But it does get lonely."

He glanced into the living room, and stopped. He supposed the large painting over the mantel had always been there, but now a shaft of sunlight broke through a gap in the curtains and illuminated it like a spotlight. The brushstrokes sparkled in relief, and the heavy wooden frame shone with ornate gilt work.

Mama Prudence stopped when she saw his reaction. "Are you just now noticing that picture, Sheriff?"

"I reckon so. Have you always had it there?"

"That's where my great-grandmother placed it, and that's where it will stay as long as I'm around."

"Is she a relative, then?"

"Oh, yes. That is the infamous Patience Bolade. Have you heard of her?"

" 'Fraid not."

"In 1864 she took her own life when she was abandoned at the altar. It was quite the scandal. And, from what the family always said about her and her ways, it was a lucky escape for the groom."

He looked more closely at the painting. The woman in it had kind eyes, or at least the artist had painted her that way. Her skin was pale, and her ample décolletage stood out sharply against her dark dress. "Was she really that bad?"

"Oh, she was a monster," Mama Prudence said vehemently. "She lived to torment her sister, my namesake."

"Prudence?"

"Oh, yes. If Prudence had anything she valued, Patience would take it away. It was a reflex for her, like drawing a breath."

"Sounds like you're still angry about it."

Mama Prudence snapped around and glared at him with an intensity doubly surprising in such an old woman. In the dim light, her eyes seemed to suddenly glow red. It only lasted a moment, and then she smiled, revealing oddly long canines. She nodded toward the painting. "I've heard about Patience my whole life, and I carry the name of her victim. I suppose I do take it a bit personally. Kind of silly, isn't it?"

"Family never lets you go," Cocker said sadly. "Not even the dead ones."

"*Especially* not the dead ones," Mama Prudence agreed. She stood on tiptoe and patted Cocker's face. He jumped at her ice-cold touch. "Now bring those groceries into the kitchen before your arms fall off, young man."

Compared to the rest of the house the kitchen was brightly lit. The brittle white curtains had yellowed so that the whole room looked vaguely jaundiced. The ancient refrigerator's compressor hummed and rattled.

Cocker put the bags on the counter and began unloading them. He put a stack of glossy periodicals on the counter. "Here's your women's magazines. People sure do look at me funny when I buy those," he said with a chuckle. He opened the pantry door and added, "Doesn't look like you've made much of a dent in last month's groceries."

She waved her gnarled hand dismissively. In this light, she looked even more like one of those dried-apple dolls for sale at the flea market. "At my age, Sheriff, I have a limited palate."

"I done told you, Mama Prudence, I'm not the sheriff anymore."

"I think most people will always think of you as the sheriff, Byron. You've certainly earned it, losing your wife the way you did."

Cocker winced slightly, as he always did when someone brought up Vicki Lynn. "That's all in the past now. I'm just a private citizen, trying to get by."

"And a movie star, don't forget."

"Now, Mama Prudence, that wasn't *me* in that movie. Bo Dan Butcher was a lot prettier than I ever was. Besides, you know I never jumped from the bed of a pickup onto the hood of a car. That's just foolishness."

He put a box of cornstarch in the cupboard, and when he turned around Mama Prudence stood right behind him, so close their bodies almost touched. He jumped, startled, and dropped a bottle of vanilla extract on the counter. It shattered.

"Lordy, Byron, I'm so sorry, I didn't mean to scare you again," the old woman said, but her smile betrayed her amusement.

"You're gonna turn me gray before I leave the house," Cocker said, laughing despite his pounding heart. He picked up the broken glass, then winced as an edge bit into the soft heel of his hand. "Dang! You got a Band-Aid, Mama Prudence?"

He turned to her, and for a moment thought her eyes blazed red again, as they'd done before. Then his vision blurred and everything went dark.

It seemed only a moment passed, but when Cocker opened his eyes again he found himself sprawled in one of the big leather chairs in the living room. The sunbeam had moved off the painting of Patience Bolade and shone almost horizontal across the room.

His body felt heavy and sore, like it did some mornings after serious drinking. His various injuries all tended to seize up when he slept, and adding a hangover merely aggravated them. But he hadn't been drinking . . . had he?

He forced himself to sit upright. The chair made loud, rude noises beneath him as the stiff leather protested the movement. He shook his head, immediately regretted it, and sagged back into the upholstery.

"Back among the living?" a brittle voice said cheerily. Mama Prudence appeared from the shadows carrying a cup of steaming liquid. "I made you some green tea. It'll help get you back on your feet."

"What happened?" Cocker asked, his voice oddly thick and subservient, like a child's. He felt weaker than he had since the last time he was shot.

"You cut your hand, saw the blood, and passed out."

"I *passed out*?" he repeated in disbelief.

"I guess anyone can be a little squeamish at the sight of blood, can't they?" Prudence said as she put the cup on the little side table.

Cocker frowned. "I never . . ."

"There's nothing to be ashamed of. Everyone has a secret fear of some sort."

He reached for the cup and saw the new bandage wrapped around his palm. It was made of gauze yellowed with age, and old tape that was coming undone. He took the cup with his other hand and said, "I'm real sorry, Mama Prudence."

"Oh, *pshaw,*" she said with a wave of one long bony hand. Except it no longer looked as bony as he recalled. Nor, he realized, did Mama Prudence's face appear quite so withered. Then again, he couldn't trust anything his brain told him at the moment. The tea, hot and sweetened with honey, seemed to muddle his thoughts even more.

"You be sure and clean that hand good when

you get home," she said as she patted his arm. "My first-aid supplies are a bit out-of-date, as you can see. Oh, and see if it still looks funny, too."

"Funny?"

"Yes. There's the big cut, and then two little cuts right beside it. Looks like teeth marks, almost." And she smiled, but her face was in shadow.

🦂 Prudence watched Byron Cocker drive away slowly and carefully, with none of his usual flamboyance. She closed the door, turned out the unnecessary lights, and walked back into the living room.

The afternoon sun heated the air, but had no effect on her. Neither did time, nor the elements. Only two things affected Mama Prudence: the blood of the living, and the proximity of her sister.

She gazed at the painting as if it might give up some secret she'd missed in the past century. Every drought caused her to anticipate this moment, but decades had passed before the right *kind* of drought, the kind that appeared only when a vampire's malevolence neared, finally occurred. She knew with certainty in her cold unbeating heart that Patience was, at last, coming home.

She sighed in almost sexual contentment as Cocker's blood coursed through her. She seldom fed anymore; it would attract too much attention in this modern world, and her choice of convenient victims was limited. But the big man's injured hand caused her hunger to unexpectedly flare, and now she understood it as yet another providential sign, like the drought.

"Soon, dear sister," Prudence said aloud, "the games begin again."

CHAPTER 5

Zginski and Leonardo stopped at a gas station just before the Shelby County line. The bell connected to the pressure hose pinged twice as Zginski parked at the gas pumps. He revved the car's engine several times, luxuriating in both the sound and the rumble that traveled through him. Of all this era's unexpected delights, the evolution of the automobile was the most exquisite. It almost made the sixty years he'd spent in hellish limbo worth it. Almost.

The night he'd first encountered "Eleanor," in the movie *Gone in 60 Seconds*, had been unusual for a couple of reasons. It was the first time he and Fauvette had attended a cinema since they'd impulsively viewed *Blacula* and *Vanishing Point* some weeks earlier. It was also the first time he'd experienced an institution known as a "drive-in," where cinemas—no, he corrected himself, they were now called *movies,* a corruption of the term motion picture—were publically displayed on a common screen before a group of people in parked vehicles. As they drove the truck into the fenced-off exhibition area, they passed a flatbed trailer with a wrecked car on it, and a sign that said, "Meet Eleanor, star of *Gone in 60 Seconds.*" At first Zginski assumed this referred to an ingenue, but once the movie started he understood that the car was the attraction. *It* was Eleanor.

And by the time the movie was over, Zginski was in love: with the speed, with the dust, with the roaring engines and the blistering movement. With Eleanor. Each crash of metal against metal, each scream of rubber against pavement, reinforced the feeling that he'd skipped the last sixty years for a reason. If he'd watched the development of the automobile, seen it grow from uncertain horseless buggies through each stage of design and manufacture, he might never have grasped how thrilling these vehicles could truly be. He had the unexpected thought that he should be *grateful* for the night Sir Francis Colby drove that golden dagger into his heart, removing him from the world for the next six decades.

That feeling didn't last, but his fascination with all things automotive did. He learned how to drive as quickly as possible, and once he'd mastered the skill looked around for a suitable vehicle. It never occurred to him that he could truly *own* Eleanor;

the vehicle on display that night bore the damage sustained during the making of the film, and would never travel the highways again. But then he realized that automobiles were, in fact, mass-produced by the thousands. He could not possess *the* Eleanor, but he could own *an* Eleanor.

The attendant emerged from the station. He was middle-aged, unshaven, clad in a brown jumpsuit with the name CLYDE stitched inside an oval patch. He spit tobacco at the ground, then said, "What kind of gas you want, Chief?"

Zginski frowned and lightly tapped the steering wheel. "Which would be most appropriate for this vehicle?"

"What's she got under the hood?"

"A Windsor 351."

Clyde's eyes opened wide. "No shit. Can I take a look?"

Zginski puffed up with pride and nodded. Clyde raised the hood and looked at the pristine engine beneath it. He let out a low whistle. "A four-barrel carburetor. This thing'll move, I bet."

"Indeed," Zginski agreed.

Leonardo joined them, still annoyed by the scene at Dark Willows. He leaned against the driver's side fender and said, "You showing off again?"

"Ain't this a beauty?" Clyde said.

"A pure metal fox," Leonardo agreed.

Clyde beamed at Zginski as if they were best pals. "What you want in the tank today, mister? Regular or high test?"

"High . . . test, I suppose."

"Fill 'er up?"

"Yes."

"Coming right up. Hope you weren't driving this thing last year when there wasn't no gas to be had 'cause of them Arabs. Yessir, be a shame for this beauty to sit idle. Thanks for letting me take a peek."

Clyde took the nozzle from the pump and began filling up the car. Zginski saw Leonardo's scowl and said, "Something troubles you?"

"Naw, nothing except the way you treat people. You messed that poor girl up good, you know. She's just a kid, she won't know what hit her."

"Your sympathy is surprising."

"Why?"

"She and her father certainly consider you beneath their station. Which, considering the depths they have sunk to, puts you very far down indeed."

"I just don't think it was necessary."

"Then perhaps you should return to console her."

Leonardo's eyes opened wide in surprise. "What, are you serious?"

Zginski shrugged. "She lives in isolation, she is young and vital, and her will is easily manipulated. She could provide you with sustenance for several weeks, if not months. If you truly wish to experience the relationship I have spoken of between one of us and a victim, this would be an ideal start."

Clyde returned and said, "That'll be five-fifty, please."

Zginski handed him the exact change. "Thank you."

"Keep it between the lines," Clyde called cheerily over his shoulder.

Zginski started the car again, sighed contentedly, and for the first time noticed the radio in the center of the dashboard. He turned the knob and a blast of trebly sound came from the speaker. The announcer was in midproclamation: ". . . home of the hits, WHBQ Memphis!"

Zginski drove off, wondering what in the world the singer meant by saying the hills that he climbed were just seasons out of time.

As he resumed following Zginski, Leonardo pondered the suggestion. When Zginski first met Leonardo, Fauvette, and the rest, he looked disdainfully on their feeding habits; he considered killing one victim a night to be egregious and dangerous, since it might attract notice. He preferred to establish a long-term relationship, seducing the victim into becoming a willing donor even though she knew that death waited at the end. He had found a new victim himself, but said little about her except that she was well educated and wealthy.

Clora Crabtree was neither, Leonardo thought. But then, his standards were different.

Gerry Barrister settled back into one of the chairs and propped his feet on a table. Since he owned the Ringside Bar and Supper Club, he could get away with that. Had a patron tried it, he would've been out the door so fast his shadow would have to hurry to catch up.

Gerry was thirty-five but looked years older. His long hairsprayed bangs hid the ragged forehead scars that were the most obvious sign of his years as a professional wrestler. He also could not fully extend his left arm thanks to a once-shattered elbow, and occasionally his vision blurred if he turned his head too fast. But he remained six feet tall and solidly muscular, avoiding most of the portliness that marked many ex-athletes.

He had wrestled for fifteen years as Gerry "King of the Ring" Barrister, on the Mid-South circuit. Most of the time he was a "face," the wrestling term for a hero, although management sometimes cast him as a "heel" to stir things up a bit. He'd toed the line, performed as required, and built a considerable fan base. But one night Jim Hogan, a fireplug Australian with a notoriously short temper, went off-script and cracked Gerry's skull with a metal folding chair. That had been enough for Gerry; he took a severance deal and used it to buy an old bar on Madison Avenue in Memphis, which he refurbished into a nice drinks-and-dinner spot. He liked the idea of being the big man dispensing free drinks to the pretty girls.

Now he regarded Patience Bolade with the same appraising look he gave every woman. She stood in the open space used for dancing to jukebox tunes, her guitar casually over her shoulder. She was pale, a bit overweight, but with the full breasts he always liked and a twinkle in her eye he suspected would appeal to a tipsy bar crowd. She had long dark hair and big eyes, and seemed perfectly at ease with his scrutiny.

"So," he drawled, "your name is Patience." His grin was accented by the mustache-less goatee on his chin. He slapped Fauvette, who stood beside him, playfully on the behind. "Fauvette here tells me you're a singer."

"I'm a musician," she corrected gently. Her full lips turned up in a wry half smile. "Singing is part of that. And I'm looking for a job, somewhere I can play regularly."

"You union?"

"No. Is that a problem?"

He smiled. "Probably. But problems exist to get solved, don't they? What kind of songs you do?"

"My own stuff, mostly."

"Who do you sound like?"

"Ever heard of Laura Nyro?"

"Nope. You got any records out?"

She shook her head. "I'm not really interested in that."

"Not interested in being a big star?"

Now she smiled all the way. "I like playing for people right in front of me. That's enough."

"What instruments do you play?"

"Guitar, mostly. Piano. Some violin."

"I don't think we'll have much call for fiddle music here," Barrister said. He turned to Fauvette, who had folded her arms impatiently. He found the barmaid almost unbelievably attractive, her little-girl looks mixing with a world-weary air to make one sweet package. She also never seemed to mind his occasional gropes or fondling, which endeared her to him even more. It never occurred to him to actually proposition her; he'd had enough barely legal poontang to do him for life, and was content these days to merely act the rogue. He said to her, "But a piano might be classy, for the early-evening crowd, don't you think?"

Fauvette shrugged. "Maybe." Gerry didn't really want her opinion, he just needed another excuse to pat her on the ass.

"Do you *have* a piano?" Patience asked.

"No, but we can rent one of those little stand-up electric ones, just to see if it's worth the investment."

"Shouldn't you hear her sing first?" Fauvette prompted in annoyance.

"I reckon I should, since you're not doing a fan dance," Barrister said with a chuckle. "So go ahead, give us something."

Patience put a glass slide onto her left pinky and ran it down the strings once. The shimmering sound commanded the bar owner's full attention. "You might know this song," she said.

When she strummed, the air around her seemed to vibrate. She delicately cleared her throat and began to sing the Drifters' classic "On Broadway," except changed to the Memphis-centric "On Beale Street."

Fauvette moved away from Barrister so she

could watch what happened. Long ago she'd realized that it wasn't physical blood she needed, but some intangible aspect of it that allowed her kind to survive. When the man told her how the Patience in his story drained the audience's energy, Fauvette immediately recognized it as some strange form of vampiric feeding. Now that Patience apparently stood before her, and was also clearly a vampire, she wondered if there might indeed be a way to feed on the intangible part without actually drinking the blood.

When Patience's voice first rang out, Barrister sat up straight, and his feet slid from the table. He leaned forward as if awaiting the signal to start a race.

Patience did not look directly at him, but stared into space toward the middle of the room. Her only movement was a slight rhythmic swaying. She was doing nothing, in fact, to hold his attention except singing in a pure, sweet voice.

But the vibration in the air grew stronger. Fauvette squinted and saw the air shimmer in waves that traveled from Barrister to Patience. She changed position so she could see more clearly, but the trembling was so delicate and subtle that she couldn't find it again.

Patience finished the song with a flourish, tossed her long hair for effect, and smiled at Barrister. "*That's* what I sound like. What do you think?"

Barrister stared at her as if he'd just seen either an angel or a ghost. His eyes even gleamed like tears were about to fall. "Holy shit," he whispered.

"See?" Fauvette said, and nudged his arm. "I told you she was good."

The contact seemed to bring him back to the moment. "Holy shit," he repeated, then got to his feet. "And you're that good, all the time?"

She nodded. "It's my job, after all."

He grabbed her hand and pumped it enthusiastically. "Well, when can you start?" Then he looked down at her fingers. "Dang, girl, your fingers are cold as ice. You'd think they'd be smoking hot after that!"

"So does she have the job?" Fauvette prompted.

"Are you kidding? If I could, I'd start you tonight. Except . . . why don't we start you on Friday? That way I can get some posters up, maybe some ads in the weekend papers. What do you say to two shows, at eight and eleven?"

Patience nodded. "That's fine."

Barrister was grinning, sweating, and shaking. "Just with the guitar at first, until I can get a piano in here." He yawned, and shook his head violently as if to shake it off. "Fauvette, honey? We got anywhere we can use as a dressing room?"

Fauvette shrugged. "We got that storeroom where we keep the extra chairs. It has a sink."

"That'll do. Well, it'll do after you get it cleaned out and fixed up. Take some of the petty cash and get a bunch of nice things, mirrors and stuff. Hell, just let Patience here give you a shopping list."

"Sure," Fauvette said with a scowl. "Waitress, janitor, and now decorator."

He yawned again, completely missing her

sarcasm. "Thanks, hon, I knew I could count on you. Look, I've got to go lay down on the couch in my office. Patience, Fauvette will show you around. Make sure you leave a phone number and address. We'll get the contracts signed next week, okay?"

By then he had gone into the kitchen and they heard his office door slam shut. Patience chuckled and took out a cloth to wipe down her guitar strings. "And that, my dear, is how I feed. What did you think?"

"I could kind of feel it," Fauvette said. "It was like the air was vibrating between you two. Like when you make a telephone out of two cans and a long piece of string."

Patience put her guitar back in its case. "That's a very good analogy. I got enough energy from him to counteract what I lost in the sun coming down here. Now I should be fine until tomorrow."

Fauvette shook her head. "And how many people have to die because I can't do that?"

Patience stopped, stepped close, and sadly touched Fauvette's cheek. "Don't do that to yourself. We are what we are, Fauvette, and it's not our fault. I didn't ask to be this, and neither did you."

Fauvette luxuriated in the touch. She could not recall ever feeling so safe with physical contact. She sighed and said, "Thank you. Do you think . . . can you teach me to do that, too?"

Before she could answer, the front door opened, admitting Zginski in a blast of afternoon heat. The door closed with a thud, and Zginski looked around the empty room. When he saw Fauvette his face noticeably brightened. But it grew closed and cautious again when he spotted Patience beside her.

"And who," he said as he threaded through the tables and upturned chairs, "is this?"

Patience looked him over and said, with a grin that clearly displayed her fangs, "I was about to ask Fauvette the very same thing."

CHAPTER 6

Zginski felt Patience brush him with her supernatural influence, then withdraw it completely, like a reflex that had to twitch before it could be restrained. It had no effect, but nonetheless he found himself staring for longer than he intended.

He'd met more vampires in his brief time in Memphis than in all his decades traveling across Europe, he thought ironically. He wondered if they'd somehow spread themselves exponentially through ignorance and deliberate malice while he was in limbo. But his instant, powerful attraction to this one took him off guard. It was not that she was beautiful in any normal way. Certainly Fauvette, standing almost demurely beside her, was far more conventionally striking. Yet this newcomer compelled his attention in a way Fauvette never had.

Before Fauvette could respond, the other woman said, "'This' is Patience Bolade." She smiled and extended her hand. The gesture was graceful, and the grip dainty and old-fashioned when he took it. He bent over it, a slight version of continental chivalry, and she likewise bent her knees just enough to count as a curtsy. She asked, "And you are?"

"I am Rudolfo Vladimir Zginski," he said formally.

"Delighted to meet you," Patience said. "It appears we're thick on the ground here, doesn't it?"

"I have had the very same thought."

"Probably not phrased the same way."

"No."

Fauvette scowled, but neither of them noticed. She was unsure who inspired this surge of jealousy: Zginski for butting in on her new friendship, or Patience for so blatantly showing interest in him. Fauvette and Zginski had not been lovers since that night in the warehouse, but that didn't mean it had faded from her mind. If anything, she was growing more certain that she wanted to do it again. She said sharply, "So did you buy your car?"

Zginski, annoyed at the interruption, snapped, "Yes, I did." He turned his attention back to Patience. "And why are you here, Miss Bolade?"

"I grew up here. Well, close to here. A long time ago, though."

"I was referring to your presence at this establishment."

"Oh." She nodded at the guitar. "I'm the new entertainment."

Fauvette interjected, "So now you have your own Eleanor. You must be happy."

Patience looked puzzled. "Who's 'Eleanor'?"

"The girl of his dreams," Fauvette said.

"It is," Zginski said to Patience but with a warning glare at Fauvette, "an automobile."

"Ooh, what kind?" Patience said eagerly. "I had a boyfriend out in California who was always rebuilding this or that. He taught me a lot about them."

Zginski's eyebrows rose in surprise. "Indeed? It is a 1973 Ford Mustang."

"What size engine?"

"351, I was told."

"Windsor?"

"Correct."

She bounced with excitement. "Can I see it?"

Zginski offered his arm. "I would be honored to show it to you."

Fauvette started to say something, but caught herself this time. What was *wrong* with her? She was an eternal creature, subject to none of the rules that bound limited mortals. Jealousy was not only silly, it was pointless. What morality controlled the behavior of the undead?

As the pair went outside, Leonardo passed them on his way in. They ignored him, deep in their own conversation, and he stared after them until the door closed. Then he crossed the room toward Fauvette. "Who was that with Mistah Z.?"

"Patience," she snapped.

"Whoa, sorry, didn't mean to interrupt. You didn't look busy."

"No, her *name* is Patience. She's our new singer."

He did a double take in the direction of the door. "But she's a . . ."

"Yeah, I know."

"Appears Rudy knows, too."

"Oh, they're already soul mates," she said sarcastically.

Leonardo chuckled. "He doesn't run out of surprises, does he? So how are you?"

"Oh, I'm peachy. Did you have any trouble with the car?"

"Sort of. Some big cracker showed up and tried to make the guy sell it to him instead of Rudy. It all worked out. Except . . ."

"What?"

Leonardo sat in the same chair Jerry had used and fiddled idly with the table's salt shaker. "You know how he's always saying we should pick one long-term victim instead of a new one every night?"

"Yeah."

"I think I'm ready to try that."

"With who?"

"A girl who lives out where we got the car. It's an old plantation house that still has the slave shacks out back, if you can believe that."

"In McHale County? That's a long way, isn't it?"

He shrugged. "If I don't like it, I can kill her and be done with it without attracting too much attention."

Fauvette nodded. She felt queasy, as if too many things had changed too suddenly. She turned away from Leonardo and said, as casually as she could, "So how long will you be gone?"

"Depends on how it goes." Then he understood her meaning. "But wait, this isn't like what happened with Mark."

Fauvette waved a dismissive hand. "You're a free man, Leo. Lincoln said so." She paused. "I'm sorry, that was tacky. Something my mama used to say to her black friends."

He stood behind her, put his hands on her shoulders, and said gently, "It *was* kind of mean."

She still did not look at him. "First Toddy, then Olive, now Mark . . . we're all that's left. Once you go, I'll be all alone again."

"Mark ain't like the others," Leo corrected. "He ain't dead."

She shrugged out from under his hands and faced him, her eyes ablaze with anger and hurt. "He may not be, but he ain't around, either. After a while, that's the same thing."

Leonardo said nothing. He couldn't dispute that.

🐾 Patience held Zginski's arm as he led her behind the building. The Ringside Bar and Supper

Club occupied a low, flat-roofed structure shaded by old maples and oaks growing in a narrow strip of bare ground between properties. On one side was a small used-car dealership, and on the other a gas station. Directly across the street was a large pawnshop, and behind the bar were the back entrances of a strip mall that fronted on another street.

From the outside, in bright summer daylight, the bar was ugly and crude, a collection of mismatched modifications accumulated through the years. At night, though, strategically placed lights hid its flaws and gave the facade enough glamour for the crowd Barrister liked to attract.

Zginski had parked the car in the shade at the back of the bar, beside the overflowing Dumpster. Leonardo had put Mark's truck beside it, which made the Mustang look even more spectacular. Zginski brushed aside a leaf that had fallen from a nearby tree; the drought had turned the foliage brown and yellow months early. "This is my automobile," he said, enjoying the sound of the words.

Patience took a moment to appreciate the vehicle. "Yes, sir," she said with admiration. "That is a fine set of wheels. And you named her 'Eleanor'?"

"No, an identical automobile in a movie carried that name. I shall choose something more individual."

"Any idea what?"

He nodded. "'Tzigane.'"

"Is that a Gypsy name?"

"It is."

"Is it a *girl's* name?"

"Yes."

She smiled knowingly. "A *special* girl?"

He frowned and did not reply. Unbidden memories burst vividly into his consciousness: her black tangle of hair cascading around her bare shoulders as she sat astride him muttering strange incantations, the smell of her sweat mixing with the incense inside her tent, and most clearly the coppery taste of blood that signaled her betrayal. And yet, were she here before him, would he destroy her again or beg her forgiveness? He would never know.

She nodded at the car, changing the subject. "Can I see the engine?"

Zginski hesitated; he knew how to open the hood on the truck, but Crabtree had done so at the barn, and the attendant Clyde at the gas station. He fumbled behind the grille for the latch, until Patience nudged him aside and opened it easily. She propped the hood on its brace and looked over the engine.

"It looks," she said after a moment, "a lot like the 351 Cleveland, doesn't it?"

"I have no idea."

She smiled and looked up at him, tossing her long hair aside. "You don't know anything about cars, do you? You were showing off for my benefit."

Her constant good nature was infectious. He shrugged and said, "I am learning."

She put her hands on her hips. "About which, cars or how to impress me?"

He regarded her carefully. "Of the two, I suspect impressing you would require more study."

She wagged a finger at him in mock-scolding. "You don't trust me at all, do you?"

"I have known you for mere minutes."

"Yeah, but I can sense things. I know what you're thinking."

"That seems unlikely."

"You think between you, me, and Fauvette, we'll draw too much attention. Because we're not as careful as you, there'll be too many bloodless corpses littering the riverfront, and people will start to notice." He glanced around to make sure the remark had not been overheard, and she laughed. "You *are* a skittish thing, aren't you?"

"I have reason to be," he snapped, the momentary spell broken. "And I do not wish to add to the list of my concerns."

"Aw. Are you sure?"

"I am sure, and not in the way you imply."

"If I told you I fed on people's energy without either touching them or killing them, would that make you feel better?"

"No, because I would then be certain that you were unbalanced. Now tell me, why are you *truly* here?"

Her smile changed to an annoyed scowl. "Well, it's true, Mr. Big Shot. And I *did* tell you. I grew up about an hour away from here."

"When?"

"I was born in 1844. I became what I am in 1864."

"And where have you been all this time?"

"All over. Europe until it got too rough, Asia until the culture got on my nerves, the West Coast until I got bored with the decadence. I decided this was a perfect time to come home."

She closed the hood, then sat back against the fender. "And what about you?"

"My history is private."

"I answered *your* questions."

"There was no quid pro quo."

"Oooh," she said with gentle mockery, "the handsome man is mysterious as well."

Despite himself, Zginski found himself smiling again. "I suppose I do sound rather pompous."

"A lot of it's the accent."

"I am working to minimize that."

"You could start by using more contractions. Saying, '*I'm* working to minimize that,' for example."

"So noted."

The scalding summer wind blew her long hair from her face, and she fingered the line of buttons down his shirtfront. "And you should pay more attention to the weather. If it's hot, you dress for it. This just makes you look strange."

He was more conscious of the contact than he expected to be. "You are filled with insights."

She laughed. "I'm full of something, that's for

sure." She looked up into his eyes, and he felt the tentative touch of her powers, trying to arouse his interest. "Will you come to see my first show?"

He could have obliterated her with his own abilities, but before he could she withdrew her energy. He realized it had again been inadvertent, and that she wanted his interest to be genuine. It was similar to the way Zginski felt about Fauvette, in those rare moments when he was honest with himself.

"I will be there," he said with a courtly nod.

"Front row?"

"Probably not. I prefer to lurk in the shadows. But it does not affect my perceptions."

"I'm sure it doesn't." She bit her lip thoughtfully, the tips of her fangs plain against the red surface. "I like Fauvette. I'll be working with her, too. I don't want to create any awkwardness."

"In what way?"

She gazed steadily at him. "If you don't know, you're not as sharp as I thought."

"Fauvette and I have no exclusive arrangements. We are not, I believe the term is, 'going together.' "

She pressed a hand to her mouth to muffle her giggles. "I could listen to you all day," she said. "Except that I have to go shopping with Fauvette to get my dressing room ready. But remember, you promised to be there Friday night."

"And I shall."

"I think," she said with a wink, "you'll find it a

real eye-opener." Then she walked back around the building, deliberately swaying her hips.

Zginski stood in the shade beside his car and stared after her for a long time.

CHAPTER 7

Fauvette turned on the light. The little room was filled with boxes of napkins and toilet paper, and the sink in the corner looked as if it hadn't seen water in a decade. "This is where Gerry wants to put you. I'll make sure it's fixed up and presentable. I hope it's okay."

"I'm sure it'll be fine," Patience said. The erstwhile dressing room opened onto the hall that went along the back of the building from the kitchen, past the exit to the Dumpster, to the door that would become the stage entrance. "Where have you put the other acts?"

Fauvette scooted a heavy box aside with her foot. "There haven't been any since I started here. Gerry's been pretty content to just have people eat and drink." She paused before asking, "So . . . do you think you'll be staying long?"

"I don't know," Patience said as she sat atop one stack of boxes. "I have a lot of history in this area. I'll have to see how much it weighs on me." She looked at Fauvette seriously. "Do you *mind* it if I stay?"

"No," Fauvette replied. "In fact . . ."

"What?" Patience gently prompted.

Fauvette looked up at the ceiling. "Well, while you're here, do you think you could, maybe, I dunno . . . teach me to do what you do?"

"Sing and play the guitar?"

"No, the thing . . . the way you feed on the energy of people."

"Fauvette—"

Fauvette couldn't stop herself. The words had been building up inside her. "I didn't believe it when that guy told me about you, but I could feel it in the air, flowing out of Gerry and into you. I even *saw* it for a second. The thing is, I *hate* the hunt, the physical contact with people I don't know, the need to get rid of the body later. But even if I *know* the person, I still hate it. I shared a girl with Zginski for a while, and I got to be . . . *friends* with her, almost. Like sisters, even." Fauvette swatted at the chain hanging from the light fixture. "It's just so easy, and it feels so good when I'm doing it, that I never believed I could stop. But watching you, I thought . . ." She trailed off, looking down at her shoes.

Patience sat quietly for a moment, then said,

"Fauvette, I can appreciate how you feel. I feel the same way. The thing is . . ."

"You don't know me, and you don't trust me," she said without looking up.

"No, that's not it. I'm not like your friend Zginski. The thing is, I don't know exactly how it works."

Fauvette looked up sharply. "You don't?"

"No. It happened by accident the first time. And I know how to do it for myself, but I can't imagine trying to teach it. I can barely *describe* it."

"Will you try?" Fauvette said in a small, demure voice. "Please?"

Patience smiled. The poor girl's desperation was heartbreaking. From her appearance, Patience guessed she'd been barely out of childhood when she'd been turned. Did her long-ago mortal youth somehow still inform her feelings? "All right, honey, I'll try. But I can't promise anything."

Fauvette nodded. Patience impulsively hugged her, and felt the girl melt, childlike, into the embrace. "Shh, it's all right," Patience said, and Fauvette snuggled even closer. As she stroked Fauvette's soft hair, Patience wondered if this, more than any future indiscretion with Zginski, would be her biggest mistake.

🔖 In his office, Gerry Barrister slept on the battered old couch. The furniture had seen some wild times, but now he used it strictly for sleeping. It perfectly fit the contours of his aging, battered body. He had one arm thrown over his eyes and one foot on the floor, while his snores could almost be heard over the window-unit air conditioner.

He sensed the door opening, and turned toward it. Fauvette stood silhouetted against the brightly lit kitchen. "Hey, Fauvy," Gerry muttered sleepily, and started to rise.

Almost at once he grew weak and immobile. The door closed, plunging the room back into the dim, amber illumination that penetrated the blinds.

Gerry blinked and tried to stay awake. Was that really Fauvette removing her blouse, showing him those sweet little boobs? She came toward him now, tits swaying, her face in shadow. She knelt beside the couch, chilled fingers unbuttoning his shirt, then crawled on top of him. The rest of her was as cold as her hands.

He barely found the strength to put one hand on her ass. "You're like ice, baby," he whispered.

"Then warm me up," she sighed, writhing against him, her lips moving up his chest to his shoulder, and finally his neck. And then a sharp pain, and sudden, deep blackness . . .

Fauvette fed with efficient, rapid ease. She knew Barrister was already weakened by Patience, but it had been two days since Fauvette had taken from him, and she was desperate as well. He was *her* victim, anyway; like Zginski said, she took only what she needed, whereas Patience had drained as much as she could.

She felt his erection through his slacks as she straddled him, his limp hand resting on her buttocks. Holding back the tide of blood from his neck was the real trick, and she realized with new irony that it forced her to purse and pucker her lips like a kiss.

She broke away from his skin and licked the tiny trickles that escaped before the bite closed up. Would this be the last time she'd have to taste blood, she wondered; was this her final act of will, breaking off before she was glutted like a woman willfully resisting an orgasm?

She quickly dressed and slipped out of the office. Vander the cook would arrive soon to get the kitchen ready for the dinner crowd, and she didn't want to start any gossip.

 "Boss?"

Vander stood in the doorway. He was black, middle-aged, and a veteran of places like the Ringside. Here, at least, he was given the respect his skill deserved, even if Barrister still referred to him as "the colored cook" when talking to people. "Got a bread shipment you need to sign for."

"Humszah?" Barrister said. He sat up, shaking his head to clear it. "Sorry, boy, can you repeat that?"

Vander sighed. "Bread. Truck. Out. Back."

"Okay, I'll be right there." Barrister got to his feet, leaned against the desk until the dizziness passed, and started tucking in his shirt. He was still rock-hard from his recurring dream about Fauvette, and he had to shift himself a couple of times to find a comfortable position that didn't also make it obvious to anyone looking at him.

He washed his face in his little private bathroom. He found it really strange that the Fauvette of his subconscious was so wanton and uninhibited, while the real one seemed almost virginal. More than once he'd wondered if she actually *was* a virgin; but virgins didn't apply for jobs in bars, did they?

He checked himself out in the mirror. He looked exhausted; he would have to give himself more time to rest. After all, he was the public face of the Ringside. And would those two places where he'd nicked himself shaving *ever* heal?

As the sun set across the Mississippi River, sinking into the distant Arkansas farmland, Zginski parked his new car in the driveway of a big home in Germantown. This area east of Memphis was where the wealthiest people lived, in big houses shaded by old, stately trees. The residents were all white, and many had lived in these houses for two or three generations, a millennium here in the New World.

He sat behind the wheel for a long time, fighting

the weakness that had settled on him. He was seldom this active during the day, when the rays of the sun soaked up all his strength and weakened his powers. But buying the car, and then meeting the woman Patience, had distracted him and now he was paying the price.

At last he summoned the strength to leave the car and walk to the door. He unlocked the dead bolt and stepped inside, grateful for the relative darkness. He leaned his back against the door and closed his eyes, which he might have done anyway considering that the wallpaper pattern consisted of two-foot-wide bright red blossoms.

"My goodness," Alisa Cassidy said with concern. "You look awful."

He opened his eyes. She stood in the entrance to her study, clad in a sleep shirt and, apparently, nothing else. She was forty, with short brown hair shot through with gray. Her body was youthful and taut; only slight smile lines and crow's-feet betrayed her age.

And only the distant, haunted look in her eyes gave away the truth that she was dying.

"I *am* weary," he agreed. His voice was even weaker when he said, "and I do not wish to wade through the usual preliminaries."

"All right, if that's what—"

Before she could finish, Zginski yanked her against him and sank his teeth into her neck. She cried out once, then fell into a swoon as her blood replenished his powers. In her mind she was young again, and healthy, and being taken from behind by a shadowy male who nonetheless hit every spot and brought on wave after wave of orgasm . . .

The moon rose over the old cotton warehouse Leonardo and Fauvette used to call home. Fauvette had originally discovered it, and then more or less allowed the others to move in. There had been five of them then: Fauvette, Leonardo, Olive, Mark, and Toddy. It was Toddy's inexplicable demise, in fact, that began the chain of events leading to their walking again in daylight.

Leonardo perched on one of the rafters, among the oblivious sleeping pigeons. He had spent untold hours here, contemplating his past and making tentative plans for the future. But any changes he sought to make were brought up short by the reality that he was, in fact, an unchanging revenant, the remains of a man who had once lived. His existence could only be on the fringes of society, where he could pass for human until someone looked too closely. And then inevitably that someone would die, and Leonardo would melt back into the shadows.

His thoughts went back to the girl at the decrepit mansion. In his time he'd known many poor white girls, who often existed on the same socioeconomic level as blacks. Raised with black folks around, some found it difficult to accept the prejudices of their parents and society; some, of course, did not. The Klan, after all, had recruited more poor whites than rich ones. And it had not been gentlemen farmers and bank presidents riding beneath those hoods, at least not in *his* mortal childhood.

But Clora Crabtree was an enigma. She clearly felt there was a difference based on race, but had gone out of her way to initiate conversation. Was she so isolated out there with her father that any stranger was a welcome relief? Leonardo knew what the typical redneck daddy might do with a nubile young daughter in that kind of solitude, but he got no sense of that, either. So what motivated her?

He dropped from the rafters to the warehouse floor. It was on this spot that Zginski, with no apparent effort, had transformed into a wolf right before his eyes, and moments later changed back. There had been no transition; one moment a man stood there, and the next an enormous, growling canine. Leonardo would not rest until he badgered Zginski into telling him how he accomplished that trick.

But on this night, he decided on another mission. Zginski was always preaching about how it was better—more discreet, more meaningful, more fun—to pick a single long-term victim at a time, gradually seducing them into craving the incremental loss of their own life. He claimed that after a few visits, the use of vampiric powers to sexually fascinate the victim would not even be necessary. They would willingly give themselves up as they grew weaker and weaker. Properly cultivated, a young, healthy victim could last as long as six months, and the victim's complicity helped insure no unwanted scrutiny.

So Leonardo decided to give it a shot. He would seduce Clora Crabtree, taking only enough blood on each visit to satisfy his immediate needs. And in the process, he might also learn what was at the heart of her paradoxically prejudiced open-mindedness.

CHAPTER 8

Clora Crabtree stood in the gabled window of her bedroom on the top floor of Dark Willows and looked out at the night. Because of the heat she wore only an old undershirt that hung to her thighs, but was too small for her recently matured bosom. She smoked a cigarette with her wrist bent dramatically, the way she'd seen her late mother do. Her reflection greeted her in the sections of glass, and she forced herself to stand up straight. A full-figured gal, her mama had told her, should never slump.

So far this had been the worst summer of her life. Isolated here with her father, it felt as if the world were rushing by in one of the expensive, fast cars her father repaired but never owned. He'd even sold the one her cousin had left to them, depriving her of even the chance to drive it. She knew he didn't trust her, and she knew he was right to feel that way. But still, he could've let her get behind the wheel once, on a hot day when the dust raised by the tires would hover in the air long after she'd roared off down the gravel drive. It wasn't like she didn't do things to help ease *his* loneliness.

The May issue of *Tiger Beat* lay on her bed, the pages dog-eared and worn. Marie Osmond was in the center of the cover collage, with hair so large Clora wondered just how much hair spray was involved. Her own hair was thin and lanky, much more like the hippie girls from ten years earlier. She would've loved that time, she thought bitterly: easy drugs, easy love, and a wide-open sense of the future. Her prospects seemed hemmed in by the doleful woods surrounding Dark Willows.

She ground out her cigarette in the ashtray and flopped on the bed, idly turning the magazine pages. Tony DeFranco, dark-haired and big-eyed, took readers on a tour of his family's new house. Freddie Prinze talked about his unhappy childhood. "Bunch of spic greaseballs," her father called them, but she liked the way their black hair fell around their soft faces. She imagined they'd smell of cologne and freshly ironed shirts.

She rolled onto her back. The pictures of Brett Hudson sent an intimate shiver through her, and she cupped her breast with her left hand. The itch grew maddening, and she felt her cheeks and neck flush red. She moaned aloud, softly, not wanting to attract her father's attention but unable to stay completely silent.

She closed her eyes and slid her knees apart. The shirt's hem crept up her thighs and gathered at her waist. She moved her right hand down her belly.

Then something tapped shave-and-a-haircut against her window.

Face burning, she sat up and yanked the shirt down to her knees. The tapping came again. She grabbed cutoffs from the floor, slid them up her legs, and went to the window.

She opened the glass. The humid night air surged in past her as she leaned out. "Bruce?" she hissed.

"Ain't Bruce," an unfamiliar voice said.

She turned toward a figure perched at the edge of the roof. It was crouched almost like one of those gargoyles in that scary movie she'd watched on TV, and she gasped and stepped back. When she did, the room's light fell on the figure's face. She recognized Leo, the black boy from that morning. "What the *hell* are you doing here, boy?" she hissed.

"Came to see you," he said quietly, and stood up. Despite the roof's slope, he seemed completely at ease.

His voice sent a tingle through her as strong as the one inspired by Brett Hudson. She had to swallow hard before speaking. "You know my daddy'll beat the nappy off you if he catches you."

Leonardo strode up the slanted roof and crouched by the window. "Do you want me to go, then?"

She licked her lips. Her knees trembled as a vast gulf of physical need opened inside her. "Well . . . no. But you gotta be quiet."

He slipped inside and hit the ground without making the wood creak. "I'm like the wind, baby."

"Well, the wind's hot tonight, so close the window before you let all the cool air out."

As he did so, she pulled out another cigarette and lit it with trembling fingers. If her daddy *did* find her with a colored boy, he'd kill the boy first, then beat her within an inch of her life. That was as certain as the sunrise. But maybe it was that very danger that had gotten her blood racing. "So how'd you get out here anyway?"

"Drove my friend's truck," Leonardo said as he moved slowly around the room, absorbing the details of her life. "Parked it down the highway and snuck through the woods."

She watched the way his muscles moved. Her voice was raw when she said, "I'm surprised the dog didn't start barking."

He smiled. "Dogs love me."

"How'd you get up on the roof?"

Leonardo turned and stepped close to her. He felt the heat of her body in the air, and could sense the young, surging blood beneath her skin. "You ask a lot of questions," he said softly. "How about I ask you one? You like coloreds in general, or just me?"

Her hand shook so much the ash fell from the cigarette as soon as it burned. She tried to sound blasé. "I thought you people didn't like to be called 'coloreds' anymore."

He took a strand of her hair and tucked it behind her ear, careful not to touch her skin. She gasped anyway. "What I don't like," he said, "is to have my crank yanked by some Goody Two-shoes with jungle fever. Is that what you're doing?"

She trembled at his nearness, at the knowledge that only the undershirt separated his hands from her skin. He had to have noticed the way her nipples stood out through the fabric. "Wh-what do you want me to do?" she said.

He smiled, showing his teeth but not his fangs. He let his power envelop her, drawing on reservoirs of desire she never knew she possessed, and focusing it all on him. "What do *I* want? The question is, what do *you* want?"

She impulsively grabbed his wrist and put his hand against her breast. She gasped in both sensual response and at the chilly touch. "Your hand's like *ice*."

He closed his fingers slightly around her breast. "You want me to stop?"

She shook her head and moved closer, pressing herself against him. His lips were as cold as his hands.

Alisa's eyes opened suddenly, as if she'd awakened from a nightmare. She lay on the plush settee in her study; the lights were dim, and the windows showed her it was dark outside.

She tried to recall the dream, or what had awoken her from it. But her fuzzy mind couldn't recover the thoughts.

She looked around the room to orient herself. She had moved her desk into the living room for convenience; after all, with Chad gone, she had no one else to answer to, and no need for a separate workroom. The prevailing color here was green, with leafy floral patterns on the couch, chairs, and curtains. Over the couch, dominating the room like a window onto a giant's garden, was an enormous painting of a cross-section of broccoli done by an artist named Close. The walls hung with certificates and photos, including many pictures of Chad. She had not been able to look at them for a long time after he died, but now that her own death was imminent they comforted her. She would see him again soon.

She sat up just as Zginski came from the kitchen with a glass of wine in his hand. He wore a white shirt and khaki slacks, and his hair was loose. Having recently fed, and now empowered by the night, he radiated confidence and authority. The thought of denying him anything seemed absurd.

She smiled. "I thought you never drank . . . wine."

"I do not. But it will do you good."

She nodded and gratefully took the glass. She swung her feet to the floor and waited for the dizziness to pass. "That was intense. How long was I out?"

"Four hours, approximately. My apologies. I had spent too much time in the sun."

She took a long drink. "I've barely seen it. I've been hunched over the *Festa Maggotta* all day. But I think I may have found the sort of thing you were looking for. Would you like to see?"

He lightly brushed her hair. The dark circles under her eyes, usually hidden by her tan, were more prominent now. "Are you sufficiently recovered?"

She smiled wryly. "I'm dying of cancer, Rudy. I am as recovered as I'm ever going to get."

She walked with his aid over to her desk, where photocopies lay scattered next to spiral notebooks. The facsimiles reproduced pages of the *Festa Maggotta*, "The Feast of Maggots," an ancient alchemical tome from the university's Sir Francis Colby collection. Zginski had, in fact, met Alisa thanks to this book: when he requested it, he was told that it was not available for casual lending, but the leading expert on it was in fact working with it at the moment. He introduced himself as a fellow scholar, and knew within fifteen seconds that she was deathly ill. Luckily she knew it, too.

She pointed to the image of a page, with a word in an unknown language at the top as a header. "That word *vrykopilo* translates as, I believe, 'vampires.' "

"Indeed. In what language?" The *Festa Maggotta* was notoriously difficult to translate;

sections were written in a mishmash of known languages, interspersed with unknown and possibly made-up tongues.

"Two, actually. Greek and Italian. The first two syllables, 'Vryko,' are from the Greek word *vrylolakes*. The last two, 'piro,' could be either Italian or Portuguese. I'll know more when I've translated some of the surrounding text. I could be completely off, but it'll be interesting either way."

He took the empty wineglass and put it aside. He had taken her that first night, seducing her with his powers and gaining immediate entrance to all aspects of her life. She was a widow, a full professor of linguistics who specialized in ancient and lost tongues. She was also dying of ovarian cancer. "Do you feel strong enough to discuss something with me?"

"As long as it's not my impending death."

"I believe we have exhausted that topic. Today I encountered another of my kind who claims she can feed, and survive, on merely the energy she draws from other people. Without touching or injuring them."

He paused, until she prompted, "And you don't believe her?"

"I do not know. It seems an absurd thing to lie about, and yet if it were true . . ."

"Then you wouldn't have to kill people to survive."

He smiled. She had discerned the truth about him that first night, and despite her initial disbe-

lief had now fully embraced it, and him. He dead-
ened the agonizing pain of her disease, and
reawakened the erotic desires that she feared had
died with Chad. "I do not kill to survive. I kill
when necessary. All creatures do that."

"I think your body count's a bit higher than
most."

"You are familiar with the world's many folk-
lores," he said, returning to the topic. "Does such
a thing sound possible?"

She yawned. "I'm no biologist, Rudy. I don't
know how your body works. You have no pulse,
no respiration, yet you don't physically decay. You
can take no sustenance from traditional food, yet
human blood not only allows you to survive, but
makes you superhumanly strong."

"Perhaps it is not the blood itself," he said
slowly, thinking aloud. "Something contained *in*
the blood. An energy of some sort. Is *that* possible?"

"Maybe. If you draw essentially the same energy from blood that she draws in some other
way, that would explain it. Like a person getting
her calories from either a steak or a candy bar."

"How would she be able to do this?"

"You'd have to ask her," Alisa said wryly. Then
she smiled and softly laughed. "It's funny to find
out there are things about being a vampire that
you, a vampire, don't know."

"Much of your own body's workings are mysterious to you as well."

"Yeah," she agreed with momentary sad irony. "I just thought that, given what you've endured—all those years in limbo, I mean—that you might know more than the average person, vampire or otherwise."

With no warning he slapped his hand over her mouth and nose, then leaned close to her and whispered, "Imagine you are in the middle of taking a breath, and suddenly you can neither finish inhaling nor exhale and take another. That is what it feels like. There is no enlightenment, no gift from a benevolent deity."

Her eyes were wide, and she tried to force his hand away. When he released her she took a deep, gasping breath and sat back in the chair. *"Fuck!"* she yelled at him. "What the hell was *that* for?"

"A hint of what I experienced," he said with no remorse.

"I'll be dead soon enough, you know. I don't need a sneak preview." Furious, she stood and started to walk away.

He caught her by the wrist. "Ask me," he said simply.

She tried to pull away, but his grip was like iron. "Ask you what?"

"To make you as I am."

"I don't *want* to be what you are. I'm just willing to give you what you need, in return for you making me forget what *I* am." She winced as a fresh stab of agony shot through her, and leaned against the desk to keep from falling.

He sent a surge of power at her and smiled

with perverse enjoyment as the blazing fury and pain in her eyes was suddenly swamped by a wave of sexual desire. He released her wrist, and with a helpless moan she began unbuttoning her nightshirt.

CHAPTER 9

Clora had no idea what had happened, or how she'd ended up this way. One moment she was on her feet, Leo's palm against her breast, and the next she was naked, facedown on her bed, too weak to even move. Her body felt both heavy and light, and the dull throb inside her told her she'd been thoroughly satisfied. But somehow she couldn't *remember* it.

Finally she opened her eyes and turned her head. Leonardo stood shirtless, looking at a poster on her wall. "Who is Vincent Van Patten?" he asked.

"An actor," she said, her voice a rasp. Had she been screaming? Surely not, or her father would've burst in with the shotgun. Unless, of course, he was passed out drunk again in front of Johnny Carson.

Leonardo picked his tank top off the floor. "Better be splittin'."

"No, please, don't go," she said, jumping up. Sudden awareness of her nudity made her flush red; she'd never been naked in front of a boy before, not this way, not under bright lights and standing up. But at that moment keeping him with her meant infinitely more than her modesty.

She put her arms around his neck and pressed herself to him. "God, why are you so *cold*?" she said, then began kissing his neck.

He took her by the shoulders and pushed her back. "Why you so anxious to keep me here?"

"Because . . ." She choked, the words she wanted to say logjamming in her throat. How *could* she love him? Yet what else but love could inspire the physical need she felt?

He smiled. "Don't worry, baby, I ain't leaving you for good. I'll be back."

"When?"

"Tomorrow night. Or maybe the next. Leave your window open for me?"

She nodded. She felt more vulnerable than ever in her life.

He kissed her, his hands running all over her body. She moaned and could not imagine denying him anything.

Then he pulled away and slipped out the window. As silently as he'd entered, he was gone.

Clora stood in the middle of her bedroom, stark naked, fighting back tears. What had just happened to her? How could she ever face . . . well, *anyone* again? For the first time she was grateful for her isolation. She'd let a black boy have her *body*, have access to all the intimate parts she was supposed to save for her true love. Hadn't she?

She paused. She really could not remember. She did not feel sore inside, the way she did when Bruce made love to her. But if she and Leo hadn't had sex . . . what *had* they done?

She turned and saw herself in the mirror. Something caught her eye, and she walked closer, tossing her hair aside as she did so.

On the right side of her neck were two tiny punctures. They were tender, and when she tried to daub them with a wet rag they began to bleed again. It looked like a *bite*, like some smaller version of the gory vampire marks she'd seen on Channel 3's late show.

The warm blood trickled down her neck, and showed no sign of stopping. She looked around for clothes. She'd have to go to the downstairs bathroom to get the Band-Aids.

Leonardo leaped from the edge of the roof and landed silently thirty feet below. He stood immobile, listening for any sign he'd been spotted. Through one of the big porch windows he saw the blue light of a black-and-white TV. Clora's father sprawled asleep in a recliner, the less-than-vigilant dog asleep at his feet.

Leonardo smiled in satisfaction. The night had gone better than he ever anticipated. As Zginski said, the thought of draining the throbbingly alive girl of her life a little at a time was infinitely more appealing that just killing her outright. When he watched her choke down the words "I love you," he felt more powerful than ever before.

He moved silently through the woods toward Mark's truck. Just as he reached it, another vehicle turned into the same isolated tractor path and stopped behind the pickup. Leonardo immediately leaped twenty feet up into the branches of a tree, careful not to rustle the leaves when he landed.

The car's headlights illuminated Mark's truck. It was no police vehicle, but Leonardo couldn't imagine who would be out this late, looking to use this spot. The door opened, emitting a blast of "Jackie Blue" and a tall, muscular teenage boy. He had long blond hair and bangs that fell down over his eyebrows. He walked around the truck, peered inside the cab and the camper shell, then examined the license plate. Finally he shut off his car and headed through the woods with the certainty of someone who knew the way.

When he was out of sight, Leonardo dropped to the ground and went to the car. The boy hadn't locked it, so Leonardo opened the door and quickly put his hand over the dome light. He found the registration in the glove compartment. He suspected that this boy was the "Bruce" Clora had expected on her roof, but the name on the certificate startled him.

The vehicle was registered to *Byron Cocker*.

He climbed out and shut the door. There was

enough room to maneuver the truck around the car and get away, but he felt a surge of possessiveness when he thought about Clora in the Cocker boy's arms. It was as if another child had taken his favorite toy on the playground.

He dashed through the forest back to the house. By the time he reached the edge of the yard, the young man was climbing awkwardly up the drain that led down to the ground from the gutter.

Leonardo paralleled him up the branches of a tall oak. He had a clear view of Clora's bedroom window as the newcomer tapped on the glass, and his vampire senses had no trouble hearing their conversation.

"Jesus, what are you doing here?" the girl hissed as she opened the window. She wore a terry-cloth robe bundled up to her neck, as if she were freezing despite the heat.

"I told you I might come by," the boy said. His voice had a high, whining quality. "Come on, let me in."

"I'm not in the mood tonight, Bruce."

"Oh, come *on,* Clora," he whined, "I came all the way out here."

She sighed and said, "All right, for a minute."

He crawled into the window, and closed it behind them.

Leonardo sat with his back against the trunk. He could leave and be back in Memphis long before dawn. Or he could see what these two talked about, and what effect he'd had on Clora.

He tried to recall the sensation of being a live teenage boy. There must have been urgent feelings, and needs, and the kind of intensity only possible when emotions are new. He hadn't experienced a new emotion in half a century.

He climbed higher to get a better view.

Clora had no patience for Bruce Cocker tonight. On a good day he was stuck-up, vaguely stupid, and treated her like a pet he owned. He refused to be seen with her in public, and she knew why: he was the son of a legend, and she was considered white trash.

Yet because of her aching loneliness, she had accepted his attention on his terms. Since the end of the school year she'd had no visitors, been nowhere without her father, and had spent far too much time alone with her thoughts. When Bruce first called her two weeks into the summer vacation and suggested a meeting, she could hear his friends snickering in the background. But the thought of another human being, whom she could talk to and touch and make laugh, was too much for her. So she agreed.

She suspected that on that first night, when she met Bruce out behind the barn, his friends waited in his car down by the highway. She thought she heard the distant sounds of laughter and car doors. But it didn't matter: he'd kissed her, and touched her breasts, and told her she was beautiful. She was glad to let him bend her over the fender of the ancient Oldsmobile parked in the weeds. For those brief minutes she felt alive and not alone.

In the weeks that followed she allowed him to visit again and again, making him scale the outside of the decrepit house like a knight visiting an imprisoned princess in a tower. When they were alone, away from his friends, he became kinder, quieter, more vulnerable. He treated her gently, and she could pretend they were a real couple.

Now, though, something was different. She stared at him as he stumbled through her room, half-drunk already, and picked up her lighter. He wriggled his hand into the pocket of his tight jeans and emerged with a badly rolled joint, creased from his exertions. "Let's relax a little, what do you say?"

"You do what you want, I'm not in the mood," she said, deliberately sitting on the little stool in front of her vanity. He sat on the bed and patted the mattress beside him. She shook her head.

"What's the matter?" he asked.

"I just don't feel like it, is all."

"Oh." He nodded sagely. "On the rag."

"I'm not on the rag, I just don't feel like fooling around. And you're not helping things. What are you doing here, anyway? You're supposed to call first."

Bruce lifted his shirt and displayed his back. A long red welt ran parallel to his spine. Clora gasped and said, "What happened?"

Bruce lowered his shirt. "My dad's getting

worse. He drinks all the time now, and then talks about how everyone's out to get him."

"Are they?"

"Some are, I'm sure. He pisses a lot of people off. Not getting reelected sheriff really hit him hard." He kicked off his tennis shoes and they hit the floor with two loud thuds.

"Quiet!" Clora hissed. "My dad might hear."

Bruce fell back on the bed, his hands behind his head. "Mom used to tell him that it didn't matter what people thought about him, as long as they respected him to his face. I think he needed to hear that. Now there's no one to tell him."

"You can tell him."

Bruce laughed coldly. "No thanks. He already smacks me enough for having a smart mouth."

"My mom used to tell Daddy that we had all we needed here. I don't think it was true, but she made him believe it."

"Did she believe it?"

Clora shrugged. "I don't know. *I* don't. That's why I can't say it to Daddy. And he knows I just want to get out of here as soon as I'm old enough."

"Does he hit you?"

"Daddy never hits me. He just gets this sad kinda faraway look and sighs a lot." *And asks me for favors I'll never tell* anyone *about,* she added in her mind.

"I wouldn't mind that," Bruce said. "Better than getting licks with a belt."

Clora lay down beside him and slid her hand under his T-shirt. "It hurts worse than you think."

"Worse than a two-inch-wide strip of leather across your bare ass?"

"Maybe not worse, then. But different."

He fondled her nearest breast with a mechanical, proprietary grip. It did nothing for either of them. He said, "Will you suck me off?"

"I told you, I'm not in the mood."

"Please, honey. I need it."

She melted at the word "honey." He seldom called her by name, let alone with any sort of endearment. She pushed his shirt up and kissed just below his navel, where the little trail of hair led down to his crotch. He unsnapped his jeans and slid them down to his knees.

As she moved to comply with his wishes, she tossed her long hair to one side. He sat up. "What's that on your neck?"

She looked up at him. "Bug bites or something. Why?"

His face darkened with rising anger. "It's a hickey, ain't it? You're seeing somebody else. Was that his truck parked down the road?"

She glared at him. "I'm about to give you a blow job, Bruce. Maybe you should pick the fight *after*."

"*Is* it a hickey?"

She sat up angrily. "No, it's not a hickey! Look!" She tore off the Band-Aids and tilted her head. "See? Something bit me. Twice."

He scowled and muttered defensively, "Well, the way you people live out here, it's a wonder I ain't got the crabs from you already."

She glared at him. "Get out of here, Bruce," she said coldly. "I mean it."

"Or what? You'll call Daddy? My daddy'd kill yours without a second thought. And get away with it." He fastened his jeans and stomped to the window. "You know why? 'Cause you're *trash*."

She felt tears in her eyes as he opened the window and clumsily crawled out onto the roof. He turned and stuck his head back. "If I find out you're seeing somebody else, I'll kick *his* ass, then yours. You just pass that along." Then he was gone.

Clora sat on the bed, then scooted off the spot Bruce's body had warmed. She cried openly, her emotions roiling out of control. And she was more tired than she could remember. She lay down and drew up her knees, then pulled a pillow over her head. The light switch by the door might as well have been in another town.

🐾 Leonardo watched Bruce totter across the roof and climb down the pipe. He felt no animosity toward the boy; he had simply behaved according to his nature, like an animal might. Nor did he experience any real sympathy for Clora. Instead, he wondered if the apparent change in her attitude toward Bruce was a result of his influence on her. It had to be; but exactly how?

He peered back in the window. Clora was curled on the bed, the pillow over her face. The soles of her bare feet were black with dirt.

When he returned to the truck, he discovered that Bruce had petulantly slashed one of the tires before he left. He sighed in annoyance, opened the tailgate, and retrieved the spare.

CHAPTER 10

Two days later, on Thursday, Byron Cocker drove slowly up the Crabtree driveway at 8:15 A.M. He wanted to catch the man doing something wrong, something Cocker could then hold over his head. He was still steamed over the lost vehicle, and while he mainly sought revenge over the Russkie who'd stolen it from him, it was Crabtree's lack of respect that allowed it to happen. That had to be rectified as well; he might no longer be sheriff of McHale County, but Cocker still had to live here.

Dark Willows appeared deserted as it came into view. He parked at the far end of the drive to keep anyone from leaving, and got out of the car. The dog galumphed from the house barking, but Cocker just snapped, "You git on outta here!" and it reversed course, dashing under the porch.

Cocker strode across the still-damp lawn. Midges danced in the sun, dispersing their clouds as he passed through them and immediately reforming in his wake. He stamped loudly onto the porch and knocked on the edge of the screen door. "Open up!" he said in his best warrant-serving voice. "Jeb Crabtree, I know you in there!"

After a moment he heard the floorboards creak, and the inner door opened. Clora Crabtree, dressed in what appeared to be just a large red kerchief tied around her torso and a pair of worn denim short-shorts, squinted out at him. "Mr. Cocker," she said in surprise, although her voice was too weary for much enthusiasm. "You're here awful early."

"I need to see your daddy, Clora."

"I don't know where he is," she mumbled. "He was gone when I woke up this morning."

"Open up, then. I need to use your bathroom." It would give him a chance to plant something incriminating that he could return and "discover" later.

"I ain't supposed to let anybody in when Daddy's not here."

His trained cop instincts immediately pegged her slurred speech and squinted eyes as something more than a reaction to the sun. "Clora Crabtree, are you stoned on the pot?"

"No, sir," she said immediately. "I'm just a little under the weather this morning. Must be the heat."

"Your daddy's got a lot of property around this

house. He wouldn't be growing a little something on the side, would he?"

The implication seemed to penetrate her fog. "No, sir. You know my daddy, he'd never do something like that."

"How about you?"

"No, sir, I swear. I ain't smoked it, and I ain't grown it. Sir."

She also still hadn't opened the door. Cocker was about to make that an issue when Jeb Crabtree's voice called, "That you, Sheriff?"

Cocker turned. Crabtree, dressed in grease-smeared coveralls and wiping his hands on a rag, came around the corner of the house and up onto the porch. "I'd shake your hand, Sheriff, but I might get it all dirty." He saw Clora through the screen and said, "Christ Amighty, girl, go put some clothes on. Wearing nothing but a dishrag, that's just plain unacceptable."

"Yes, sir," Clora said demurely, and scurried off into the house.

Crabtree smiled, forcing his voice to stay casual. His eyes betrayed his fear, though. "What can I do for you this morning, Sheriff?"

This time Cocker did not correct him. "I need some information from you, Jeb."

"If I can."

"How would I find that fella who bought that car the other day?"

Crabtree chuckled. "I don't rightly know. He paid cash, took the title, and skeedaddled. I never even got his phone number."

Cocker slammed the heel of his right hand into the nearest porch column. He hit it as hard as he could, and it creaked under the impact. Dust and debris drifted down on the two men. The nerves in that hand hadn't worked properly since he'd been shot up, so Cocker felt little of the pain he should have. And the look on Crabtree's face was enough to justify it anyway. "So you don't even know where he took the car once he bought it?" Cocker asked.

"Nossir, I don't. Although I believe the truck he drove out here had Shelby County plates."

"What was his name again? Ziggie-inski?"

"Something like that. I got it written down inside."

"Then go fetch it. And anything else that might help me find him."

"Yes, Sheriff," Crabtree said quickly. He grabbed the handle of the screen door, but it was still latched inside. He rattled it in confusion, then scurried in one of the floor-length windows that opened onto the porch.

Cocker flexed his fingers and rubbed his knuckles. Sometimes, he reflected, you just had to punch something to get things done. He sat down on the steps and lit a cigarette.

Before he'd taken three drags off it Crabtree returned with a piece of notebook paper. "Here you go. This is all I know about him."

Cocker folded the paper without looking at it. He stood, and even two steps down he was taller than Crabtree. "Thank you, Jeb. By the way, is your little girl feeling all right?"

"She was a little peaked at breakfast. I figured it was her monthlies. She gets 'em as bad as her mama used to, God rest her."

"She been keeping company with anyone?"

"Clora? Naw, she never leaves the house. I don't know what she spends all day doing, but with that red hair and freckles, she just about bakes if she goes out in the sun very long."

"I'd keep an eye on her if I was you." He mimed smoking from a joint.

Crabtree looked down as he nodded. "I'll do that. Thank you, Sheriff."

When he returned home, Cocker entered his house and paused in the living room. When money from the movie deal first came in, Cocker hired a decorator from Memphis to redo the house and remove any hint of Vickie Lynn's presence. Taking Cocker's hypermasculine sensibility into account, the decorator lined the living-room walls with thin slices of logs, and brought in furniture made of unfinished wood with solid, square-cut corners. It was a bit like living in a hunting lodge, and suited Cocker and his son just fine. Well, he assumed it suited Bruce; he'd never really asked, and Bruce hadn't volunteered an opinion.

But even redecorating hadn't helped. Vickie Lynn's presence still filled the place, as if her ghost still roamed whenever he was absent. He imagined her drifting through like smoke, frowning at the changes and itching to give him a piece of her mind. Yet as soon as he came home she vanished again, leaving only the vague sense that he had just missed her.

And each time, it broke his heart a little more. If it wasn't for Bruce, he didn't know what he'd do.

He should've sold the house and moved him and Bruce into something nicer. He could certainly afford it, now that *Swinging Hard* was a huge hit and there was talk of a sequel. But this was his home, and to leave it would mean letting the bastards who'd killed Vicki Lynn win, even though they were now all dead. And that would never happen.

He went to his son's door and leaned close. He heard faint music. "Son, it's a pretty day," he called. "You want to go fishing?"

There was no response. He tried the doorknob, but it was locked. He wrapped his huge hand around it, tightened his grip, and turned with all his strength. The puny mechanism gave way. When he pushed, the door got stuck on a rolled-up towel stuffed under the bottom. It ripped when he yanked it aside.

Bruce sprawled on his bed, fully dressed, enormous headphones on his ears. The music blaring through them was more of that hard rock nonsense that Cocker had forbidden to be played aloud in the house. He found its glorification of raunchiness and antisocial behavior entirely unacceptable, and was close to joining his minister in the belief that it was, truly and literally, satanic.

Cocker slapped his son's foot. Bruce's eyes opened, then he sat up suddenly and yanked off the headphones. The music was so loud it made Cocker wince; he couldn't imagine that cacophony pouring directly into his ears. "Turn that racket off!" he bellowed.

Bruce scurried to stop the turntable and turn off the stereo.

"Stand up," his father said.

Bruce did so. The boy was almost as tall as Cocker, and his shoulders were as broad. He was more slender, though, a trait inherited from his mother.

Cocker backhanded him across the face so hard it knocked him onto the bed.

"What was *that* for?" Bruce cried. His face felt numb and hot.

"Bad enough that I know you're out there dealing dope like some Memphis pusher-pimp, but now you done got that Crabtree girl hooked on it, too."

"What are you talking about?" Bruce cried. The whine he knew his father hated crept into his voice despite his best efforts. "I'm not selling anything!"

"I just saw her, son. She looked like a junkie, and I know you been keeping company with her on the sly."

"I ain't had nothing to do with that ol' Crabtree trash."

"Son, I was a policeman for a long time. I know where you been, and what you been up to. You ain't smart enough to put something past me yet."

Bruce was silent for a moment. Then he began to laugh.

"You best show some respect," Cocker said darkly.

Bruce continued to guffaw. "Tell me, Daddy, were you using that same brilliant detective mind when you took Mom along on that stakeout?"

Cocker froze. Bruce continued to giggle. Then Cocker deliberately unbuckled his thick leather belt and slid it out of the loops.

By the time it hung free in his hand, Bruce was no longer laughing. He said nothing, though; experience had taught him there was no dissuading his father once he'd set his mind on violence.

Cocker doubled the belt in his hand and slapped it against his other palm. It sounded like a pistol shot. "Boy, this is gonna hurt me more than it hurts you," he said. "And it's gonna hurt you a *lot*."

"Hot enough for you?" Cocker said to the clerk at the Shelby County Motor Vehicles office. Cocker's smile had once charmed the ladies from Mobile to Louisville, but the plastic surgery after his chin was shot off made it far less endearing. One woman told him he now looked like a possum baring its fangs.

Charlene Hanks would have been immune to

Cocker's smile anyway. She knew of the former sheriff through her cousins in McHale County, many of whom had spent the night in Cocker's jail back when he wore a badge. He made no secret of his dislike for black people, and considered any who crossed his path to be "guilty until proven more guilty," as he put it. One cousin would never walk right again after a particularly vicious blow from the sheriff's famous baseball bat shattered his ankle.

The back room of the DMV was filled with the chatter of typewriters and adding machines, interspersed with the occasional clang of a metal license plate against a wooden desktop. Two dozen desks, most manned by women, processed the forms provided by the clerks at the customer windows.

Charlene opened the file folder, which held page after page of recent vehicle registrations. "If the car you mention has been registered in Memphis in the last week, it would be on this list. You're welcome to go through it. I can't imagine there's too many . . ." She glanced at the note Crabtree had given Cocker. "'Zginskis' in here." She looked up at Cocker. "Is that a real name?"

"As real as Latrelle or Melvis or some of the names you folks give your babies," Cocker said with a laugh. Then in a vaudeville accent he asked, "Now why don't you check that list for me, chile?"

Charlene sighed and shook her head. Cocker had no right to the information he sought, but he also was a celebrity and had plenty of friends in medium-high places. She flipped through the forms, looking for names that started with Z. She found *Zeigler, Zamboni,* and *Zidack,* but no *Zginski.*

As she worked, a perky little blonde tapped Cocker on the arm. "Mr. Cocker," she said in a voice so high-pitched with nervousness it could make dogs howl, "could I have your autograph?"

"Why, sure, hon," Cocker said. He took the offered pen and paper, and asked in a deep purring voice, "Now who should I make this out to?"

The blonde giggled, and Charlene rolled her eyes. She reached the end of the list, and waited for Cocker's attention to return to her. He signed three more autographs for simpering women before he turned back to Charlene and asked, "Any luck?"

"There's no Zginski on this list. He's riding with bad tags."

Cocker shook his head. The man could not simply vanish, that wouldn't be fair at all. God wouldn't do that to him. "Thanks. Will you let me know when he shows up?"

"Mr. Cocker, I have an awful lot to do around here besides running errands for you. And as I recall, you're just a civilian now anyway. Any cooperation you get is strictly a courtesy."

Cocker scowled in frustration. "I'm pretty sure this fella was a foreigner, one of them dee-fectors from Russia. How would I go about tracking that down?"

"You asking me?" Charlene said dubiously.

"Surely y'all must have dealt with illegal aliens

before. How do you go about keeping up with them?"

"If they're illegal, we have to wait until they get caught."

Just loud enough for Charlene to hear, he growled, "Are you getting mouthy? Don't you be getting smart with me, girl."

That was the final straw. Charlene jumped to her feet and put hands on her hips. Her chair rolled into the desk behind her. She barely came up to Cocker's chest, but her anger made her seem much taller. "And don't you be treating me like I'm damn Mrs. Butterworth, then," she bellowed. "You may have lots of important friends, but it don't give you the right to march in here and act like you own the place!"

The rest of the room fell silent. A Shelby County deputy sheriff, so young his face was still pink from his morning shave, appeared beside Charlene. "Is there a problem here?"

Cocker, aware that he had an audience, shook his head and patted Charlene on the cheek. "Just another sign that ol' desegregation might've been rushed a little." Then he gave Charlene a quick kiss on the forehead, which left her speechless as he sauntered away, his enormous frame drawing every eye. He waved to the room as he went out the door.

"Just a friendly warning, Charlene," the deputy said after Cocker was gone. "That's not a man you should piss off."

"Well, I ain't gonna sit here and be pissed *on*,"

she snapped. "If he thinks he's getting any more information out of *this* office, he's a bigger honky fool than he looks like."

"That's enough of that!" called out Mr. Biltmore, the supervisor. He stood in the door to his office. "I won't stand for racial slurs in this workplace. Charlene, get in here right now!"

In his car outside, Cocker waited as the air conditioner cooled the interior. He should just let it go, he knew. Really, it was just a car.

And yet Zginski's arrogant sneer, the utter lack of *respect,* just would not fade from his memory. Who the hell did that foreign bastard think he was, anyway, swiping a car out from under a real American?

He'd come all the way to Memphis on the hottest day of the year so far, and it had been a bust. He wanted a drink before starting the long drive back to McHale County, and maybe a real man's lunch. He knew just the place to get it, too.

CHAPTER 11

The lunch crowd packed the Ringside when Byron Cocker entered, and he paused in the door to let his eyes adjust. As they did, he heard the usual wave of whispers spread through the room. Even people who hadn't seen *Swinging Hard* recognized him.

"Byron!" Gerry Barrister called as he worked his way through the crowd. He was pale and haggard, but his good nature was undimmed. The two men shook hands. "Didn't know you were in town. Come on over here and have a drink."

"Think I can get a sandwich, too?"

"Sandwich, hell. Byron Cocker gets the best steak in the house!"

Barrister led Cocker to the bar and waved Fauvette over. "Fauvette, this is the world-famous

Byron Cocker, inspiration for the movie *Swinging Hard*. We wrestled together back before he turned to law enforcement. I pinned him in less than a minute one time, too."

Fauvette looked from Barrister to the much larger Cocker. "Really?"

"That's 'cause the promoter decided he'd be a better heel than I would be," Cocker said. "I was more the handsome baby-face type. Well, back then, at least."

"Listen to him," Gerry said. "He used to have the women crawling all over him. Couldn't keep a jock strap for girls stealing 'em for souvenirs."

"Not my fault them tights showed off what God gave me," Cocker said with a grin. Then he took his first real look at Fauvette and frowned. "Honey, are you old enough to be working in a bar?"

"Oh, yes, sir," Fauvette assured him. "I just *look* young."

"Now, Byron, you think I'd be hiring underage girls?" Barrister said. "This is a respectable business. Hell, starting this weekend we'll even have live music."

"What's your poison today, Mr. Cocker?" Fauvette asked with her best disarming smile.

Barrister waved her close and said just loud enough for Cocker to hear, "Give him a silver bullet in a jacket."

"Anything you say, boss." Fauvette knelt and took a can of Coors beer, illegal east of the Mississippi, from a special cooler hidden on the bottom shelf. She wrapped a fake Budweiser label around it and presented it to Cocker. "Compliments of the house?" she asked Barrister.

"Of course. And have the kitchen whip up a steak for my friend, too."

Cocker took a drink and sighed contentedly. "Man, that's good stuff."

"Good thing you don't carry a badge anymore, isn't it?" Barrister said, his laugh just a hair too forced.

Cocker sipped the beer and nodded his thanks to Fauvette. The instant their eyes met he felt an odd, vaguely familiar chill from her, and the cut on his hand tingled.

And then, as Barrister droned on about their shared wrestling past, Cocker felt *another* tingle, the one that unmistakably warned him of danger. He turned toward the door.

Rudy Zginski entered, paused, and looked around.

Cocker couldn't believe it. After convincing himself he'd never find the stuck-up Russkie again, here he just walks into the same bar, big as life. What were the chances? Clearly the good Lord was on his side, as always.

Cocker hunched his shoulders and tried to duck down out of obvious sight. He was the tallest person in the room, which was usually a good thing except when he wanted to be discreet. He peered at Zginski through gaps in the crowd. Barrister obliviously continued his story.

Zginski stood rigid, hands formally clasped behind his back. Despite the heat he wore a black polyester suit over a white shirt with the top two buttons undone. A simple gold chain hung loose around his neck. A white handkerchief peeked from the coat's pocket, almost hidden by the wide lapels, and matched his white belt. His shoes were white leather with stacked heels. His gaze traveled methodically around the room like a radar antenna.

Then he turned and looked directly at Cocker.

Cocker's throat constricted with the sudden certainty that the smaller man *scared* him. Those eyes gave him the same shudder as the girl bartender's.

Then he realized that Zginski wasn't looking at him, but *past* him at Fauvette. The girl gazed back, as if some unspoken communication passed between them. Both stood perfectly still; for them the loud, crowded room seemed not to exist.

Cocker's attention flicked from one to the other. There was definitely a resemblance: both were pale, seemed unnaturally calm and slightly removed from the world around them. And both had the same cold, slightly creepy eyes. True, the girl didn't have his accent, but could they be *related*?

Then Zginksi turned away and disappeared into the crowd. This broke the moment, just as Barrister said, ". . . and that's the truth. Ain't that right, Byron?"

"Sure thing, Gerry. 'Scuse me for a minute, I need to visit your facilities."

"Well, hurry back, that steak'll be up in a minute."

Cocker moved through the crowd, accepting handshakes and back pats with as much graciousness as he could. He saw no sign of Zginski, but was certain the man had not gone back out the front door. He looked in the men's room, but only a fat man in a cowboy hat stood at the urinal and all the stalls were empty. Where had he gone?

He stood at the back of the dining room and looked over the crowd until he noticed a door marked EMPLOYEES ONLY. It opened onto a service hallway, and he quickly slipped inside. He heard voices ahead of him and moved quietly toward them.

He stopped when he saw Zginski standing in the doorway to a small room with a metal star tacked to the door. Inside was a young woman with long black hair who was restringing a guitar. Cocker stayed perfectly still and strained to catch their conversation over the restaurant's muffled noise.

The dark-haired woman looked up at Zginski with a wry little smile. There was something recognizable about her, too, but in a different, more tangible way: she *looked* familiar. She was too old to be a friend of Bruce's, and too young to be any of the women he'd once dallied with. She was a musician, so it was possible he'd seen her photo on a poster or record sleeve. Yes, *that* was it: he'd seen her picture. But where? He closed his eyes and tried to decipher their conversation.

It was no use; he could not make out the words. He quietly backed away and returned to the main room.

Patience smiled wryly at Zginski. "Why should I tell you what Fauvette and I talk about?"

"Because it would be in your best interest to establish me as an ally," he said.

"Ooh, a threat, how sexy." She plucked the guitar strings and adjusted the tuning pegs. The room was now freshly wallpapered, with a vanity and mirror in one corner. Only the industrial sink with attached mop-wringer remained to hint of its former use. "Are you being all male-chauvinist-pig because you're afraid of a liberated woman?"

"Hardly."

She batted her eyes at him. "Well, then, it must be because you think I'm pretty."

Zginski scowled. It was the closest a vampire could come to blushing. "I assure you, I—"

"So you *don't* think I'm pretty?"

"That is entirely beside the point," he snapped. She was making him sound foolish, and he hated that.

"Are you sure?" She lay the guitar aside, stood, and put a hand on his chest. "I've met a lot of men over the years, and I know when I make one's heart beat faster. And in your case I mean that metaphorically."

Zginski started to speak, but before he could Patience pressed even closer. She slid one hand around his waist, while the other tickled lightly at his goatee. She said, "We could reduce each other to quivering little puddles of desire, you know. That might be a lot of fun."

He gently pushed the hand away from his chin, but did not break the embrace. "I am afraid not. Not until I know more about you."

She took his wrist and flicked her tongue over the lifeless pulse point. "What is it you want to know?"

Something stirred within him. She was not using any vampiric influence, either; it was pure seduction, which he had never experienced as a vampire. He was both intrigued by her courage, and infuriated at the ease of his own response. "How," he said, his voice steady despite her ministrations, "did you become what you are?"

She pulled away, looking anywhere but at him, and smoothed her dress. "That might be a story for another time. I'm not saying I won't tell you, just not here. Not like this, standing in a closet while people eat and drink twenty feet away." She looked up at him seriously. "Can you accept that?"

He nodded.

"But it's quid pro quo. I want to know about you, too. You're clearly from Eastern Europe, and for some reason you talk like you've been shut up in a drawer for the last century. There must be a good story behind that."

That isn't far from the truth, Zginski thought.

It also meant Fauvette had been discreet, which pleased him. He said with a courtly nod, "I will also explain my background."

"Good. Then maybe I'll know why Fauvette's in love with you when you act like she's not even there." At his scowl she added, "Oh, come on, I'm a girl, too. We can spot these things."

"Fauvette and I have a mutually acceptable relationship."

She giggled. "Wow, with an attitude like that you must have the girls lining up. Even without being able to seduce them with a glance."

"Your own attitude is just as perplexing."

"It is? Why?"

"You seem to take nothing seriously."

"Oh, that's not true. Not at all. It's just that, as time passes, the list of serious things gets shorter and shorter. Haven't you found that to be the case?"

He suddenly wanted to end this conversation. She treated him as an equal, and more, seemed to find his discomfort amusing; he needed to regroup. "We shall talk later. I *am* looking forward to your performance tomorrow night, however."

"Groovy," she said with a smile, then before he could move she stepped close and kissed him. At first he merely let her, then with as much surprise as arousal he began to respond. She broke it off before it went too far.

"It's even better," she whispered, "when you help."

"Indeed," he said. She giggled.

He took her chin lightly, then tightened his grip. "I should warn you, though. I will tolerate no behavior that constitutes a danger to me. If you intend such, you would be well advised to find another location for it."

He released her, and for a moment her eyes flared with anger. Then the amusement returned. "You certainly do take yourself seriously, Mr. Zginski. But I promise you, what I 'intend' is of no danger at all to you."

"We shall see."

She put her hand on his chest again. "Of course, what I 'intend' for *you* might be considered dangerous. By some." She touched her upper lip with her tongue and said softly, "Care to close the door?"

"I do not feel that would be advisable," he said seriously. Then he added, "At this time."

She smiled, displaying the tips of her fangs. "And we have plenty of that, don't we?"

"We do," he agreed.

Gerry Barrister sat behind his desk, digging frantically through the scattered papers in search of his Polaroid camera. He wanted a shot of him with Byron to go on the "wall of fame" beside the front door.

He looked up and yelped in surprise. Zginski stood in the office door. Behind him, the kitchen crew worked to keep up with the lunch orders.

"Dang, Mr. Z., you keep slipping up on me like

a copperhead, you'll give me a heart attack one of these days." He sat back and took a few deep breaths.

"How are the ledgers for this month?" Zginski asked with no preliminaries. With the kitchen's bright lights behind him, Barrister couldn't see his face.

He smiled and said casually, "Well, we've had some expenses I didn't count on, and the price of everything's gone up, so . . ."

"Will you turn a profit?"

Barrister couldn't bring himself to look at Zginski. "I don't think so. We'll get close. But . . . no."

"I invested in your establishment with the idea of increasing my wealth, not watching it dwindle," Zginski said. His tone was even and calm, but the threat was there.

"Look, I know you own a big chunk of me—"

"I own thirty percent of your restaurant; I have no interest in owning any percentage of you."

"That's just a figure of speech. We use those here in America. But really, I got plans. I've found this amazing musician who's starting here tomorrow night, and once word gets out about her, the place will be packed to the gills."

"The place is 'packed to the gills' right now. Acquiring patrons does not seem to be the problem. The trouble seems to be in the management."

Barrister swallowed hard. "Hey, look, I'm doing the best I can."

"I am certain of that. But is it good enough?"

Barrister got to his feet. He was a foot taller

than Zginski and sixty pounds heavier. "Listen, you ex-Commie bastard, you think you can come in here—"

"If you wish to be rid of me," Zginski said calmly, "simply return my investment, in cash, and I shall depart."

Barrister forced down his anger. "Now, don't get crazy on me, we can work this out. This place is a gold mine, you know? We just have to dig down to the vein." He mimed using a shovel.

"We will talk again soon," Zginski said, and left.

Barrister's hands shook as he continued looking for the camera. Letting Zginski buy in to the Ringside had been the dumbest thing he'd ever done; the more he thought about it, in fact, the less sense it made. What the hell had he been drinking that day?

CHAPTER 12

Zginski emerged into the afternoon sun and immediately put on his dark-lensed glasses. Recently he'd seen a film on television, one of the innumerable versions of *Dracula,* in which the title character crumbled to dust at the mere touch of a sunbeam. It amused him anew to think that Fauvette and her friends also once believed that they, too, would perish if sunlight struck them. Perhaps he erred by letting them learn otherwise.

He had invested a large amount of Alisa's money in the restaurant, subtly using his powers to overcome Barrister's resistance. Barrister really needed no additional capital, since he was well on his way to becoming profitable, but Zginski had long-range plans that involved acquiring an establishment like this. The Ringside already had a regular clientele, and before the end of the year he intended to be its sole owner. It was the main reason he had, with equal subtlety, steered Fauvette toward Barrister as a victim. Barrister's fate did not concern him.

He shut the delivery door behind him. Tzigane, once again parked by the Dumpster, gleamed in the light. Crabtree had done a fine job polishing the car, and not even dust from recent driving had dimmed the reflective chrome. He sighed contentedly.

The door opened again and Fauvette said, "So that's it, huh?" She stood beside him and shielded her eyes with one hand. "It's definitely . . . shiny."

"She is," he agreed. "I call her 'Tzigane.' "

"What's that mean?"

"It is a woman's name in my country."

"The name of . . . ?"

In a moment of weakness, Zginski had confided more about his past to Fauvette than he'd ever told anyone. "Yes, if you must know. For good or ill, the first Tzigane changed my life. I suspect that this Tzigane will do the same."

"Oh," Fauvette said. She moved closer, wishing the sun wasn't so damned bright. It might not kill her as she once believed, but it certainly left her feeling drained. "You ran off before we could talk earlier."

"Did we need to speak?"

"Well, we didn't talk the other day because you were showing off for Patience, and now today . . . I don't know, I guess I thought you might *want* to."

He looked at her. She saw her reflection in his sunglasses. "Because of that night in the warehouse?"

His cold, superior tone made her angry. "Would that be a bad reason? I thought it meant something, you know? To us both."

He smiled. She had always been a simple creature, and now that she so blatantly wanted him to herself, her simplicity was somehow pathetic. Still, he had a tiny affection for her, the way a huntsman might for a favorite dog. Or so he convinced himself. And she was still useful to him, so he allowed her to nurse her little crush.

He touched her cheek paternally. "It is a perfectly fine reason. Alas, I cannot accommodate it at this time."

Her eyes blazed with anger at his condescension, but before she could knock his hand away he walked across the parking lot to the car. When he settled into the seat he smelled leather and petrochemicals, and the rumble when he turned the ignition made him sigh with contentment. When he looked back at the building, the door was closed and Fauvette was gone.

He pulled carefully out into traffic and headed across town to rest at Alisa's.

Cocker sat in his own car. The steak Barrister had promised him, secure in its take-out box, filled the hot interior with its delicious odor. He could see the Mustang's front bumper from where he was parked, and stared at it so intently that when it suddenly moved forward he jumped. The car pulled past him and into traffic without a glance from its driver.

Cocker followed, keeping at least one vehicle between himself and Zginski. The distinctive Mustang was easy to trail since Zginski drove tentatively and slowly, like an old lady.

Cocker's plan was simple and linear. If he discovered where the disrespectful foreigner lived, he could work with the local police to arrange an arrest, and if he could get Zginski arrested, he could then get him transferred back to McHale County. Although he was no longer sheriff he still had the keys to the jail, and the current head man had once been his deputy. No one would stop him from visiting Zginski in his cell, or from giving his trademark baseball bat a good workout.

He clenched his teeth and felt the now-familiar jolt of pain where his shattered jawbone had been spliced together. He had been on a similar mission the night Vicki Lynn was killed, and for a moment her presence beside him in the car was almost tangible. *That* stakeout and pursuit had ended in horror, and he got a chill at the thought this one might. But that was silly; what threat could the slight, no doubt light-in-his-loafers foreigner pose to him?

Fauvette wandered into Barrister's empty office, closed the door, and sat on the couch. With the lights out and the blinds drawn, it was almost like a refuge. She tried to calm her racing thoughts, but too much had changed too quickly and it all logjammed in her mind.

For decades she had roamed the shadows of Memphis, taking lives as needed from among society's lowest tiers. Then along came Zginski, who showed her that her greatest fear—the light of the sun—was essentially harmless. He gave her back the daylight, and her world altered irrevocably.

And then . . .

The night she became a vampire, dying wasn't the worst thing that happened. The old vampire who killed her left her body lying in plain sight, and her virginal corpse was raped by those awful Scoval brothers while it was still warm. Vampires who died and rose as virgins were spared any of the emotions of physical desire, but Fauvette died a virgin, then rose as a deflowered woman. As a result she felt desire as much as anyone, but her virginity was restored each time it was taken. She was doomed to an eternity reliving the pain that most women felt only once.

Until, that is, Zginski also gave her back her sexuality, by using his powerful vampiric influence to arouse her to such a level that the pain of losing her maidenhead was lost in the roar of her lustful blood. It had been an amazing experience, and she desperately wanted it again.

But Zginski seemed to think no more of it, or her, than he did his latest victim. And she knew how truly little that was.

Still, there were times when he looked at her and the hard selfishness in his eyes melted just enough to give her hope. He would smile or touch her face with unexpected gentleness. Perhaps, she thought, he was as confused by his own feelings as she was.

That is, until Patience, full of music and mystery, showed up.

But she couldn't hate Patience, could she? She'd practically begged her to share the way she fed on energy instead of blood, and the woman's embrace had been the most comforting thing Fauvette had experienced since becoming what she was.

No, she couldn't hate Patience. Or Zginski. She could only hate herself, for being too weak and insubstantial to hold his attention, and too needy and childish to ever be Patience's equal.

She hung her head and sighed.

Because he was both preoccupied and sun-weakened, at first Zginski did not realize that someone followed him. But finally he sensed the danger, and a glance in the rearview mirror showed him the nondescript car two vehicles back. He immediately recognized it as Byron Cocker's.

Zginski frowned. This was both worrying and perplexing. He had very deliberately put the onus of the transaction on Crabtree so Cocker would blame him and forget about Zginski. So why was Cocker now following him? And when had it started? Did the man already know about his connection to Alisa?

He suddenly changed lanes to verify his suspicions. Someone in another car honked a horn. At first Cocker's vehicle stayed where it was, then slowly it drifted behind him again.

Zginski flexed his fingers on the steering wheel. The man clearly had skill at this sort of thing, something Zginski lacked. And, with the sun beating down from the arid sky, his powers were too weak to compensate. But he'd seen *Vanishing Point, The Seven-Ups, Grand Theft Auto,* and of course *Gone in 60 Seconds.* Surely he'd learned something.

The interstate highway loomed ahead, passing over the street on which he traveled. At the last moment he accelerated and cut across two lanes, eliciting horn blasts and unmistakable hand gestures. He shot up the ramp, barely avoided rear-ending a pickup, and quickly merged into traffic. In the rearview mirror he watched Cocker make a similar maneuver, barely missing a Trans Am that blared its disapproval. In moments Cocker was behind him again, this time making no attempt at pretense.

Zginski grew anxious. What was this all about? Surely not just the car. He began weaving again, and Cocker stuck to him as if attached by a string. He would have to try something unexpected, and the thought filled him with a frisson of fear.

Another exit was ahead, and as he approached he saw that the grassy shoulder extended down a gentle slope to the bottom of the ramp. He turned the wheel hard to the right and gunned the engine.

The Mustang hopped the curb, dug ruts as it shot down the hill, and finally bounced into the traffic passing under the interstate. Almost at once he cut back onto the next ramp and ended up back on the highway, headed in the opposite direction. He took the next exit at sixty miles an hour, barely avoiding collisions when he merged into traffic on Airways Boulevard.

He parked in the lot beside a shuttered building that had formerly been a barbecue restaurant and waited. He neither saw nor sensed any pursuit, and after half an hour decided he had, indeed, lost his pursuer.

But that was only the immediate problem. Somehow Cocker had tracked him down at Barrister's establishment, and considering his investment of both money and time, this presented a problem. He would have to phone Fauvette and tell her to report any of Cocker's further visits.

And, he realized with surprising disappointment, discretion might force him to miss Patience's show the next night.

Cocker sat at the red light fuming, both from the heat and his temper.

The fucking foreign dipshit asshole had *lost* him. That insane turn down the grassy ramp had completely surprised him, and by the time he'd reached the street below Zginski had vanished. He spent thirty minutes searching for the Mustang parked in some lot or driveway. He had not found it.

Finally he pulled in at a convenience store and bought a quart bottle of Miller. He sat in his hot car and drank it, feeling his tension dissipate as his head grew fuzzier. He ate the still-warm steak with his bare hands. Eventually he had to pee, so he went inside to use the restroom.

As he stood at the urinal, reading the graffiti scratched on either side of the condom machine, he decided on his next move. He might not be able to follow Zginski, but the man had been talking to Gerry's new musical act, and Cocker knew where to find *her*. She would lead him to Zginski, either willingly or otherwise. He had ways of making women talk.

He stopped urinating as his penis stiffened at the thought.

CHAPTER 13

When he arrived at Alisa's, Zginski parked the car in the backyard and came in through the kitchen. As always, it made him pause for a moment. He had been in some of Europe's gaudiest dwellings, from the palace of Versailles to London's Hyde Park mansions, but even these paled in comparison to the sheer audacity of common home furnishings in this new era. It seemed that the ability to decorate in a manner previously reserved for royalty had bred an utter lack of restraint in the populace. When every home looked like a palace, none of them were.

Alisa's kitchen was a prime example. The wooden cabinets were painted orange and lacquered over so that they gleamed like plastic. The wallpaper was a cubist pattern of interlocking black, brown, orange, and yellow blocks, while the ceiling used the same colors, but in a different pattern. The floor's tile was cream-colored, with hexagonal starburst patterns in each square. The overall effect, he mused, was what it must feel like to stand inside a tangerine.

He went into the living room, where he found her at work. From behind her desk Alisa looked over her glasses at him and almost gasped in surprise. She had never seen him look *worried* before. "Rudy?"

"I have put my car in the rear," he said as he drew the curtain across the front window, then peeked out around the edge. The late-afternoon sun was golden and intense. "I apologize if I have damaged the lawn, but the grass is so dry it seems unlikely."

She stood and put her notebook aside. She wore sweatpants and a Memphis State T-shirt too large for her, which made her look even more wan and wasted. "Why?"

Zginski took off his sport coat and draped it across the back of the recliner. "The drought, most certainly."

"No, I mean, why did you put your car back there?"

He debated whether or not to tell her, and finally decided in favor of it. "I found myself pursued earlier today."

Her eyes opened wide. "By who? The police?"

"No."

She said more quietly, "It wasn't a vampire hunter or anything, was it?"

Zginski smiled. She asked with such seriousness that it became absurd. "No. I believe my pursuer was once with the police in some capacity, but is no longer in their employ."

"Why?"

"Why does any man leave a job? Perhaps he was dissatisfied, or wished more payment for his services."

She swatted his arm. "*Stop* that. You know what I mean. Why were the ex-police chasing you?"

He undid the top button of his shirt. Fashion in this era may have been simpler, but it remained just as uncomfortable. "I believe it was the man who attempted to buy the car. I told you about him before."

Alisa's eyes opened even wider. "Byron Cocker? *Byron Cocker* was chasing you?"

"Indeed." He sat on the couch and unzipped the leather stack-heeled boots.

She looked out the window herself at the empty residential street. "That's *insane*. He's not a sheriff anymore, he lost the last election. I remember reading about it. That movie embarrassed everyone in McHale County, so they elected one of his former deputies instead."

Zginski sat back with a sigh. "Then perhaps he is merely a man who reacts badly when he feels wronged."

Alisa sat down beside him. "He's trouble, Rudy.

Back when he *was* sheriff he pulled over a pair of my black students, and beat them so badly one lost the sight in his right eye."

"I am not worried about his physical prowess."

"No, but he also doesn't give up. Ever. Even after his wife was murdered and his face was blown off, he didn't give up."

He looked at her suspiciously. Had Cocker found him through Alisa? "How do you know so much about him? Is he an acquaintance?"

"No, I saw the movie."

"Ah, yes. The gentleman who sold me the car mentioned it."

Alisa nodded. *"Swinging Hard."*

Zginski picked up the newspaper from the ottoman. "Perhaps I may learn something by seeing the same film."

"It's probably not playing anymore; it came out a couple of years ago. My point is, the man is *crazy.* I don't know how you got him on your trail, but he's a good one to avoid. Especially for a man like you, with so many secrets."

Zginski found the movie listings, but as Alisa predicted there was no mention of *Swinging Hard.* "What is the plot of this movie?"

"Well, Cocker was the sheriff over in McHale County. There were a bunch of bootleggers and crooked gamblers settled in along the state line, and they tried to bribe him to look the other way. When that didn't work, they ambushed him, killed his wife, and shot him in the face. He survived, and then beat the main villain to death with a baseball bat. Hence the title."

"And this is a true story?"

"I'm sure they simplified it so it was pure good-versus-evil. The real Cocker was—is—a racist red-neck thug, by all accounts. But his wife *was* killed, he *was* shot in the face, and he *did* clean out the gang."

Zginski went back to the window and watched a car pull into a driveway on the opposite side of the street. There was still no sign of Cocker, and his sense of pursuit told him he'd made good his escape.

"Is he out there?" Alisa asked.

"No, I have eluded him." He turned to face her. "And I will deal with him, so you do not have to worry."

"Right," she said wryly.

Zginski, annoyed by her sarcasm, reached out with his power. Softly but with great fury he said, "If I say you should not worry, you will do as I say."

Alisa swallowed hard, her priorities instantly realigned. She ached for him now, both intimately and emotionally. The pure sexual lust he first inspired in her had now, with time, become something she could only classify as love. It left her craving more, even the moment after an orgasm. There was never enough to satisfy her. She reached for the bottom hem of the T-shirt to pull it off.

He held up his hand. "I must rest. I will attend to you when I return."

Alisa hated the pleading whine in her voice. "What? You're just *leaving* me this way?"

"The next time I give you an assurance, you would do well to accept it without the irony." He headed toward the cellar door.

Alisa stared after him, her body on fire with sexual need. She could minister to herself, she knew, and it would dim the intensity a bit. But only the touch of his icy skin, and the sensation of his teeth penetrating her neck, would cause this arousal to dissipate.

She slid her hands beneath the T-shirt and squeezed her breasts. "Oh, you *bastard,*" she breathed, and sank back onto the couch. Not since she'd been a teenager had she so wantonly touched herself.

As she endured the effects of his power, she also felt absurdly grateful. He'd completely removed the pain from her consciousness.

Zginski padlocked the cellar door behind him and descended the stairs. The basement was a small concrete room containing the water heater and assorted boxes of miscellanea belonging to Alisa's late husband. The one small window had been boarded over, which rendered the room pitch-black. For Zginski that was not an issue.

A faux Oriental screen separated the rest of the room from the cot where Zginski slept. On the back of the screen, and the concrete wall opposite, he'd taped up pictures from various magazines of the devices that seemed central to his new era. It was a silly affectation, but somehow waking among these images helped him grow more acclimated. He still did not understand all of them, such as the "pet rock," or why "linear tracking" made a modern gramophone work more efficiently. But most of them were of automobiles, and the shiny surfaces and exposed engines filled him with energy whenever he awoke to them.

He settled onto the cot, feet crossed at the ankles and hands folded across his chest. A vampire's sleep rendered him indistinguishable from a corpse: his joints would stiffen like rigor mortis, he had no pulse or respiration, and his skin was cold to the touch. If discovered in this state he would be helpless, so finding a secure spot was crucial.

Folklore said that vampires must return to their graves to rest, and for some he knew that was true. Many simple peasants, disoriented and confused by their new vampiric state, did exactly that. It took a certain mental sophistication to accept that one had become a vampire, and not everyone could accomplish it. Many embodied every vampire cliché because they thought they were *supposed* to behave that way. Fortunately, because of this they were often quickly destroyed. As Leonardo once said in his peasant patois, play by the rules and you're sure to lose.

Even Fauvette and her friends were gullible enough to believe what the movies, the modern equivalent of folklore, told them: sunlight would destroy them, they must kill each victim, and the universe's morality damned them for all eternity simply for being what they were.

Zginski, too, had fallen prey to these delusions—for about a minute. He had been disoriented and puzzled after he clawed free of his coffin and emerged from his grave, but never once believed the superstitious nonsense about the moral state of his new condition. He had changed, irrevocably and permanently, but he was no more bound by the laws of God and man than he had been as a mortal human being. He quickly realized the advantage, though, in using these superstitions for his own ends, such as revenge on the woman who had inadvertently turned him.

Until Sir Francis Colby, and that night in Wales sixty years earlier.

He would adjust his schedule, he decided. Over-confidence had been his downfall before, and now it led him to move about more and more in day-light, when his powers were weakest. Now he would resume a mainly nocturnal existence, and prowl the day only when it was unavoidable.

His mind drifted as his body transitioned into corpse-sleep. As always, for just an instant before he lost consciousness, he felt a jolt of terror that he might in fact awaken in that ghastly limbo again, that his resurrection had been simply a vast cosmic hallucination or dream. It was one of the few things that completely and utterly terrified him. But then the usual nothingness took him over, and like all dead things, he had no worries at all.

❧ Alisa, her naked body soaked with sweat, stood just outside the cellar door and pressed her cheek to the wood. This was her house, hers and Chad's, but since Zginski took over her life she felt like a guest in her own home. He used her car, her money, her resources, and especially her body whenever he felt like it. And he made her *want* it.

She wanted it now, that was certain. She wanted to feel his weight on her, wrap her legs around his wiry form, and pound up against him until the need within her was sated. But try as she might, she could never conjure an actual memory of them having sex. Surely they must have; whenever she awoke after he'd fed on her, she felt satisfied and a little sore in that unmistakable way. But why couldn't she actually *recall* it?

She had been working frantically on the *Festa Maggotta*'s section on vampires, but progress was slow. For most of the years she'd plugged away at the translation, she considered the book a mere collection of folk tales. Now that her worldview included undead lovers, though, she saw it as a source of useful, practical information. If she learned more about vampires, she might be able to adjust the balance of power, which at the moment tipped entirely in Zginski's favor. She would love to see him as desperate as she was, just once before she died.

She scratched her fingernails on the wood. It sounded pitiful and plaintive, like a trapped kitten. He was down there, immobile and asleep, as helpless in his way as she was. She could free her life from this parasite simply by knocking down the door and driving a stake through his heart. Would he wither and crumble as she watched?

But she knew she wouldn't do that. If he left her, the pain would return. Her death was a foregone conclusion, and she didn't fear it; but she dreaded the deep agony as her body devoured itself. Since he arrived she'd lost weight and grown weak, but her hair was back and she was able to work with a reasonably clear head. Without him she would be bedridden, bald, and so doped on morphine she would barely know day from night.

The wooden door felt cool against her heated skin, and she squirmed against it with an unmistakably sexual rhythm. "Please," she whispered, "wake up soon."

CHAPTER 14

Barrister unplugged the jukebox, stepped up to the microphone, and said, "Howdy, everybody. Hope you're enjoying your drinks and dinners, and don't forget to tip your servers, they work mighty hard."

"Then you ought to pay 'em more," someone called out.

Barrister chuckled, enjoying this brief return to the spotlight. Here at least he didn't have to worry about being blindsided with a folding chair. "I've got a special treat for you tonight. The Ringside is about to start featuring live music with our drinks and world-class steaks, and tonight I want you to see the reason for that. She's an amazing performer, and I can almost guarantee you've never seen or heard anything like her. She'll flat-out take your breath away. Folks, I give you Patience Bolade."

He gestured to the side of the stage. Patience stepped up to polite applause. She wore a macramé vest with a palm tree pattern on the back, and tight-fitting dark blue slacks. A Native American-style choker encircled her throat. Her pale face sported deep blue eye shadow. She carried her acoustic guitar, and as she put the strap over her head she said, "I'm not sure I can live up to that introduction, Gerry. But I'll sure do my best."

She strummed once and said, "Like Gerry said, my name is Patience. And it's true, I have a lot of it. But you know what they say." She smiled, sly and sophisticated and totally in command. "That's a lot of patience to *lose*."

There was some laughter, but she didn't wait for the joke to settle in. Instead she began to play rapidly and confidently, barely glancing at her hands. She hummed, loud and deep, and it was like a signal going out that locked the attention of every person in the room on her.

Then she began to sing.

Barrister watched from the bar, and Fauvette had to peer around him. Every face was rapt and attentive; no one looked away or spoke, and no silverware clinked. Even the waitresses and bus-boys stood immobile, a couple of them in midmotion. She felt a tingling as the energy from the crowd found its way to Patience. No one supplied very much, but the combined surge was strong enough to make the air shimmer in her vampire vision, like waves of summer heat over a highway.

There was no question of seeing it now, it was as plain as trees waving in a storm.

"Holy shit," Barrister whispered. "She's *amazing*."

"She's built like a brick shithouse, ain't she?" another man at the bar said admiringly. His friend immediately shushed him.

Fauvette grew more excited at the prospect of learning to do this herself. Except . . . how? Would she have to sing or perform in some way? Or could she learn to do it by just willing people to send energy her way?

When the first song ended there was a moment of total, complete silence. The air conditioner, the compressor on the refrigerators beneath the bar, even the traffic outside could all be heard. Then as if someone threw a switch, every person in the bar began to clap, whistle, and cheer. Most of them got to their feet. Patience stood with a shy smile, accepting the approval with apparent bemused delight.

Only Byron Cocker did not join in. He stood in the shadows at the back of the room, fighting to keep his attention on the task at hand and not the enchanting Patience. He could not explain why he was suddenly so exhausted, since he'd deliberately had no alcohol. But he knew Zginski would show up, and he was not about to let the man slip past him this time.

• • •

Zginski placed the bouquet of roses in Patience's dressing room, making sure the note was plainly visible. He went back into the hall and opened the door to the dining room just enough to catch a glimpse of her onstage. From this angle he saw both her and the rapt faces of the crowd. She was telling a story to introduce her next song, and it was as if everyone in the audience was hypnotized by her words; they stared, some with bites of food halfway to their mouths.

Her voice needed very little amplification to fill the room, and she played the guitar expertly. Halfway through she stopped singing and admonished, "It's okay to clap along, you know," and everyone immediately did.

Zginski smiled. He was well rested, well fed, and at his full power. He had slept through the day and emerged with all his vampiric abilities at their strongest. Nothing happened around him of which he was unaware, so he knew that Cocker was in the restaurant, no doubt with his eyes peeled for him. The ex-lawman would end the evening sorely disappointed.

Something moved in the corner of his vision, and he squinted. For a moment the air seemed to tremble and swirl around Patience, as if she stood in the eye of a storm. He wondered if it was indeed the strange energy effect Fauvette had described, or just the result of the rumbling air conditioner sending its vibration through the building.

Zginski closed the door and returned to the

kitchen. Vander the cook waved at him as he went out the back door. "Float on, Mr. Z.," he called.

"And you as well," Zginski replied. He'd gone out of his way to befriend the cook, because he intended to keep Vander when he took over from Barrister. He wanted as little discontinuity as possible; change drew attention.

He found Cocker's car in the lot and considered sabotaging it; an automobile accident might end this nuisance once and for all. But he should be able to avoid the big man long enough for him to abandon his vengeance, and that would be the most discreet way to handle it.

A premonition of danger had caused him to park Tzigane down the street, in the lot of a convenience store. When he returned to it he found three black teens walking around the car, looking it over. They started to behave belligerently as he approached, but he sent a wave of fear at them and they quickly backed off.

He drove away into the night, to await Patience at the appointed location. On the radio, a sultry female singer enumerated the many promised pleasures of some oasis at midnight. Zginski smiled at the irony.

Mama Prudence, carrying a candle through the dark mansion, opened the front door. "Goodness, who's banging on my door at this time of night?"

The pale redheaded girl stood demurely, hands twisting before her. She wore cutoffs and a faded blue T-shirt, with an incongruous orange scarf tied around her neck. She swatted at the mosquitoes. "I need your help, Mama Prudence."

Prudence put the candle on the table beside the door. "Clora Elaine Crabtree, does your daddy know you're out prowling on a night like this?"

Clora shook her head. "No, ma'am. But I need to talk to you." She looked up pitifully, the candlelight sparkling on her sweaty cheeks. "I'm afraid something terrible has happened."

"Something your daddy doesn't know about?"

Clora nodded, eyes downcast.

"Well, come out of the heat then, child," Prudence said, and gestured for her to enter. "I've got some cold lemonade in the kitchen, and you can tell me all about your troubles."

Clora followed Prudence through the dark house. It was cooler inside, but also clammy, the way a basement might feel in the summer. It smelled heavily of dust, with a vague underscent of mildew. She remembered a Girl Scout field trip to a nursing home, back when her mother was alive and took her to the meetings, and the odor was very similar. She associated it with human decay.

The kitchen, although stocked with appliances at least thirty years out of date, was warm and cozy once Prudence turned on the lights. She used the candle to light the gas stove, then put a kettle on the eye.

"I thought you said there was lemonade," Clora said.

"I did, but now that I think about it, I believe it would be better to have some tea."

"Hot tea? In the summer?"

"Didn't your mama ever teach you that if you warm your body up, you won't feel as hot?"

Clora looked down at the gleaming Formica tabletop. "My mama died before she could teach me a lot of things."

"Oh, that's right, child, I plumb forgot," Prudence said. "Please forgive me for being so insensitive." She patted the girl on the arm.

"It's okay," Clora said, recoiling a little at the cold touch.

Something else was odd about Mama Prudence's hand. It was not wrinkled and covered with age spots, the way other old people's were. Arthritis hadn't turned her knuckles into hard little knobs. Clora couldn't recall for certain that it had always been this way, but how could it be otherwise? Perhaps, given the arrogance of her own youth, she'd just never looked closely before. Until now, that is, when she needed the old woman's help.

Prudence pulled out a chair and sat opposite the girl. "What can I do for you tonight, Miss Clora?"

"I need a reading."

"Then it's a good thing I made tea."

Clora suddenly realized it *was* a good thing, as if Prudence had known what she wanted before she even arrived. That would make sense; the woman's reputation as a fortune-teller and diviner (or witch, as some said) gave her credit for being able to do everything except fly on a broom. "Yes, ma'am."

"What sort of trouble are you having?"

Clora stared down at her thumb, sliding back and forth across the slick Formica tabletop. "I met a boy."

"Oh," Prudence said knowingly. "I'd heard you were seeing that Cocker boy."

"No, not Bruce," Clora said dismissively. "It's another boy."

"So are you . . . *in trouble*?" Mama Prudence's meaning was plain.

"No! I mean . . . see, that's part of the problem. I don't know if we did 'it' or not. I have a hard time remembering."

"Were you drinking?"

"No, ma'am. And no drugs either. The thing is, he's . . ." She stopped, looked anywhere but at the old woman, and tried to get the words out.

"What?" Prudence urged.

Clora blushed, her pale skin turning bright pink and highlighting her freckles. "Colored."

There was a long silence. Finally Prudence said, "Is this a local boy?"

"No, ma'am, he's from Memphis. He drove all the way out here to see me."

The kettle began to whistle and Prudence stood to attend to it. Clora continued as if she couldn't stop. "He treats me really nice, a lot better than the boys around here do. He makes me feel special and beautiful. I just need to know if it's right or not."

Prudence poured hot water into a waiting cup. "You know it's not *right,* young lady. I don't need tea leaves to tell me that. If the good Lord meant for whites and coloreds to mix, He wouldn't have made *us* in His image." She put the cup in front of Clora. "I think you want to know what will happen if you keep doing it."

"Yes, ma'am."

"Drink it down, then. I can't read the leaves until you finish."

Clora winced as the hot liquid touched her lips, but something in Mama Prudence's demeanor kept her on task. In moments she had finished the tea and placed the cup aside. Mama Prudence slid it across the table and peered down into it.

"Oh, dear," she said after a moment.

"What?" Clora gasped. Her heart tried to leap into her throat.

Prudence tilted the cup slightly. "I don't know if I should tell you."

"No, tell me, please."

Prudence looked at her seriously. "The leaves say that if you continue on the path you've chosen, your lover . . ." She stopped.

"What?" Clora almost sobbed.

"He will become your executioner. You will die at his hands."

Clora was silent while this sunk in. Finally, in a whisper, she asked, "Which one? Which lover?"

Prudence looked into the cup. "I can't say from this. Only *you* know which one you simply dally with, and which one is truly your lover."

Clora started to speak again, then put a hand to her head. "I'm a little dizzy."

"It's some serious news," Prudence said.

Clora tried to stand. "Oh, wow," she whispered, and then sat back down as her legs collapsed. Her head hit the table with a loud thump. She did not move.

Patience sat and waited to be sure the girl was indeed drugged. She took the cup to the sink, washed it out, and placed it in the drying rack. Then with no effort, she lifted the girl as if she'd been a tiny child and carried her upstairs.

In the dark bedroom, she stretched the girl out on the bed, unused in years. Clora was tall and gawky now, but Prudence knew she would mature into a beauty if left alone. She recalled the girl's mother, Elaine, and remembered that she, too, had been a tall voluptuous redhead.

Prudence reached back and undid the catch on the back of her musty old dress. It slid to the floor, revealing her faded white silk undergarments. She stepped out of her shoes, then knelt beside the bed and gently brushed the hair back from Clora's neck.

She untied the orange scarf to expose the girl's pale throat. Clora moaned in her sleep but did not awaken. Prudence leaned forward, toward the heated artery, then stopped.

For a long moment there was no sound in the room except Clora's gentle, heavy breathing. In the night outside, an owl hooted. Something scurried along the baseboards of one of the other rooms.

Finally Prudence reached out one hand and touched the tiny wounds on the side of Clora's neck. They were unmistakable, and she could not place their presence into any reasonable context. *She* was the only vampire in McHale County. She had made none herself, and if another had settled in the area, she would know. Wouldn't she? She *had* gone an awfully long time without regular feeding. Had her powers withered along with her body?

Then she remembered Clora's description of her encounter with the colored boy. *I have a hard time remembering,* she'd said, and swore no alcohol or drugs had been involved. It *could* have been a vampire's attack.

But Prudence had never heard of a Negro vampire. Such a creature would no doubt feed on its own kind, fearing the risk of exposure that would accompany its visits to a white woman. Some lines just should not be crossed, she knew, and a nigger vampire was still first and foremost a nigger.

Then Prudence laughed and brushed a strand of the fine red hair from the girl's cheek. In her worries about miscegenation, she had completely missed the obvious. Only one vampire would dare come this close, feeding on a victim practically within shouting distance of Prudence. *Patience.* Her dear sister had indeed returned.

It explained everything, and confirmed what the unnatural drought had implied. Prudence assumed the accident with the broken glass that led her to drink Byron Cocker's blood had been coincidence, but it was clearly fate announcing the return of the prodigal sister. She thought the taste of fresh blood after months of withering away had been the source of her sudden rejuvenation, but now she knew it was Patience's proximity. She giggled, then began to laugh, then sat on the floor holding her sides as she descended into hysterics.

When she finally got control, she took off the girl's T-shirt and bra so no blood would accidentally stain them. Then she positioned her mouth over the bite left by her sister, and settled in to feed from the fount that had recently nourished Patience.

And as the blood seeped into her, she began to plan.

CHAPTER 15

"Hey. Byron. *Byron.*"

Barrister shook his friend's shoulder very carefully. A man who'd been through the things Byron had might wake up with fists flying.

But Cocker only opened his eyes and raised his head from the table, where saliva had pooled. "Wha . . . what time is it?"

"Midnight, son. We've got to lock up, and that means you have to go home. Are you okay to drive?"

Cocker sat up, shook his head, and waited for the cobwebs to fade from his vision. "Midnight?" he said, and looked around. The bar was empty. The bright overhead lights revealed the detritus of the evening, and the air was as hazy as his brain. Fauvette and another waitress were stacking chairs, and a young giggling couple stood at the door, struggling to get enough composure to go outside.

"The witching hour," Gerry said. "And you have to grab a broomstick and head home."

Cocker looked around. "Did he show up?"

"Who?"

Cocker's face was numb from sleep and the residue of his plastic surgeries. He realized either Zginski hadn't shown or he'd slept right through it. Christ, he only had one drink. But despite the confusion, his cop brain quickly switched gears. "The girl . . . is she still here? The singer."

"Patience? She's back in her dressing room. Why?"

"Dressing room," he repeated, and put his hands on the table to rise.

Barrister gently pushed him back down. "Come on, she's not your type. She's one of those women's libbers, I'm pretty sure. She'd probably slap you if you held the door for her."

"Need to see her," Cocker growled. Even half-awake and kitten-weak, he resented being told what to do.

Barrister hoisted Cocker to his feet and made a show of straightening the big man's clothes. "There's a place about three blocks down where you can get some coffee for the road. Might be a good idea, considering how far you have to go to get home."

Cocker shook his head again, slapped himself,

and blinked. "No, I'm . . . I'm okay. So Patience is still here?"

"Yes. But really, Byron, she's not—"

"What? Oh, yeah, I know that." He did not want to unduly draw Barrister's scrutiny, so he mentally counted to three, smiled, and said with apparently genuine cheer, "Wow, Gerry, I'm sorry. I must've been more tired than I thought. Let me use your restroom and I'll get out of your hair, okay? Thanks for the drinks."

"Sure thing, Byron. You know where it is."

Barrister watched Cocker walk to the men's room, his gait steady. He was immediately suspicious, though. Byron Cocker wasn't the kind to apologize and make nice unless he was up to something. The sooner he was out the door, the better Barrister would like it. He most definitely did not want Cocker bird-dogging around Patience; a heartbroken chanteuse was useless to him.

Cocker emerged a few moments later and waved as he headed toward the door. "Thanks again, Ger. See you next time I'm in town."

"Anytime, Byron." He tried to hide his relief.

Patience closed her guitar case and checked a final time to make sure she had left nothing personal behind. The dressing room might be all hers, but she'd been around enough not to take it for granted yet.

She smiled at the flowers, and ran a finger along one silken petal. My God, she was being *romanced*. The note read, *I have a gift waiting for you, a token of apology for being unavoidably detained and missing your performance.* It was signed simply, *Z,* and listed the address of a motel just beyond the city limits. Giddy excitement ran through her at the prospect of being alone with Zginski.

She looked up as Fauvette appeared in the door. Her waitress outfit was wrinkled and stained with the night's work. "Hi," she said. "Are you leaving?"

"Yeah," Patience said. "I've got some things to do before I go down for the night."

"Oh," Fauevtte said, making no effort to hide her disappointment. "I was hoping we could talk some more."

Patience touched the other girl's cheek. "We will, sweetheart. Soon, I promise."

Fauvette scowled. "I know you mean well, but please don't treat me like a child. I just *look* like one. I'm actually sixty years old."

Patience was silent for a moment, then said, "What's wrong? Really?"

Fauvette nodded at the flowers. "Did Rudy give you those?"

"Yes. Is that a problem?"

Fauvette crossed her arms. "If you mean, am I jealous, then yes. Rudy seemed to . . . I thought he and I were on the verge of something, but I can see it was simply his normal self-preservation

disguised as tenderness. That's a bitter thing to chew on. If you mean, do I blame you, no."

Patience said quietly, "I won't go if it will cause trouble."

"It won't. He's free, you're free." The irony of her situation rode heavy on her; just weeks ago, she had been in Zginski's position, with both Mark and Zginski battling, subtly and without apparent malice, for her affection. Now she felt abandoned and more alone than ever, and Mark's disappearance no longer seemed so inexplicable.

She managed a smile. "I thought your show went great tonight."

Patience nodded in appreciation. "Thanks. It did what it was supposed to do."

"I could feel it. And see it."

"Good. Maybe doing it won't be as hard for you as I thought."

"Maybe." She looked down at her shoes. "I still wish you didn't have to go. That you wanted to spend time with me instead of . . ." She waved her hand in disgust. "*Boys.*"

Patience took Fauvette's hands. "Sweetheart, I'm not picking boys over you. We have all of eternity to get to know each other. One night won't change things."

"It only took one night to make us what we are. That was a big change."

"You know what I mean."

Fauvette nodded. "Yeah. Well, have fun. Rudy knows how to treat a woman, I promise. Just try not to get your heart involved."

Before Patience could reply, Fauvette pulled away and rushed back into the dining room. Patience sighed, picked up her guitar, and turned out the light. She left the flowers behind, but the note was safely tucked into the guitar strings.

Cocker went to his car in the Ringside lot, started the engine, and turned on the air conditioner. Besides his own, only three cars remained. He knew Gerry's Trans Am, so one of the other two must belong to Patience. And the singer, no doubt, would head straight to her boyfriend, Zginski.

Patience suddenly appeared out of the darkness next to the long, low black LTD. She put her guitar in the trunk and pulled out into the almost-deserted street. Remembering his failure with Zginski, Cocker stayed far enough behind her that she couldn't possibly know he was there. He turned on the radio, and the first song was some of that obscene jungle music, in which the singer berated a woman for not following through on a promised tryst. "I gotcha," he gloated, and Cocker smiled.

Patience kept going into the run-down neighborhoods off Lamar Avenue. This was where the pushers and pimps skulked about with impunity, and where Cocker's white face was as rare as a black one back in McHale County. She turned down a street with no working lights and finally parked in the driveway of a run-down faux antebellum mansion, the kind that were often cut up into welfare-family apartments. Cocker drove past and saw her put her key into the door and go inside.

He parked across the end of the driveway, blocking her in. When he got out, he heard music and laughter from one of the other houses, and watched a low rider drift past checking out the big white guy. He went to the front door, knocked authoritatively, and said, "Open up! Sheriff's office!"

He waited. There was no response. The single mailbox indicated that the house had not yet been subdivided. He saw no sign of life beyond the dark windows.

He tried again. "Open up or we'll break down the door."

He was about to knock a third time when the door suddenly opened, and his hand met no resistance. Instead it thudded against flesh, and a female voice cried, "Ow!"

He jumped back, and the porch light came on, momentarily blinding him. Patience stepped out, one hand to her face. Furious, she yelled, "You punched me in the eye, you *asshole*!"

Startled, Cocker blurted, "I'm sorry, I didn't know—"

She glared up at him with her good eye. "And you're no sheriff, you're that drunk who passed out at my show tonight. How about I call the *real* sheriff and get you locked up for assault?"

The threat cleared his confusion, and he was back on track. He put his hand on her sternum and pushed her back inside, closing the door behind them. "Turn on the light," he snapped.

After a moment a single overhead bulb came on, revealing Patience in a simple black cocktail dress. She had one hand over her eye, but the other still blazed with fury. "Look, pal, I don't know who you think you are—"

"I'm the man looking for Rudy Zginski, bitch," he said. "And since you're dressed to go out, I figure you're going to meet him. So you're going to tell me where he is."

Patience stared blankly at him, then laughed. "Is that right? No, I don't think I am. I think I'm going to ask you to leave, and since that won't work I'm going to *make* you."

He smiled. He was twice her size, and had no moral problem forcing a woman to do anything. "Sweet thing, you best start saying 'yes, sir' and 'no, sir' if you don't want that pretty dress torn. Now where is he?"

She lowered her hand. The eye behind it showed no sign of injury. Then she turned away and went into the sitting room. The walls were faded and water-stained, and except for an old couch and stacks of unopened boxes the room was empty. She turned on another lamp and faced him again.

"You're used to getting your own way, aren't you?" she said casually. "Using aggression and violence to accomplish things. I've known a lot of men like you. A *lot*."

Cocker smiled coldly. "You ain't known nobody like *me*, hot stuff. Now where is Rudy Zginski?"

"You're thinking that if you threaten to beat me or rape me, I'll tell you." She mimicked his heavy drawl. "But you ain't known nobody like *me*, either."

"Are you threatening me?"

She continued as if he hadn't spoken. "Maybe I like the thought of being raped by a stranger. Maybe I want you to slap me around." She fingered her neckline and licked her lips voluptuously. "Did you ever think of that?"

Cocker said nothing.

"Or maybe I just want you to do enough so that when I kill you, it's clearly self-defense. Maybe close enough to kiss is close enough to kill. Maybe I'm just waiting for you to make a move."

Cocker's eyes flickered around the room. He saw no weapons, but the girl's mocking tone and blatant sexuality had him off-balance.

Suddenly he froze. A painting propped on the mantel, barely visible in the light, transfixed him. He tilted the lamp shade so more illumination shone on it.

The face, the blond hair, the regal cheekbones, all looked familiar. It was unmistakably Mama Prudence as a young woman, beautiful and cold and somehow frightening.

His eyes opened wide and he stared at Patience. *Now* he knew why she had seemed familiar; the painting in Mama Prudence's living room was clearly *her*, dressed in the fashion of a century or more ago.

"Who is that?" he whispered, nodding at the painting.

"That? It's my sister, Prudence."

"Your *sister*?"

She smiled. Her canine teeth looked abnormally long. "Yes. Beautiful, isn't she?"

Cocker began to back away. "Stay away from me, bitch."

Patience laughed. "'Bitch'? You mean little ol' me has scared big, strong *you*?" She looked at him in an odd, new way that truly did terrify him. "Friend, you don't have any idea how scared you should be of me. If there's a lick of common sense in that dense redneck skull of yours, you'll leave now and never come back. Not here, not the bar, maybe not even to Memphis."

Cocker's back was to the door, and he fumbled for the knob. "I got friends on the force," he said, but it sounded weak and pitiful. "They can make life real hard for you."

"And I've got friends out in the night," Patience hissed. "Friends who leave bloody pulps where there used to be human bodies. Friends who aren't half as scary . . ."

And here she stepped close so quickly she seemed to vanish across the room and reappear right in his face. "As I am," she finished with a whisper.

He wrenched the door open and fled down the drive. By the time he reached his car the door was again closed, and all the lights were dark. He roared off into the night.

CHAPTER 16

Patience watched out the front window for a long time to see if the man would return. At one time this sort of encounter would have sent her fleeing the city, possibly the country. But the man clearly had no interest in her except as a way to Zginski. That certainty allowed her to brush off the encounter, but it also meant she couldn't risk putting Zginski in danger by keeping her date with him. Still, he was bound to approve when he learned of her reason.

Zginski was a handsome devil, and his manners reeked of a bygone time. He was certainly sure of himself, in a way that both infuriated and fascinated her. He reminded her of Vincent, in fact, and that thought made her hands slide slowly up and down her thighs.

Vincent. Young, dashing Colonel Vincent Drake . . .

Why must we wait until our wedding night? he whispered as his hands slid over her corset. *You will be my bride, and surely a few days can make no difference?* She could barely breathe as he unlaced the garment, and her body blossomed with desire as his lips traveled from her shoulders to the curves of her breasts. She had no idea that a grown man would *want* to suck on a woman's nipples, let alone that the sensation would practically immobilize her. By the time she lay naked on his cloak in the summer night, she was too overwhelmed to resist. And once the initial sharp pain of his penetration had faded, she had not *wanted* to resist.

Oh, Vincent, you damned fool, she thought now, *if you'd only been as true as you claimed to be.*

She gazed at her sister's portrait. Prudence was tall, slender, with Grecian features and the haughtiness that accompanied them. Beside her, Patience always felt fat and dumpy. *That's the only thing that isn't right,* she thought for the millionth time. *Prudence, your eyes were* never *that kind.*

They certainly weren't the night before Patience's wedding, when her sister looked up from beneath Vincent, her pale thighs spread wide for him, his firm behind clenching as he poured his seed into her. Prudence's eyes were triumphant, looking over Vincent's shoulder at her sister frozen in the garden shed's doorway. Then Vincent, oblivious, had said, "You are so much more a woman than your fat sister." Prudence's eyes had turned triumphant with delight, and her laugh made Vincent say, "Oh, my love, my love," just as he had done to Patience beneath the summer moon mere days earlier.

Patience traced the frame's beveling, feeling the weight of the cherry wood and its varnish. Their father had commissioned separate paintings instead of the usual one of both sisters together. "You two are so different you might not even be related," he'd said often, "if I wasn't so completely sure of your mother's fidelity." And for a long time Patience had pretended they weren't, that she was a changeling born of a Gypsy princess and a disgraced nobleman, sent to America for her own safety.

But truthfully, there *was* a resemblance. Both were smart, capable of great deviousness, and able to see through the lies of most everyone around them. Except, in her case, those of her fiancé and sister. They were bound by blood, now in more ways than one.

She sighed and went upstairs to the master bedroom. She'd placed clothes in the closet, and filled the dresser with lingerie, but otherwise the room was bare. She needed no bed: she rested on the floor, usually naked, her limbs neatly arranged. She required nothing else.

She'd tried sleeping in a coffin once, for a week. It had been both uncomfortable and pointless. She'd researched the folklore and understood the desire to return to the grave, but for her it was simply a waste of time. She knew what she was and understood her limits. She did not fear discovery.

As she lay on the floor, feeling the grain of the wooden slats beneath her, she recalled the night she had been turned. Her final mortal memories were all sensations: the weight of Vincent's pistol in her hands, the cold metal barrel against her soft bosom, the flash of light, the smell of powder and burnt meat, and the incredibly anticlimactic, muffled bang. Then the agony of the round bullet tearing through her bodice, her flesh, the bone beneath it, and finally her heart. She had fallen atop the hill, where the morning sun would reveal her body for all to see.

But before the sun rose, there was the moon. It was full, and cold, and merciless. It carried magic that she never anticipated, charms sympathetic in the worst way to the impulses that drove a girl to suicide. More than just the bite of another vampire could create its kindred; the universe itself, if the conditions were right, could spawn one just as it had once spawned life from a sea of primeval chemicals. Instead of journeying to heaven, or hell, or the nothingness she truly expected, the moonlight fixed Patience's soul to her body and left her with an irresistible urge for the only substance that would anchor her to the earthly plane.

And before her lifeless corpse could be found by her family, she awoke beneath the stars with a chill in her heart and a hunger greater than anything she'd ever known. With a certainty so great it was as if God himself had ordained it, she made straight for the one thing that could appease her new appetite: Vincent.

There was no hesitation, no stealth, no subtlety. She burst through the window of the guest room and pounced on him without a word. Her teeth had grown long and sharp, the better to rend the flesh she'd once coveted. He managed to fire a pistol at her, striking near the wound she'd inflicted on herself. But except for the thump of impact she felt nothing, no burning or pain or weakness. If anything, it made her more furious.

She crushed his hand while it still held the pistol, driving splinters from the wooden hilt into his palm. His screams were high and girlish. Then she slammed him back against the wall, tilted his head to one side, and buried her teeth in his neck. She had not understood the nature of her need, and instead of simply piercing his vein she'd ripped out a fist-sized chunk of flesh. She spat it to the ground, and then the ecstasy of the blood found her. She put her face into the wound, uncaring that it flooded her nose as well as her mouth, grateful only for the sense of completion she now felt. *This* was what she needed. *This* was her reason for living.

Except that she wasn't living. And when the door flew open, and her father and male cousins stood frozen in horror, she realized she was no longer Patience Bolade. She was a monster.

Her cousins tried to restrain her, but she killed two of them instantly with blows to the head, and a third was left crippled after being hurled out the window. Her father tried to shoot her but could not bring himself to pull the trigger, and stepped aside for her to emerge from the room and ascend the stairs. She bellowed her sister's name like the cry of some rabid beast.

But when she found Prudence huddled in her closet behind her petticoats, she felt a cold certainty that stayed her hand. "I will never die, Prudence," she had warned, her voice wet and gurgly. "For the rest of your days I will haunt you. You will never know when I will strike. No prayer can save you from me." And with that, she left her family and her life behind. She bore them no ill will, and no anger; with all eternity before her, she saw Prudence's actions as those of a limited, selfish mortal.

Or at least she tried to. Because the next night, while the moon was still full, Prudence also killed herself on the same hill. And when she arose, she eliminated the rest of the Bolade family and swore eternal vengeance on Patience.

Patience tried to reason with her sister, to convince her that vampires had no need for grudges over things done during their mortal existences. But Prudence was adamant that someday, somehow, she would avenge what Patience had done. So Patience left Tennessee, putting as much of the planet between her and Prudence as possible. Discreet inquiries subsequently told her that Prudence still occupied their ancestral home, a dim shade spoken of in whispers by those who lived nearby. "Mama Prudence" they called her, and came to her for fortune-telling and crude magic spells. Isolated, with no one to feed on regularly, she withered and shrunk so that she resembled a storybook crone. No one truly believed she was the same Prudence Bolade from a century earlier; most assumed she was a slightly dotty relative, content to live among the relics of the past.

As her limbs grew rigid and her consciousness faded, Patience's last coherent thought was, *Soon, sister. We shall settle this soon. You know I'm close, just as I know you are. Because I'm weary of running and hiding. I'm tired of not being able to come home.*

Clora kissed Leonardo hungrily, and her body squirmed against him almost of its own volition. She couldn't wait to get naked with him; it was all she'd thought about since sundown. He never specified which nights he would visit, so every night became a sleepless, humid battle against her raging body. The sleeplessness was beginning to tell on her, too: she'd lost ten pounds, and now had dark circles under her eyes.

On the nights he didn't come, she thought about Mama Prudence's warning. There was no question which of the two boys in her life was truly her "lover." Yet could Leonardo seriously pose that sort of danger? He never asked to meet her out anywhere, and if she couldn't be safe in her own bedroom, where could she? No colored boy would dare injure a white girl in her own home. Not in McHale County, for certain.

"Touch me," she said, reaching for his wrists and putting his palms against her breasts. "Please, touch me everywhere . . ."

He smiled, but she was too close to him to see it. "Don't worry, girl, you'll get what you want." He squeezed gently, and she moaned in gratitude.

He could tell there was less life in her than before. The air around her used to be heated by her body's thriving energy, but now it was cooler and weaker. It wasn't yet dangerous, but before long it would become so. He would have to decide then what to do about her.

She took his right hand from her breast and began to kiss his fingers. She said breathlessly, "Daddy and I went to town today. I got you a present."

"Really?" he said, his free hand roaming over her body through her clothes. If she sensed how clinically detached he was from the process, she gave no indication.

"Mm-hm," she said, and pulled away enough to open the night-table drawer. She retrieved a small, velvet-covered ring box. "Open it," she said when she handed it to him.

He did, and took out the plastic ring with its wide oval stone. He held it up to the light. "What is it?"

"It's a mood ring," she said.

"What does it do?"

"You know what a mood ring does, don't you?"

She had seen commercials for them on Channel 5 out of Memphis, so surely everyone in the city knew all about them.

He shook his head. "Tell me."

Maybe he was just testing her, to see if she was really with it or not. Bruce would do that, quizzing her on the latest music. "It changes color based on your mood. Well, really, based on your body temperature. For example, when you're here with me, mine turns blue." She held up her left hand, where she wore an identical ring. The stone was deep blue. "Now let's try out yours."

"I don't think it'll work on me," he said.

"Oh, come on, give it a try." She took his left hand and slid the ring on his finger. They both watched it for several moments; it remained the same neutral gray color.

"Sorry," he said, and took it off. "I told you it wouldn't work."

She sighed, and wanted to cry. It had been such a minor thing, but to have it collapse this way left her feeling as useless and stupid as she did around Bruce. She took the ring and hurled it through the open window into the night. Then she turned back to Leonardo.

The next thing she knew it was dark, and she was alone.

She sat up in bed. She was still dressed in her panties and T-shirt, but she ached inside as if she'd had sex. As always, though, there was no memory of it, just a nagging sense that something had happened. She looked at the window, which stood open to the night; the tops of the trees were visible in the moonlight. She stood, intending to close it, but a wave of dizziness struck and she sprawled back on the bed. *Just a moment,* she told herself, *until this passes, and then I'll close the window.*

In less than ten seconds she was asleep again.

Outside, on the roof, Leonardo sat on the peak beside one of the chimneys and looked up at the moon. He knew he should get going, in case Clora's other boyfriend came around. But he needed to think and regroup, because he'd learned something tonight that was totally unexpected.

Another vampire had fed on Clora.

Whoever it was had been careful to use his fang marks, and had clearly not taken much. But the taste of strange saliva was there, altering the essence of Clora's blood for those first few draughts. He had shared victims with Fauvette and Mark, as well as Olive and Toddy before they were destroyed. He recognized the change, but not the taste.

That left two candidates: Zginski, and the new girl singer Patience. Or it was a vampire he knew nothing about. That was a long shot, since there simply weren't that many vampires around, and they tended to congregate in cities, not sparsely populated rural areas where their predations would attract attention.

He wrote off Patience as a possibility, which

left Zginski. It also brought up the unanswerable question of *why*.

Zginski pulled back the curtain and again checked his watch by the streetlamp outside. It was three in the morning, and he had to accept the fact that Patience wasn't coming. Instead of the usual rage at being treated so cavalierly, he felt something unexpected: disappointment.

He turned to the motel bed, where a teenage boy lay asleep in the darkness. Clad only in his white jockey shorts, his erection straining against the cotton, he murmured and tossed but did not awaken. In his dreams he was reliving his deepest sexual fantasy, but was unable to reach completion despite his best efforts.

Zginski touched the boy's sweaty chest. He was handsome, with brown hair and a dimple in his chin. He played football, an American sport of great violence, so his body was muscular and supple. Zginski intended him to be a gift, something he and Patience could share the way a mortal couple might go out to dinner. Now Zginski was, as he'd overheard on occasion, stuck with the check.

And yet he couldn't believe Patience would simply ignore him this way. He would reserve judgment until he spoke to her about it, he decided. He would give her the greatest, rarest gift that Baron Rudolfo Vladimir Zginski could give anyone: the benefit of the doubt.

But that still left him with the moaning boy. He considered the alternatives. He could leave him here, and assume he would return home too ashamed to speak about how he'd awoken in a strange motel in his underwear. He could not possibly connect this to Zginski; after all, he had only seen the vampire for a few moments in the gas station bathroom, before the vampire's influence had rendered him helpless and oblivious.

Or Zginski could kill him.

The boy tossed his head, exposing his jugular. "No," he whimpered, so softly it was barely audible.

Zginski smiled. Sometimes the universe made decisions for you.

CHAPTER 17

Beams from the orange sunset shafted almost horizontally through the frames of the long-shattered windows. In the dusty, pollen-heavy air they made irregular patches of illumination on the debris-covered floor. Pigeons trilled in the rafters. Rats scurried in the walls and under the warped floorboards. And the corpse of a stranger, someone who had overdosed alone and forgotten long ago, was now little more than rags and a skeleton in the oppressive heat. His bony fingers still clutched the remains of a violin, the punch line to an obscure joke.

Patience stood on the crumbling loading dock as she looked over the abandoned, decrepit cotton warehouse. She wrinkled her nose at the smell. "So this was your home?"

"Yeah, I guess," Fauvette said, suddenly embarrassed. She scuffed one tennis shoe self-consciously. "It was just where we slept, really. I found it, and the others joined me after a while. We used the basement and the boiler room for our coffins."

Patience carefully picked her way around the debris, looking up at the roof. "And you picked this place because . . . ?"

Fauvette shrugged. How to describe the sense that when you're a walking corpse, the corpse of a building can actually be a comfort? "It seemed appropriate."

"For a cockroach, maybe." She instantly regretted the comment. "I didn't mean that literally."

Fauvette, shuffling along behind her, kicked at a piece of broken glass. "For a long time, that's what I figured I was. Something that only came out at night, that had to stay in the shadows and run from the sun."

Patience shook her head. "So you really thought the sun would burn you up if it even touched you?"

Fauvette nodded. "I never had anyone explain to me what I was. So the only information I could find was in the movies and on TV. I didn't know if it was true or not, but under the circumstances it seemed kind of silly to put it to the test."

"That must have been a terrifying way to live. So lonely."

"I wasn't living. And I wasn't alone. I had friends, at least until Rudy came along."

Patience's eyes opened wide. "He *killed* them?"

"No, actually he saved us. And taught us what we are. But . . . some of them *did* die around the same time, but it wasn't his fault. Not entirely."

Patience looked out through the big, empty window frame at the overgrown field that surrounded the abandoned warehouse. She swatted at the gnats that filled the air. "He's very intriguing, isn't he? Your Mr. Zginski."

"That's one word for it."

Both were quiet for a moment. Another rat scurried along the wall, its passage loud in the silence. Finally Patience said, "You said he saved 'us.' I met Leonardo, the colored boy. Who else?"

"Well, there was Olive, a colored girl. She died. And Toddy, who was a crazy white boy from the country. He died. And Mark, who . . ."

"Died?"

"I don't know. He said he needed to find out some things, and that he'd be back when he could. It wasn't like him, but at the same time, with all the changes, maybe it was."

"Were you and he . . . ?"

"I think we were about to. Then Rudy came along."

Patience idly lifted a board, sending a fat corn snake slithering for new cover. "And what did Rudy do?"

Fauvette thought about the answer for a long moment. "He made me forget what I am."

Patience looked up in surprise. "In what way?"

Fauvette stared into space as she spoke. "The vampire who made me took my life when I was still a virgin. This was up in the Kentucky hills, fifty-some-odd years ago. He didn't mean to make me a vampire, I don't think, he just didn't take any precautions to keep me from rising. Only before I rose, but after I died, I was raped."

It took a moment, but it finally registered. Patience's eyes opened wide. "While you were *dead*?"

Fauvette nodded. "The Scoval brothers. The joke around the hollers was that no farm animal was safe when the Scovals started drinking. I was a sheltered little girl, I thought it meant they might steal them and eat them." She smiled bitterly. "Apparently no corpse was safe, either."

Patience could think of nothing to say. A virgin vampire was eternally spared any sexual feelings, remaining in a kind of prepubescent netherworld of amused detachment. But Fauvette seemed anything but that.

"Because of that," Fauvette continued, "I have all the sensations you do. But my virginity is still there. And if I lose it, it comes back the next night."

"Oh, my God, honey," Patience said as she comprehended the horror of the situation. "That's awful."

She nodded. "It hurts, too. When I lose it. It's the only thing that does. And it bleeds."

"It *bleeds*? Like you were still alive?"

She nodded. "I don't know why. I don't know the 'why' of anything."

Patience knelt and wrapped her arms around Fauvette. It reminded Fauvette of the way her mother would come to wake her up, the way she'd snuggle her body against her mother's full, strong form. She closed her eyes and tried to recall the way that little cabin smelled, the way the wood creaked in the wind or her father's footsteps across the hard floor. She could see them in her mind's eye, but the actual memories seemed like mere photographs.

Patience stroked Fauvette's soft hair. "Honey, I can't change what's happened, but I'll try to make what's coming a little better for you. I promise you that." She stood back, kissed Fauvette on the forehead, and said cheerfully, "Now, enough of this. Let's go back to town and get started on your first lesson."

🐾 "Clora! *Clora!*"

Clora came down the stairs from her room, having to stop on the second floor as a wave of dizziness hit her. She'd visibly lost weight, although she'd made no changes in her diet or exercise. Along with the weight, it seemed she'd lost the energy or desire to do anything except at night, when *he* came to visit.

She stumbled into the living room. It was the hottest day of the year so far, and her father had turned off the window-unit air conditioner to save money. The windows were open, but the immobile curtains testified to the lack of a breeze. It was dusk, and the daytime flies were joined by mosquitoes that found every tear and opening in the screens. It often seemed to Clora that they might as well have lived out in the yard.

Jeb sat in his recliner, staring at the TV even though it wasn't turned on. The only light came from a dim lamp on the side table. A dozen beer cans littered the floor around him. "Yes, sir, Daddy?" she said.

When she saw his teary eyes, Clora knew what he was about to ask. Jeb's voice was small and pitiful when he said, "Honey, you know what I need, don't you?"

Clora licked her lips, tasting salt from the sweat. "Daddy, please, I'm awful tired."

Despite his unruly hair and stubble, he looked and sounded like a little child when he whimpered, "Clora, baby, you're all I got. Please?"

She felt a pit open in her belly, a mix of fear and excitement. "It ain't right, Daddy," she mumbled, hoping this time he'd let it go.

"What?" he snapped in the rage that only came with alcohol. "Are you talking back, girl?"

"No, sir," she said. The man in the chair now, soaked in beer and lost in the past, was not the father she loved. This man would chase her down and beat her savagely if she back-talked. The other man would reappear in the morning, contrite and apologetic, but that wouldn't make the pain any less. "I'll be right back."

She went into the downstairs bedroom, where Jeb slept when he bothered to leave the recliner. She closed the door and looked at the bed where her mother and father slept, and where she had been conceived. She stripped off her tube top and shorts, then opened the dresser and removed her mother's sheer black nightgown.

Elaine Crabtree had been dead four years now. The first time Clora had tried on her mother's clothes, she had felt grown-up and sophisticated, and flounced into the living room to show her father. His reaction had both puzzled and frightened her, and led to the little ritual she was about to enact.

She pulled the garment on, careful not to tear it: she was wider-hipped than her mother. The bottom hem came to the middle of her thighs, and she replaced her own white cotton panties with the matching black ones from the drawer.

She adjusted herself in the mirror, then took the headband that her mother always wore and used it to hold back her bangs. She really *did* look like Elaine now; the picture on her father's nightstand could easily have been one of Clora, if it had been taken years in the future and somehow sent back in time.

She turned, and a rush of nausea and dizziness hit her. She sat down heavily on the bed, startling several flies attracted to a stain she didn't want to think about. She waited for her head to stop spinning. This was the fifth time in two days she'd nearly passed out. Was she sick? Or . . . worse? She'd know about the second option in three more days, since she was as regular as the sunrise. Until then, she did her best to put it aside.

She stood, shook her head to clear it, and turned out the light. Then she went back into the living room.

She stopped in the shadowy entrance and said in a throaty voice, "Turn out the light, Jeb."

The recliner protested as he leaned over to hit the light switch. Her father could barely see her, but that was part of the trick. She leaned against the edge of the kitchen doorway and began to hum "Ode to Billie Joe," her mother's favorite song. Then she began slowly to dance.

"Oh, sweetie," Jeb said, shifting in his chair. She heard his zipper slide down.

Once when she was a little girl, she had hidden in the dark under the kitchen table and watched her mother dance for her father. Jeb was handsome then, and proud of his wife, and when he took her there on the couch Clora had watched in both horror and wonder. The next time she tried to spy they caught her, but the image was already burned into her memory. Now she mimicked it perfectly, sliding her hands over her own body just as Elaine had done. She looked at the water-stained ceiling, the warped hardwood floor, anything to avoid seeing what her father was doing in his chair.

Thankfully, it never took very long. When he finally croaked, "That's enough, baby," she scurried back to strip off the dead woman's negligee and retrieve her own garments. Her father inevitably passed out after this routine, so she knew she'd have the rest of the night to herself.

This time she tossed the nightgown and panties

back in the dresser, grabbed her own clothes, and rushed naked up the stairs to her room. She slammed and locked the door. She was dizzy again, and it was hard to breathe, and for some reason the bug bites on her neck throbbed and itched.

She pulled on a clean T-shirt, grateful for the crisp coolness against her skin. She wanted a shower, but needed to wait until her head stopped spinning. And the place on her neck continued to throb, the way it did when *he* was near.

Something scratched softly at the open window. "It's me," a voice said.

Leonardo was right outside, perched on the roof and running his fingernails lightly along the glass. He smiled when he saw her. She hurriedly opened the window the rest of the way, and he gracefully slithered in.

She threw her arms around him. "I'm so glad to see you," she cried. "I was so afraid you wouldn't come tonight."

He held her loosely, surprised and disconcerted by her intensity. "Why? What happened?"

She shook her head. She couldn't possibly tell him. "Nothing, honey. I'm just glad to see you." She raised her face to him, eager to kiss his cold lips again.

And then suddenly they were in bed. She was naked, on her stomach, and he sat shirtless on the edge of the mattress. She was breathing heavily, and tingles ran through her muscles indicating she'd experienced a strong climax. But she couldn't remember it.

She rose on her elbows. Her hair was matted with sweat, and the hot little room smelled of bodies. He'd left the light on again, which meant he must have watched her as they . . . whatever they did. She blushed with shame at the thought.

He smiled down at her. For just a moment, the image of his extra-long canine teeth and the sudden tingle in her neck made her think something so absurd she almost laughed aloud. But it passed in a wave of fresh weakness.

"How was that?" he said, and kissed the tip of her nose.

She couldn't speak for a moment. "I never knew I could feel all those things."

He laughed. "That's what they all say."

She blushed and said pitifully, "Don't laugh at me."

"Why not? If it's funny, why shouldn't I laugh?"

"Because it's *not* funny. I love you!" Immediately she looked away, unable to believe the words had just burst forth like that. She didn't see the sadness cross his face, or regret battle with indifference. She only heard him say, "Man, you white girls. You get a little taste of chocolate and it's all she wrote."

Clora's eyes filled with tears and she scooted away from him. "Why are you being so mean to me? I gave you everything."

He looked at her clinically, as if her emotions were somehow alien to him. He had no real desire to hurt her, but at the same time it was oddly fascinating to witness her crumble this way. In the past his victims only had time for one emotion: terror. Then they died. He said, "I best be going."

She grabbed frantically at him. "No, please, not yet."

He untangled her hands and said firmly, "Yeah."

He pulled on his shirt while she sat up and clutched her girlish, lace-edged pillow to her chest. "I'm sorry, I shouldn't have said that. Please don't go."

He smiled. "Don't worry, Snow White, I'll be back."

Still clutching the pillow with one hand, she grabbed his arm. "Then take me with you."

He looked into her desperate eyes. Death hovered there now, nearby and patiently biding its time. "No," he said.

Tears poured down her face. "Why are you doing this? How can you not believe I love you after all the things I did for you?"

He kissed her lightly, perfunctorily. "I believe you, Snow White. Maybe I just don't care."

She collapsed to the floor, her face buried into her pillow, sobbing. Leonardo crawled out the window and closed it behind him.

CHAPTER 18

Leonardo leaped from the roof to the closest tree and quickly shimmied to the ground. Through the open living-room window he saw Clora's father passed out in his chair, the dog asleep beside him. The TV displayed a carrier signal, its whine low and insistent.

Leonardo was confused now, and that annoyed him. As a human, he'd hated white folks, a simple and clean emotion that was neither unique nor unjustified. He'd seen the results of carpetbagger racism, watched it feed the self-pity of the poor whites around him, and experienced firsthand the violence that sprang from it. His hatred spared neither young nor old, rich nor poor, male nor female. He hated pretty white girls as much, and for the same reasons, as ugly white boys.

After becoming a vampire, though, his hatred had changed. No longer needing to fear for his life, he prowled the night with an arrogant confidence that often drew the ire of whites. His own brutal revenge on any who dared accost him was one reason he'd ended up in Memphis so far from his birthplace in rural South Carolina. In the city, a single death drew little attention. But eventually the hatred had, if not faded, become something that was more amusement than anything else. How could he *not* laugh at the certainty that he could quickly and easily kill any of the so-called superior race? How could that not be funny?

And yet Clora stirred something unfamiliar inside him. He had no doubt the girl was as racist as those white-sheeted community leaders he'd witnessed as a child, but he wondered if there was something more to it. Perhaps the racism was just a sense of isolation, expressed the only way she knew how. It wasn't, he pondered, that different from his own existence. He, too, was isolated, and spoke only in the language of his kind, which in its view of the living was every bit as prejudiced.

But was that a valid comparison? And if it was, what did it explain about his confused, and confusing, feelings for the girl?

He was so engrossed in this that he walked right into the ambush.

The blow across the back of his legs knocked him down, and he tasted dirt as he landed face-first. There was no real pain, just the odd sense of being suddenly out of control. He lay still for a moment, listening as the attackers left their hiding places. There were four of them, and they had him surrounded.

"I got him," an excited male voice cried, almost cracking with excitement. "Did you see that? I got him!"

"Shut up, Tiny," a more authoritative voice said.

"Holy shit, it's a fuckin' *coon,*" said a third.

"She's banging a nigger," the last one said with more surprise than anger.

Leonardo got to his knees, but was struck across the back with the bat. "Stay down in the dirt, nigger, where you belong!" the one called Tiny said.

Leonardo did as ordered. It was so dark a normal person would make out only shadowy forms, but he had no trouble seeing their faces. They were all teenage white boys. Leonardo even recognized one of them: Bruce Cocker.

"What you want to do with him, Bruce?" a tall, acne-spotted boy said. He had the swagger of a schoolyard bully, and the smile of someone who enjoyed hurting people.

"Yeah," added the fat one called Tiny. "If he needs another smack, let me know."

Bruce crouched in front of Leonardo. The boy's gaze was cold and completely sober. "Depends on his attitude, I suppose."

Leonardo had seen that look before, the gaze of a white man certain his woman had crossed the color line. He smiled. "Hard for me to tap-dance for you while I'm down here, massah."

Bruce didn't change expression. The acne-ridden boy appeared over his shoulder and whispered in his ear like some devil. "You've eyeballed him enough. Let's teach him a lesson, like we planned."

"Clora's my girl," Bruce said to Leonardo. "And you been putting your hands all over her, haven't you?"

Leonardo raised one hand, the palm dirty from the ground, and looked at it in mock surprise. "This hand? Lordy, massah, I swear I ain't."

Bruce smacked him openhanded. The blow wasn't particularly powerful, and Leonardo absorbed it with ease. But he acted as if it hurt, and yelled in mock pain.

"Integration was the worst thing ever happened to this country," Tiny said in disgust. "These stuck-up darkies need a fucking lesson. Ain't that right, Travis?"

"You know it, Tiny," the bespectacled one named Travis said, and slapped hands with the fat one.

"Tie him up, Travis," Bruce said as he straightened. "But don't use the long rope. We'll need that later."

Travis grabbed Leonardo's hands and crossed his wrists at the small of his back. He tied him badly, using multiple pointless loops. Even if he'd been bound well, Leonardo could've easily broken free; but now he was curious to see if they'd really go through with what they clearly intended.

"Get up," Bruce said, and nudged him with his

foot. Leonardo got to his knees, his eyes open extra wide to convey mocking minstrel-style fear. Bruce nodded to his pimply friend. "Dave?"

"All the way up on your feet, you stupid tar baby," Dave said, and kicked him for emphasis.

Leonardo complied, head down to hide the attack of giggles building in him at the situation's absurdity.

Bruce grabbed a handful of Leonardo's Afro and jerked his head back. "Something funny, nigger?"

"Not a thing," Leonardo managed to say with a straight face.

"So how'd you meet Clora, anyway? Her daddy don't let her out of his sight."

Leonardo's lip trembled as he tried not to laugh. To Bruce it looked like terror.

"Don't matter how," Dave said. "He knew not to cross the line. Your daddy never told you what used to happen to niggers who even looked cross-eyed at a white girl?"

"Oh, lawsie, sir, I never knew who my daddy was," Leonardo said with a grin.

Dave punched him awkwardly over Bruce's shoulder. Again Leonardo reacted quickly, rolling with the slap to keep from breaking the boy's hand. Dave then spat in his face.

Leonardo clenched his teeth and fought the desire to rip his hands free. He glared at Dave and said, "You mighty tough when you're in a bunch. How about you untie me and try that one on one?"

Dave just grinned. "Fuck you, nigger."

Leonardo wrenched his head free from Bruce's grip. This game was quickly losing its charm. "Yeah, I been all over your pretty little Snow White up in her tower. I wrung her out so good, she begs me not to go every time I leave. She ever beg *you*?"

Bruce stared at him, his expression more hurt than angry.

"Cut his nuts off, Bruce!" Travis urged.

At last Bruce asked calmly, "Do you know who I am?"

"Just some pasty white asshole with a dick the size of my pinkie finger," Leonardo said with a grin.

"C'mon, quit talking, let's teach this jungle bunny a lesson," Dave said, jumping around in his fury.

Tiny smacked the bat against his open palm. "Let me work on him some more."

Bruce stepped close to Leonardo and said, just loud enough for him to hear, "I'm Bruce Cocker. My daddy is Byron Cocker. That means I can pretty much do anything I want in this county and get away with it. You understand me?"

Equally soft, Leonardo said, "Takes a big man to hide behind his daddy."

Bruce scowled, then spit in Leonardo's face. Dave howled with laughter, while Travis and Tiny slapped high fives. Bruce whirled and said, "Keep it down, you dumb-asses. And bring him on."

They pushed Leonardo through the woods

until they reached a clearing where a large oak tree rose into the night sky. "You know what this place is?" Dave asked Leonardo. "My daddy told me they used to hang uppity niggers from this-here tree. If you look close, you can see the scar in the branch where the ropes dug in."

With his vampiric night vision Leonardo had no trouble seeing the mark. He'd seen plenty of them on old trees throughout the South. He looked around at the boys. None of them was out of high school, and only Dave seemed to really be motivated by genuine racial hatred. Bruce acted out of jealousy, and the other two simply wanted the approval of their cool friends.

Dave took the long rope and began expertly tying a hangman's noose. "My daddy showed me how to do this. Said sometimes a man has to take the law into his own hands, because some folks just need killing. Know what I mean, nigger?"

Leonardo stared at the noose, recalling the swinging bodies of slain men from his childhood. The reality of the situation drained the last bit of the humor from it. He stood up straight, looked Dave in the eye, and said coldly, "My name is Leonardo. *You* can call me Mr. Jones."

Dave smacked him across the face with the rough noose. "Your name is whatever I call you, boy. I am a white man, and you will *respect* that."

This time Leonardo did not pretend the blow hurt. "I don't see a *man* anywhere around me. Just a bunch of chicken-shit cracker boys."

The rage in Dave's face was something to see, but before he could respond Bruce got right in Leonardo's face. "We'll see how funny this is when you're dancing in midair."

"Hey, y'all, wait a minute," Travis suddenly said. "You know where we are? This is old Mama Prudence's property. That's her house over yonder." He pointed to a dark house through the trees. "They say she's a witch. Maybe we should, I dunno, go somewhere else?"

"Jesus Christ, are you six years old?" Bruce said. "She's just an old lady. My daddy has to take her groceries to her."

"Maybe this ain't a good idea in general," Tiny said, his voice trembling. "I mean, he's colored and all, but this is still, like, *murder*, ain't it?"

Dave ignored them and said, "Somebody put that bucket under the noose."

Travis put the metal bucket in place. Dave tossed the rope over the branch, then put the noose around Leo's neck. As he cinched it tight he said, "Beg for your life, nigger, and you might see the sunrise."

Leonardo laughed. "I wouldn't beg you to piss on me if I was on fire."

Dave spat in his face. He pulled on the rope, forcing Leonardo to climb onto the bucket. Bruce tied the loose end of the rope around the tree trunk, and Leonardo stood on tiptoes to keep the pressure off his neck.

The boys silently watched him. The reality of

their act registered on Tiny and Travis, but Dave was positively gleeful and Bruce remained enigmatic.

"Last chance, nigger," Dave said. "Beg for your life, and we'll let you down."

Leonardo laughed, and directed his words to Bruce. "You know what your girlfriend told me about you, big man? She said, 'Lordy, he got this thing between his legs that looks just like a man's dick . . . only smaller.'"

Bruce's face went cold with rage, and he kicked the bucket out from under Leonardo's feet. "That's it, man!" Dave cheered.

The rope yanked tight. Leonardo gurgled and kicked.

"Hey, I think the joke's, like, over," Tiny said. "He's gonna get hurt."

"Fuck him," Dave said, eyes alive with amusement.

"Yeah," Bruce muttered. "Fuck him."

Tiny and Travis exchanged a look, but neither had the courage to face Dave and Bruce.

Leonardo made the convulsions weaker, until he finally hung limp, his tongue hanging out. He swung in a slow arc, his feet grazing the bucket.

For a long moment the only sounds were insects and wind. Finally Dave stepped up to the hanging body and put his ear to Leonardo's chest. He listened for a long moment, then said, "He's dead, all right."

"Shit," Travis said, his voice trembling. "We gotta get outta here."

"Just hold it right there," Bruce commanded. "Nobody's panicking. We did this, and now we're gonna walk away. Nobody seen us, there ain't nothing to tie us to this boy, and believe me, the sheriff ain't gonna look too hard at one more nigger suicide."

"That's right," Dave said. He stepped behind Leonardo, uncinched his hands, and pocketed the twine. "So let's just get back to our car and have a beer and a toke."

"And if any of you say a word about it, remember we can all be charged as adults. Remember that." Bruce glared at his two friends, trying for the expression his father used on recalcitrant informants. It seemed to work.

He went over to Leonardo and gave him a shove. His body swung in the night, the tree branch creaking under his weight. "Fuck you," he spat. Then he walked away without a word. His friends quickly followed.

CHAPTER 19

"Young man. *Young man!*"

Vampires did not lose consciousness in the standard way, but their minds could wander so that it appeared to outsiders that they had, in fact, passed out. Leonardo's mind had wandered that way, into memories of humid South Carolina nights and the terror of white-hooded figures moving through the Spanish moss. Now he was yanked back to the moment by a sharp blow from a stick.

"*Ow!*" he said, startled rather than hurt. He opened his eyes, and for an instant his swaying view of the world disoriented him. Then he remembered.

"Don't ignore me when I'm speaking to you," the woman standing below him said in a thick drawl. She waved the stick like a rigid schoolmistress.

It was still dark, but Leonardo saw her clearly. She was white, and wore an antique black dress with lace at the collar and wrists. Blond hair was piled high on her head in an outdated style. Despite these antiquarian signs, she appeared around thirty years old, and was beautiful in that cold European way. He instantly knew that she, too, was a vampire. She barked, "Now you come down from there this instant and tell me what in blazes you think you're doing hanging there."

Leonardo reached up, grabbed the rope holding him with both hands, and pulled until it snapped. He landed silently and tossed the noose aside. "Lady, some crackers *lynched* me."

"I know, I saw that."

"And you didn't say anything?"

"You could easily have freed yourself, had you wished to do so. I'm wondering why you didn't."

He brushed detritus from his jeans and felt his neck. The rope left little ridges in his skin. "Seemed easier to just go along with it."

"Really?" she asked dubiously.

"And I wanted to see if they'd actually do it."

"You had any doubt?"

He looked up at the rope end still swaying above him. "I guess not. Just hope, maybe."

She scowled, so that her face took on a pinched look as if she'd smelled something foul. "Hope for your kind is a misplaced and pointless indulgence."

He turned to her. "*My* kind? In case you hadn't noticed, we're the same."

She snorted. "Oh, hardly. You and I are very different, as anyone can see."

So as he always suspected, even the undead had a color line. After what he'd just been through, it surprised him but didn't enrage him as it might have otherwise. He managed a slight smile and said, "Right. I'll just be on my way, then, Missus Massah." He was glad he parked the truck in a different place, where perhaps the rednecks hadn't found it.

"Wait," the woman called after him. "I'm sorry, I'm not behaving like a lady. My etiquette tutor would turn in her grave. You're right, making an issue of mortal demarcations is pedantic. You've been mistreated here, and it's my duty to see that you're taken care of."

He stopped and looked at her skeptically. "Why yours?"

"This is my land. This old tree was planted the same year I was born."

Leonardo started to reply, but something struck him anew. As she moved into a clear shaft of moonlight, the woman looked uncannily familiar. "Do I know you?"

She laughed at his presumption. "I don't believe we move in the same circles."

He took a hesitant step toward her. *Man,* she did look familiar. "My name's Leonardo Jones.

Ma'am," he added, with fake but hopefully passable humility.

"I am Miss Prudence Bolade," she said haughtily. "Owner of the Bolade mansion and plantation you see through the trees."

They looked at each other for a long moment. Each was ready to fight should the other attempt to exert any vampiric influence, but neither did so. Finally Prudence said, "To make amends for your treatment on my property, Mr. Jones, why don't you come in for a cup of tea?"

"You drink tea?"

"No, of course not. But I find the aroma delightful."

He smiled. "You inviting me in to sniff your tea?"

"I'm inviting you in to get to know you. Since you and I are distinctive creatures operating in the same area, it behooves us to be civil, and to understand each other. The tea just provides a social structure."

"I got a friend uses big words like that," Leonardo said. He sensed no danger, and if he was wrong, he deserved whatever happened. "Sure, I'll sniff your tea."

She curtsied. "I am truly obliged."

He followed her through the woods to the back of the big, dark house. It sent shivers of memory through Leonardo as he recalled similar houses of his mortal youth, and the fear associated with them. Even though most white people were kind to him, or at least benignly indifferent, the knowledge that they *could* mistreat him with impunity poisoned all relationships. This night's experiences brought all that vividly back.

Suddenly he realized where he was. This was the very house where he and Zginski had gotten directions that day they picked up his car. Now he knew why the woman looked familiar: she had answered the door that day, and even though she'd been old and wrinkled, he knew it had been her. Vampires didn't age in the traditional sense, but if they went too long without feeding they withered, which often looked the same. And because it had been broad daylight, when his powers were weak, he hadn't realized what she was. And because he was a Negro and thus beneath her notice, she didn't recognize him now.

He kept all this to himself. Zginski would be proud.

They entered through the kitchen door, which would've been the servants' entrance in earlier times. Leonardo was totally on guard, but nothing appeared from the darkness to attack him, and Prudence puttered around the kitchen exactly as she might have had she been mortal. She did not offer him a seat, however, and he stood by the door, hands in his pockets.

"You know, there was a time when a young man of your race wouldn't have been allowed in this house as a guest," she said as she put the kettle on the stove. "Times have certainly changed for your people."

"I'm real tired of that whole subject for tonight," Leo said wearily. He noted that here among the faded finery, her clothes looked appropriate. "So how long you been in this house?"

"I was born here. This house is over a hundred years old, and I can remember when different things were installed in it. The spiral staircase in the foyer? My daddy had it shipped from a plantation in Murfreesboro. It doesn't quite fit, so he had to cut one corner off the door that opens under it."

She handed Leonardo a saucer and cup. She took her own, closed her eyes, and inhaled the steam rising from it. "Nothing like the smell of mint tea on a summer night," she said.

Leonardo sniffed his. There was a coincidental similarity to the cologne one of his erstwhile murderers wore, but he ignored it. "Not too bad. You do this a lot?"

Prudence laughed. "You must cultivate a taste for the small, gentle things, Mr. Jones. The gross and vulgar are so easy for our kind. We could become animals, rending flesh and bone indiscriminately. Our human traits need constant nurturing."

"Maybe." He put down his saucer. "Look, I got to ask you something. Have you been keeping company with a tall redheaded white girl named Clora?"

Prudence made a great show of putting down her own cup, which gave her time to choose her words. So it had *not* been Patience after all. "As a matter of fact, Mr. Jones, I have. She visited me the other night, and I confess to noticing your presence as well. I'm known as a bit of a seer to the local folks and she came to me to ask about her future. I saw in the tea leaves that a lover would be her murderer. Now I understand why it was so clear."

Leonardo pondered this. "Well . . . yeah, I figure she'll die eventually because of me."

"I suppose I should apologize for trespassing on *your* property, then. Will you make her one of us when her time comes?"

"Naw. There's enough of us running around."

Prudence smiled. "Then we agree, at least, on that. Come, let's sit in the parlor. It's so much more comfortable."

Leonardo followed her into the lush, musty front room, still alert for any trap or danger. They passed through the door modified by her father, beneath the unwieldy spiral staircase and into the once-luxurious sitting room. Here the faded, dissipated quality of everything felt stronger, and he worried that the ancient furniture might be dry-rotted and fragile.

Prudence turned on a light and gestured to one of the big wingback chairs. "That's the seat of honor. It belonged to my daddy; it was where he received obeisance from his sharecroppers."

Leonardo settled carefully into the seat. "And his slaves?"

"Now, Mr. Jones, that borders on the crude. I am showing you hospitality and kindness, and you wish to provoke me. Those are not the manners of a gentleman."

Leonardo couldn't hold back a smile. It was like talking to a female version of Zginski. "I apologize, ma'am. My mama did teach me better, it's just a long time since I had need of it."

"Your gracious apology is accepted."

"So do you live here alone?"

"Oh, yes. Very little needs tending, and I maintain just enough contact with the outside world to avert suspicion of my true nature."

"How long have you been here?"

"Since my dear sister made me what I am." Her words grew cold as she spoke. "We were in love with the same man, a handsome young colonel of the Confederacy. He chose me, and as revenge she chose eternal damnation. She murdered him, and left me to rise after my death."

"No one can hurt you like family."

"A true thing, Mr. Jones."

She sniffed her tea again. "A man once wrote a song about us, did you know that? It was quite the popular tune for a brief time." She cleared her throat and sang in a low, flat voice:

"Listen to what I tell you, son, every word is true
The sisters haunt the night, and might fight over
   you
Nothing can steal your soul and stamp it in the
   mud
Like being the new play-pretty for the girls with
   games of blood."

"I don't know that song," Leonardo said.

"I didn't expect you would. Its moment of notoriety was brief."

"So where's your sister now?"

Prudence shrugged. "She left. She saw her damned state as a license to become a libertine. She always loved music, so I imagine somewhere she's parading her flesh to the 'lascivious pleasings of a lute,' as the Bard says."

She gazed up at the painting over the mantel. "And yet I still miss her. Before Vincent came along, we were as close as it's possible for sisters to be. Whatever happened between us was ages ago; now I would just like to press my cheek to hers one more time, and allow the past to wither and die."

Leonardo followed her glance, then did a double take. "Whoa," he blurted. "*That's* your sister?"

She nodded. "Patience Annabella Bolade."

"I *know* her."

Prudence kept all excitement from her voice. "That seems an unlikely coincidence."

"Yeah, but dang. There's this girl that looks just like her, and she's one of us. She's a singer at this bar where a friend of mine works. The Ringside, in Memphis."

Prudence delicately placed her cup on the table. Inside explosions of emotion tore through her, but outwardly she was as calm as if discussing the weather. With a polite smile she said, "Then perhaps I will visit the city to see this woman for myself."

Leonardo nodded, suddenly wishing he'd kept the revelation to himself. Even though she did her best to hide it, there was an eagerness in Prudence that seemed too strong for the moment. Zginski would've held back, parceling out the knowledge slowly to make sure he gave away only what was necessary. As Prudence betrayed her excitement, he would've kept her off-balance and floundering, the better to retain the position of power. Leonardo used to mock him for that sort of thing, but for the first time he understood its use.

"I'm probably wrong," he said. "Now that I look at it again, it's just a vague similarity."

Prudence wasn't fooled, but she had the information she needed: Patience was appearing as a musical act at an establishment called the Ringside. "Well, it was a moment of hope, at any rate."

"Misplaced and pointless?" he said.

She sighed with heavy sadness. "It always is."

CHAPTER 20

Gerry Barrister lay asleep on the couch in his office. It was long past closing, and he should have gone home. But something compelled him to stay.

He'd had that compulsion a lot lately. It would strike with irresistible certainty just as he was about to leave. He would wake thirsty, horny, and too weak to do more than drive home and collapse on his other couch.

Now he snored peacefully as Fauvette and Patience stood over him in the darkness. Patience shook her head. "*This* is your victim?"

"Yes," Fauvette said. In sleep, Barrister's features softened and he looked almost like a large, hairy baby.

"You could have any handsome young man you want. Why pick him?"

Fauvette ran her fingers lightly through Barrister's hair. He smiled in his sleep. "Rudy said my first long-term victim should be someone close by, so that when I fed on him my comings and goings wouldn't seem unusual. He said there was always the chance that someone would recognize that he was being used by one of us, and this way I'd be close enough to know about it."

Patience shook her head. To her the man looked lumpy and coarse with the scars of his former career. She couldn't imagine the physical intimacy required to feed on him as a traditional vampire. "Do you like him, at least?"

Fauvette shrugged. "He's all right. Sometimes he cries, which is a little awkward. He's known a lot of women, but none of them have treated him very well, I don't think. But most of the time he's content with whatever's happening in his head with me."

"He doesn't think it's real, does he?"

She shook her head. "On his own, he's never approached me."

"He patted you on the ass right in front of me."

"He does that with every girl who works here. He'll do it to you eventually."

"He'll draw back a nub if he does."

"But that's just it, he only does it when people are watching. It's part of his act. In private, he's a perfect gentleman."

"Do you always feed on him at work?"

She nodded. "Rudy says that's best. Do it where your presence isn't out of place."

Patience sighed. Zginski's influence with Fauvette reminded her of the way some of her old relatives felt about God. "You know, Rudy doesn't know everything about being a vampire."

"He knows more than I do."

"He *says*."

"He's never lied to me."

Before Patience could reply, Barrister shifted on the couch. Fauvette's influence would keep him asleep indefinitely, and normally she would feed from him during this time, taking just enough to sustain her until the next session. But tonight there would be something different.

Patience decided to drop the whole Zginski issue. She didn't trust her own motives for berating him to Fauvette, and until she did a dignified silence was best. "Are you ready, then?"

"Yes," Fauvette said. "How do I start?"

"I don't know exactly, honey. It happens for me when I'm singing, and everyone's focused on me. You have to sense the moment when all his attention is entirely, willingly on you, and learn to latch on to that energy. Does that make sense?"

Fauvette nodded.

Patience kissed her forehead. "I won't stand over you and watch. I'll be out in the dining room working on a song. Come get me if you need me."

Patience left, closing the office door quietly. Fauvette knelt on the floor in front of Barrister and brushed his hair back from his face. If she could master this, then he might live to see another birthday.

Patience stood in the darkened kitchen outside the office. Only traffic and the steady hum of refrigerator compressors broke the silence.

She *could* go and work on her music, as she'd said. She did want to learn the rest of the verses to "American Pie," as well as polish some of her own work. She understood that people wanted music they recognized with their dinner, and "American Pie" had that chorus eminently suited for singalongs. But some audiences wanted the surprise of originals. After all this time she had a good sense of when to change things up, since her life literally depended on it.

Something else gnawed at her, though. She drifted down the hall to the waitresses' lockers. All were padlocked, but when she idly flicked the one on Fauvette's the lock turned out to be unlatched. She looked back at the closed office door, and felt terrible for what she contemplated. But that didn't stop her.

She opened the locker door, wincing at the squeak, and stared into the rectangular space at a sliver of the girl's life.

Two things were taped to the inside of the door. One was a postcard that showed sunrise over the ocean, faded so that the only color left was a pale yellow. "Greetings from Gulf Shores" was printed in one corner. No doubt this had been the only sunrise in Fauvette's life before Zginski came along, and the pity of that made Patience choke a little.

The other was cut from a newspaper, recent enough that the paper had not yellowed. She squinted at it, trying to decipher the significance.

The headline over the photo had been torn in half, but the words "teen racial slaying" were still readable. A bloody body lay on a stretcher in the street while policemen restrained the mostly black crowd. But there, at the front of the crowd, behind the barricade, was a vampire. Even in a photograph, one vampire could always spot another one. A black girl vampire, Patience thought; it must be Olive, one of those who died when Zginski appeared.

She touched the paper over Olive's face. Patience had made and lost human acquaintances, but until meeting Fauvette she had never befriended another vampire. Was that sort of loss different? Had Fauvette and Olive been friends longer than human lifetimes? Would she and Fauvette still be friends in a century, when all the mortals around them had gone to the dust?

She looked through the other items. Most were directly related to Fauvette's job: skirt, blouses, apron, shoes. But in the bottom, beneath a folded towel, she found something she couldn't identify. After another check of the office door, she pulled out a plastic bag, tied with a metal wire, that contained some sort of dark powdery substance.

She untied the bag and sniffed. It smelled loamy and dank. With a smile, she reached inside and withdrew a pinch. When she held it close to her nose, she recognized it at once.

Dirt. Grave soil. One of a vampire's few creature comforts.

She shook her head but didn't laugh. There were no rules for this sort of thing; the transition from coffin to bed did not have to be made all at once. She carefully replaced the bag and closed the locker, feeling even more like a heel for her snooping.

Fauvette kissed Barrister lightly on the lips. His eyes opened and tried to focus. "Fauvette?" he said fuzzily; in his dreams her lips were also cool against his own.

"It's me," she said. "How do you feel?"

He blinked a few times, then smiled. She was naked, and his eyes took in her youthful form, all soft hair and gentle curves. "Tired. But pretty groovy. Did we do it?"

"Just like we always do, baby." She kissed him again, and let him touch her breasts.

"Dy-no-mite," he murmured with a smile and closed his eyes. His hand fell away.

She leaned closer and nibbled his earlobe. "Don't go back to sleep, honey. Look at me." She turned on the little desk lamp for illumination.

He rose on one elbow, shook his head a little, and gazed at her. She stayed as still as death, trying to sense the little shiver that meant energy was flowing from Barrister to her. She'd practically seen the air reverberate with it the night of Patience's show, but now there was nothing. Unless it was the slight, almost imperceptible tingle that faded almost at once.

Barrister watched her for a few moments longer, then closed his eyes. His head sank down, and he went back to sleep.

"Honey?" she said, and then more firmly, "Gerry?" But he was too far gone into dreams of carnal excess to respond.

Fauvette sighed and stood. She walked to the window and looked out at the deserted street. After a moment a Gran Torino went past, the *hooga-chakka* chorus from "Hooked on a Feeling" blaring from the 8-track. She winced at the intensity.

The office door opened, and Patience silently entered. She stood behind Fauvette, her hands on the girl's bare shoulders. "How'd it go?" she whispered.

"I don't know," Fauvette said aloud, still watching the world outside the window. "I think I felt something, but he wouldn't stay awake."

"You may need to do more. I sing; it's something to make people focus on me."

"I can't sing."

"Can you do anything *like* singing?"

"What's 'like singing'?" Fauvette snapped, whirling so fast her hair smacked Patience's face. "Should I belly dance? Read a poem? Dance a jig?"

Patience held up her hands. "Don't get defensive, honey. I just mean, because of what we are, it's easy to make people do things. It's more difficult to make them *want* to do something. It's the difference between looking at a painting because someone tells you to, and looking at one because it's so beautiful you can't look away."

Fauvette gestured at herself. "Then I don't think I can ever do it. No one looks at me that way."

Patience lifted the girl's chin. "I'm no classical beauty either, hon. Nothing quite like realizing you're stuck for all eternity with those twenty extra pounds that the world now considers unattractive. But *how* we look has nothing to do with it. It's about being . . ." She searched for the word. "Compelling."

Fauvette stepped around her, gathered her clothes, and began dressing. On the night she died, she was traveling home through the woods alone because Junior Caldwell ignored her at the revival. That humiliation, like her virginity, seemed doomed to repetition. "I don't know that I can ever master that. I'd probably be a dried-up old maid by now if I hadn't become what I am."

Patience knew better than to push the issue. Despite the years and experiences, something in Fauvette remained fundamentally childlike and easily hurt. And much like feeding on energy, no one could be taught how to overcome that; you either matured, or you didn't.

On the couch, Gerry Barrister moaned and rolled onto his back. His erection pressed firmly against his olive sans-a-belt slacks. To Patience, it seemed pitiful and sad.

• • •

🦌Zginski looked down at Alisa asleep on her bed. She wore a sheer nightgown, and her skin glistened with unhealthy sweat. The cancer had begun to eat into vital organs, and her body tried desperately to communicate its agony through the haze of Zginski's influence. So far, it was unsuccessful, but he knew that soon he would be forced to finish her. Their contract said he would let her feel no pain.

A book lay open on her chest. The spine read *Looking for Mr. Goodbar*. He picked it up and read the page where she had stopped. He grimaced; this modern American fiction struck him as more gynecology than literature. And when the body, the instrument of love, held no mystery, love would inevitably become as base an emotion as jealousy or hate.

He unbuttoned his patchwork shirt and stepped out of the platform shoes. The footwear made him two inches taller, which secretly pleased him; he had once been of average height, but during his time in limbo people had grown taller in general. A short man stood out almost as much as a tall one, and the shoes helped him blend in.

It was almost dawn, and now that he was on his traditional schedule he should descend to the basement to rest. Yet something kept him at Alisa's bedside. She moaned softly, and intermittently tossed her head. He knew what was happening in her mind, and felt oddly sad at its pathetic unreality. Chad would never be beside her when she awoke.

At last he said firmly, "Alisa, awaken."

She opened her eyes at once, and stared up at him with the desperate, on-the-verge look of a woman distracted at the worst possible moment. Her surroundings gradually replaced the landscape of her dreams. "Rudy," she whimpered, tears welling in her eyes. He touched her cheek. She swallowed hard, emotions churning within her.

"I wish to feed," he said.

She nodded and turned her head to display the bite marks over her jugular.

He felt the tug of her blood, but held back. When she finally noticed she said, "What?"

He shrugged out of the shirt and stood bare to the waist. He put his thumbnail to his chest and dug it deeply into the skin. When he finished, a three-inch gash cut across his pectoral muscle.

Alisa gasped and with difficulty rose on her elbows to stare at the wound. "What are you doing?"

"The vampire in that Irishman's famous book did this," he said. "I thought you would appreciate the literary allusion. It allowed him to control one of the female characters."

"You already control me pretty well," she said.

"It was also the first step in transforming her into a vampire."

Alisa said nothing. A thick drop of blood, so deeply crimson it was almost black, seeped from the wound and poised, tearlike, for descent down his torso.

"We have discussed this numerous times," he continued. "Your answer has never wavered, and I respect your consistency. But I have never presented you with the reality of the option."

She watched the play of light on the drop's surface. "Drink from you and live forever?"

"I cannot promise 'forever.' But I can insure you will not die of your disease, and that your pain will end. And you will have free will."

Alisa sat up slowly. The drop swelled; surely it must fall soon. "Why are you doing this now?"

"I fear it may be the last time for you to consider it with a clear mind."

She understood his meaning. He could sense the cancer's progress from the qualities in her blood. She got to her knees on the bed and leaned close to his chest. The drop began its slow track down his skin, and another swelled behind it. "I swore I wouldn't. I don't want to be a corpse walking around. I don't want to live off death."

"As I do?"

That got her attention. She finally looked into his eyes. "You could make me do this, couldn't you?"

"Yes."

She licked her lips, suddenly torn. She had made the decision after their first night together, when he had consumed her blood and left her wet, and drained, and sated. It had been their agreement ever since, and although he occasionally inquired, he never demanded a choice until now. "I'd be alone forever."

"Loneliness and solitude are not the same."

"Are you alone?"

"I was. I am no longer." Even as he said this, though, he wondered where the idea came from.

She had no illusions that he referred to his time with her. She knew there must be other vampires, but she never inquired, and he never offered.

She sat back on her heels. She was weak with disease and desire, and the decision seemed so plain, so obvious. Yet she could not do it. "No," she said. "I won't."

He said nothing.

"It's not that I can't," she continued, speaking as much to herself as to him. "It's that I choose not to. Death is natural. I don't fear it."

He nodded. "I will respect your decision and not offer again."

She was about to say thank you. But before she could form the words she was suddenly back in that mental realm where orgasmic lust overwhelmed her, and she barely noticed when Zginski sank his fangs into her neck.

Later, as the sun rose, Zginski stopped at Alisa's desk on his way to the basement. He perused the copies of the *Festa Maggotta* pages, marveling anew at their intricate, impenetrable script. The author, known only by the odd name Kiniculus, was as much a mystery as his tome: some sources called him a necromancer, others a char-latan, still others a fallen angel or risen demon. Certainly his mastery of the world's tongues, and his ability to combine them to both convey and protect arcane information, implied a more-than-human knowledge. Zginski often wondered if he were a vampire, not necessarily more intelligent than men but simply longer-lived, able to absorb more information over a longer period of time.

He picked up the latest bit of completed trans-lation. *The vampire,* it said, *does not exist in time as mortals do. Unless he possesses extreme will, his new state traps him in the moment of his death, unable to move forward or back in his existence. If he does possess the will, he may become more cunning than any mortal man by virtue of his ability to experience more, and thus learn more than a normal life span allows.*

Zginski smiled. Kiniculus indeed understood why some vampires became shambling mindless revenants, while those like Zginski found their own path in the world. Fortunately this informa-tion would never become public; he would make certain Alisa's notes were never published, but instead hidden where only he might refer to them.

At the thought of her impending death, he felt an uncharacteristic and unexpected pang of re-gret. Where were these emotions coming from? The only possible source was the blood-bond he'd used to save Fauvette and her friends. When his strength bolstered them, some of her empathy and morality must have infected him.

That had to be it. The alternative, that these were somehow his own feelings, was absurd.

He winced at the first full ray of sun through the window. He was tired, and the cut on his chest continued to ooze despite the towel he pressed against it. It would heal as he slept, and be gone when he rose, so he checked the locks on all the doors and descended into the cool darkness.

CHAPTER 21

The apartment was in run-down public housing covered by the new Section 8 provisions, where Zginski stood out far more prominently than he liked. He was about during daylight again, but only barely; it was late afternoon, and while the sun baked everything with a final surge of intensity, it also steadily sank toward the horizon. It would not debilitate him much, or for long.

Fauvette's new home was affordable on her limited income, and a logical first step away from the decrepit warehouse. When she was ready to move into a real house, it would be simple enough. Her pale skin and odd demeanor drew attention, but suspicious onlookers no doubt thought she was a drug user spiraling toward her end, or a runaway trapped by circumstances. The truth would by its nature be very far down the list, and her uneducated neighbors seemed the last ones likely to divine it.

Four black teenage boys sat on the broad hood of a Cadillac listening to a song urging them to be a "shining star." To Zginski their sullen stares were very much the opposite of "shining." He nodded to them as he passed, aware that their gazes followed him.

A boy sporting an enormous Afro slid off the car, belligerently stuck his chest out, and called to Zginski's back, "What you looking at, honky?"

"Man, you better shut up," another said seriously. "I bet he going to see that creepy-ass white girl."

"Aw, I ain't afraid of her," the first boy said. "I don't believe in all that voodoo-witchcraft jive."

Zginski paused, his back still to them. He concentrated and sent a wave of terror-inducing power into their psyches, ferreting out whatever scared them most. He sensed their antagonism turn to fear so quickly it was almost comical. He smiled as he entered the four-story building.

The hallway smelled of urine and dust. Various sayings and symbols marred the walls, some painted over and then remarked. Somewhere a TV blared, "Today on *Donahue*," only to be drowned out by a crying baby.

Fauvette lived on the ground floor, in the back beneath the stairwell. She opened the door wearing only a white bathrobe. It made her normally death-pale complexion look almost normal. Her wet hair hung past her shoulders. "I'm just about ready," she said. "Come in."

He did so, closing and bolting the door behind him. The living room was entirely bare, its walls pockmarked and stained. Drawn blinds covered the single window. He followed her down the equally Spartan hallway to the single bedroom.

She went into the bathroom and began brushing her hair. "Thanks for offering me a ride to work. Cabs get expensive, and some won't even come into this neighborhood. So what did you want to talk to me about?"

He looked around the bedroom. The door had four dead bolts on the inside and the heavily curtained windows were closed with three enormous latches. In the movies vampires used mortal slaves to guard them during their rest, but Fauvette preferred to rely on strong locks. The bed was a saggy single mattress and box spring with only a sheet and thin blanket; she had not yet acquired even a pillow. "I have not seen your friend since she stood me up," he said. "I wondered if you had."

Fauvette smiled. "Yes, as a matter of fact. And she had no choice on that, someone followed her home from the club and she didn't want to risk involving you. I said you'd appreciate that."

Zginski looked at the walls. They were decorated with posters featuring handsome young men, apparently star athletes and popular entertainers. He shook his head; poor Fauvette was trying to mimic what she imagined a girl her apparent age might have in her room. "Then please inform her I would like to reschedule our meeting."

"You can tell her yourself, she'll be at the club tonight." She leaned out the bathroom door and grinned knowingly at him. "Isn't that why you offered to take me to work? So you'd have an excuse to see her?"

"I do not employ such subterfuge."

"Of course not." She withdrew and, in a moment, the hair dryer's whine drowned out any other noise.

Zginski sat on the edge of the bed. When the dryer shut off he said, "I would like to ask you a question."

"Sure," she called.

"Since our sharing of blood at the warehouse, have you felt anything . . . unusual?"

She leaned out again. "How do you mean?"

"Out of the ordinary. Different from how you were before."

She thought for a moment. "No, I don't think so. Why, have you?"

"I am uncertain," he said honestly.

She came out of the bathroom, her hair blown dry and enormous. She went to the closet, dropped the robe to the floor, and stood naked as she selected her clothes. Not that it mattered, since she'd change into her uniform once she got to work, but having a wardrobe made her feel so grown-up.

Zginski gazed openly at her bare form. He recalled the night in the warehouse when he'd taken that body, using his influence to arouse her so much that the breaking of her maidenhead was no more than a twinge instead of the agony she usually experienced. He'd touched her there, and there, and kissed her there; the passion had been brutal and rapacious, but also genuine. Yet now he felt, not feral lust, but a kind of tenderness that he could barely comprehend. He wanted to take her again, but he also wanted *her* to want it. He had no clue how to express that feeling.

She dressed quickly in bell-bottom jeans and a red button-up blouse tied above her navel. She slipped sandals on and said, "How do I look?"

"Typical," he said.

She grinned. "Perfect, then. Let's go." She headed for the front door without waiting for him.

He stood to follow. From beneath the bed where he'd sat, a fine cloud of something drifted into the air. Curious, he lifted the ruffly, secondhand mattress skirt.

Dirt dribbled out from between the mattress and box spring. A layer of soil had been evenly spread there.

"You coming?" she called from the front door.

He smiled. The grave soil was pathetic. And oddly, also touching.

🐾 Byron Cocker sat in his rented '74 Chevy Impala down the block from the Ringside. He sipped soda from a cup and munched his way through an order of McDonald's french fries. His rebuilt jaw sent familiar twinges of pain through him as he chewed. He'd gotten used to that, because the doctors only wanted to treat it with pills that made him dopey. Getting drunk was one thing, but he wasn't about to get hooked on drugs, legal or otherwise.

The stakeout was not an investigative task at which he excelled. It was late afternoon, and he'd been here since before lunch. He knew Zginski would spot his normal vehicle at once, so he'd rented the Impala as a disguise. It handled okay, and the air conditioner kept the heat at bay, but what Cocker really wanted was to kick in a door and bust some heads. His failure to get information out of Patience, and the ridiculous fear that seized him in her house, chagrined him. *You don't have a badge anymore,* he kept reminding himself. *You could go to jail if you did that, and most likely your cellmates would include some of the men you once sent there.*

At last the tricked-out Mustang appeared at the red light, and moments later pulled into the bar's parking lot. Zginski got out, walked to the passenger side, and opened the door.

The little jail-bait waitress Fauvette emerged. There was no way to hear at this distance, but they were in midconversation, the kind that only people who knew each other well conducted in public. Cocker wondered exactly how these two were connected.

• • •

"It will never work," Zginski said.

"It works for her," Fauvette replied. "Why are you so against it?"

"Because it leaves our victims . . ." He paused as a couple emerged from the Ringside and walked to their car. When they were safely out of hearing range he concluded, "With too much free will. I do not know exactly how she does what she does, but I suspect it is all a charade, and she secretly feeds in the traditional way."

"I've seen her do it. I've felt it."

"The power of suggestion. You told me you heard about it before you saw it, so were primed to accept it. I was here briefly on her first night, remember, and I saw nothing."

Fauvette shook her head at the absurdity. "And why would she fake something like that?"

He looked at Fauvette seriously. "People often do inexplicable things in order to feel unique. Becoming one of us does not necessarily change that urge."

"So you think she's lying?"

"Or deluded."

With a jealous whine even she found distasteful, Fauvette said, "I thought you liked her."

"Finding someone attractive does not blind me to their faults."

She glared at him. "I'll be sure to remember that."

"She was to teach you her technique. Have you been able to replicate her results? That should tell you something."

Fauvette felt a surge of shame and anger. "You know, I think you have a problem with anyone who doesn't agree with you. You felt the same way about Mark."

Zginski held up his hand. "That is a different, and unrelated, topic."

"It's an *unfinished* topic."

"And will remain so until Mark returns from wherever he has gone."

Fauvette started to fire back a reply, then thought better of it. "Well, I have to get to work. Are you coming in?"

"No."

"Are you at least coming back to see Patience's show tonight?"

"Possibly. I have not decided."

"I'll plan to find my own way home, then." She stamped toward the door, then looked back at him. "Rudy, tell me the truth: do you ever want to have another time like we did in the warehouse basement?"

He kept his face impassive, even as his emotions churned and roiled. "I do not believe that is an appropriate conversation for the five minutes before your shift begins."

"It's a yes or no question. That only takes a second."

"No, it is a question that masks the true question."

"Huh?"

He was stalling, and doing it badly. He snapped, "We will discuss this at a later time, Fauvette," and turned to walk away. Then he stopped. His tone softened. "But I will say this: it has become one of my fondest memories."

She shook her head and snapped, "I swear, sometimes I wish I'd never met you." She slammed the door behind her.

Byron Cocker watched the Mustang pull out into traffic. His urge was to follow it, but he had no idea what the Impala's 4093 six-cylinder engine would do in such a situation. The Mustang was a V8, and chasing it now would be as pointless as it had been the time before.

Instead he forced himself to consider what he'd seen. Zginski had dropped off Fauvette, and they'd had some kind of intense discussion before she went inside. Surely they weren't a couple; the age difference was just too much. Besides, a man like that wouldn't allow his woman to work, let alone take a job where she was publicly ogled. What then?

Father, he decided, *and daughter.*

He leaned back against the seat and smiled. Well, that was handy. As a parent himself, Cocker knew one undeniable truth: nothing he could do to Zginski, no humiliation he could inflict, would compare with the pain of seeing his *child* hurt. Fathers protected their sons, but they *treasured* their daughters. And Cocker knew just how to hurt a girl so that she would never be able to look a man, even her own father, in the eye again.

He drained his soda in triumph. There was no need to sit here anymore; he had time to drive home and clean up before returning for the evening show. And this time, he was damn sure he'd stay awake to follow little Fauvette.

CHAPTER 22

Prudence gave herself a final once-over in the foyer mirror. According to the magazines Cocker brought with her groceries, she now looked like a slightly eccentric, old-fashioned version of a typical modern woman of her apparent age. Thanks to the relatively youthful, vigorous blood of Clora Crabtree and Byron Cocker, that age was now somewhere around twenty-five. Since she was nineteen when she was turned, it was certainly closer than her recent withered, dried-up self. Fresh blood could do wonders.

She spent the previous night after Leonardo left scavenging the many closets full of ancient clothes, in search of something that would look at least somewhat contemporary. She settled on a pink top with billowing angel sleeves and matching pants. A belt emphasized her tiny waist, and made her recall how much Patience hated having her own round form laced into a corset. She wore a necklace of dark brown wooden beads and matching earrings. Her eye shadow was also dark, and heavy. She did her best to match the effect on the model's face, but worried that she'd actually made herself look rather raccoonlike.

She winced against the afternoon sun as she went to the freestanding garage beside the house. A call to Privitt's gas station in town had gotten slack-jawed old Herm Privitt to come out and charge the battery, check the oil, and do whatever else needed to be done to get her seldom-driven 1958 Ford Thunderbird ready for the trip to Memphis. It would be her first journey to the city since the car was new.

The T-bird started on the first try, and she pulled the long, narrow shifting lever down until the little indicator stopped over the "D." It was completely unlike the first car she'd owned, and her left foot still sought the clutch. She eased the vehicle out so slowly it barely raised the dust along the unpaved driveway, and when she pulled onto the highway she soon had four other annoyed drivers bumper to bumper behind her.

🎔 Byron Cocker unknowingly passed Prudence going the opposite direction. He parked the Impala behind his own car in the driveway. He yelled "Bruce?" as he closed the front door behind him and leafed through the mail waiting on the side table. The TV in the den was on, as were the overhead lights in all the rooms. A loaf of bread and jar of peanut butter were out on the kitchen counter. "Bruce!" he yelled again.

"In my room," came the muffled voice.

"Get down here and clean up this mess!" he yelled. Then he went to his own bedroom, undressed, and took a shower.

As he toweled off, he noted each of his scars. There were the puckered bullet holes: one in the dead center of his chest, deflected by his sternum so that it missed his heart, another in his left thigh, and a final one just above his right wrist. The thin, raised lines on his belly showed where a drunk stabbed him four times, so rapidly that Cocker barely registered the first before the final one drove home. His jaw looked pink and smooth where the skin had grown tight over his reconstructed bone. His farmer tan, which left his torso pale white while his arms and face were sunbrowned, only accented these souvenirs.

By the time Cocker emerged from his room the bread and peanut butter were gone and the lights turned off. Bruce slouched in his dad's armchair clad only in his running shorts. "Whose Chevy is that in the drive?" the boy said without taking his eyes off the TV.

"Mine," Cocker said. "It's a rental."

Bruce turned to inquire further, but did a double take instead.

Cocker wore a high-collared shirt unbuttoned

down to his first bullet scar, with a gold chain displayed just above his graying chest hair. His brown polyester pants were tight, and the stacked shoes added another inch to his already-formidable height. His hair was slicked down, the part ruler-straight.

"Have you got a *date*?" Bruce said in disbelief.

"I'm going back into the city," Byron said as he checked himself a final time in the foyer mirror. "Don't wait up."

"You *do* have a date," Bruce said, his voice tinged with disapproval. He didn't know when it would be okay for his father to start seeing other women, but he was sure it wasn't time yet.

Cocker blushed. "I'm visiting a *friend*. Gerry Barrister. We used to wrestle together, remember? He's opened a place in Memphis."

Bruce snorted. It occurred to Cocker that their whole relationship could have been summed up in that one contemptuous noise. He said in what he hoped was a reasonable tone, "Son, please don't cop an attitude every time I talk to you. I don't have a date, but even if I did it wouldn't mean any disrespect to your mama's memory."

Bruce didn't look at him. "Yes, sir."

"You and I, we're all we've got. We're the whole family now."

"Yes, sir," he repeated in the same tone.

Cocker clenched his fists. The disrespectful little shit deserved another whipping, but he didn't have time right now. "All right, then," he said as he left. "Have it your way."

"Yeah, I'm fucking Burger King," Bruce muttered as the door closed. The setting sun blazed through the windows, turning the now-silent room deep orange.

He pulled a joint from the waistband of his shorts and looked around for a lighter. He sucked the smoke down and held it while the TV played a black-and-white rerun of *Gilligan's Island*.

He'd stayed stoned as much as possible since that night in the woods, trying to keep the vividness of what they'd done from truly settling on him. The thought that it was cold-blooded murder lurked at the edge of his brain, but the dopey haze kept it from moving to the front of his thoughts. Sooner or later, though, he would have to acknowledge it and figure out what, if anything, there was to be done about it.

Every morning he listened for the gunshot smack of the newspaper hitting the driveway, and rushed to check it before his father woke up. Was it seriously possible that the boy's body remained hanging from the tree, undiscovered and unmissed? Or had something fortuitous happened, like the rope breaking and wild dogs eating and scattering the corpse? Would that be proof that God truly did look out for him?

He'd talked to Dave once since that night, but his friend was even more messed up. Dave had been to California earlier in the summer and brought back enough heroin to get him through until the start of the school year; he called it an "ice cream habit," which apparently meant he would quit as soon as he was sure the trouble had passed. Travis and Tiny had not returned his calls; he worried they might panic and confess.

There was only one thing to do, he knew. He would have to go see for himself, and if the corpse was still there, he'd have to bury it where no one would find it. Which would involve *touching* it, a possibility that scared the hell out of him.

He once snuck into his father's office and saw crime-scene photos of his mother's corpse, a sight that gave him nightmares for months. Her face was intact, but the whole back of her head was gone; she looked mildly startled. There was also a huge exit wound just below the hollow of her throat big enough to hold a softball.

He imagined what the black boy would look like now: distended tongue protruding from swollen lips, eyes bulging and probably swarming with gnats. Insects would be all over the place, flies and midges and other things that normally fed on carcasses. They did not discriminate between humans and animals; they were completely unbigoted. For some reason this made him feel even worse.

But that would all have to wait until after dark. By then he hoped to be too stoned to get off the couch, as he had been every night since the lynching.

Then he realized that going to hide the body would also take him close to Clora Crabtree's house. That had not occurred to him before. Memories of his times with her began to dissipate the dope. He stretched and smiled to himself; maybe his famous daddy wouldn't be getting any that night, but it didn't mean *no* Cocker would.

🦇 Leonardo waited for Zginski behind the Ringside. He'd changed from his usual tank top into a pullover shirt, and felt unaccountably awkward in it. He sat on the curb beside the big metal trash bin, unoffended by the smell and certain that no one would bother him. One more poor black kid getting drunk in the shadow of a Dumpster wouldn't raise an eyebrow in Memphis.

Just past sunset Zginski backed the Mustang into the alley and parked facing out, toward Madison Avenue. He emerged wearing a black turtleneck under a tan sport coat, with black bell-bottom slacks. He noticed Leonardo immediately. "Are you waiting for me?"

"Yeah," Leonardo said as he stood. He brushed dirt and leaves from his jeans. "I need to talk to you."

"You are doing so."

"Oh, that's a good one. Nothing gets past you."

"What do you wish to tell me?"

Leonardo looked around to make sure they weren't overheard. Even as he did it, he realized it was the kind of thing Zginski might do, and for the first time he understood that level of caution. When he was sure they were alone he said, "I met another one of us. Out in the country close to where we bought your car."

"Where your victim lives?"

"Yep. Remember that house where we asked for directions?"

Zginski was suddenly grim. "Indeed? Tell me about him."

"Her. Her name's Prudence, and I think she's Patience's sister."

Zginski was now seriously focused. "Tell me how this meeting came about."

Leonardo gave him the short version, and was relieved that Zginski's concern over yet another vampire popping up apparently canceled out the expected lecture about the whole lynching incident. "And what did you tell her about us?" Zginski asked when he finished.

"You mean what did I tell her about *you*? Nothing. But I let slip that Patience worked here. Sorry about that."

"Is this woman planning to make an appearance?"

"I don't know. She had a weird vibe going on, like she'd been shut away talking to herself for too long. Very old-fashioned; she reminded me of you, actually."

Zginski ignored the comment. "Thank you for providing this information." He smiled wryly. "And other than the mob execution, how goes your relationship with your new victim?"

He should've known Zginski couldn't let that pass without comment. "She's okay, I guess. I see what you mean about the whole experience being intense, but I think I can do better next time."

"That is a good realization to have."

"How about yours?"

"The relationship is progressing the way I anticipated. And the results will be as I wish."

"Have you done that wolf thing for her yet?"

Zginski's smile widened, blatantly displaying his fangs. "You are a persistent devil. What would you say if I told you it was a simple trick of the mind, easily replicated with a bit of concentration?"

"Is it?"

"What else could it be?"

Leonardo closed his eyes and rubbed his temples. "Okay, how about we don't talk about this until you're ready to stop acting like a damn teenage girl with a secret?"

"As you wish. Are you staying to watch the evening's entertainment?"

"That's why I put on a clean shirt. Course, I'll have to stay in the kitchen with Vander and peek through the door. I can't get into the dining room unless I'm working as a busboy. Tell me, is she any good?"

"I believe you will be pleased. Her voice is pleasant and she has true musical aptitude."

"I bet she just melts when you tell her things like that."

Zginski chuckled, and rubbed the top of Leonardo's head. Leonardo stared after him, openmouthed, as Zginski went in through the kitchen door.

CHAPTER 23

By showtime the Ringside was packed. Besides word of mouth from the earlier show, the first ad had appeared in both the *Commercial Appeal* and *Press-Scimitar* newspapers, and Barrister even sweet-talked a commercial onto WHBQ during the morning drive show. He'd learned promotion during his wrestling career, and this was no different really, except that hopefully no one would end up bleeding.

Barrister stood outside Patience's dressing room. He wore a brand-new suit with a pattern shirt and two gold chains. He had to lean close to be heard over the expectant crowd. "Listen to that. I've got people waiting for tables even though they know it'll be over an hour, and they ain't waiting for our steak fries, baby. It's all for you."

Patience stroked her eyelashes with the mascara brush. Already she felt the surging, writhing pool of anticipatory energy just waiting to be tapped. "I'll sure do my best, Gerry. And I appreciate you getting me a piano."

"All an investment in the future. You have to spend money to make money. Colonel Tom Parker says that, and he's a man who knows."

She stood and kissed him on the cheek, quickly so the coldness of her lips wouldn't register. He smelled of Old Spice. "Thank you."

"Here, let me look at you." He held her at arm's length. She had on a black sleeveless dress that fell to her ankles, the skirt decorated with images of large red flowers and leaves. Her hair was loose, and she wore no jewelry. Her décolletage was prominently displayed. "You look like the bell at the end of a cage match, honey."

"Is that a good thing?"

"If you're inside the cage, there's nothing better."

"Then thank you again." When he continued to stare at her cleavage she said patiently, "Shouldn't you go introduce me?"

"Hm? Oh!" He turned and rushed down the hall. The noise swelled when the door opened and faded as it shut.

Patience shook her head, turned, and yelped. Zginski stood right beside her.

"Good *God*!" she cried. "Don't do that!"

"My apologies," he purred. "I merely wished to see you before your engagement began."

She could hear Barrister's indistinct voice. Something he said made the crowd laugh. "Well, you've got about ten seconds."

"Fauvette explained to me why you did not keep our rendezvous. I wish to express my thanks and appreciation. You seem to have a level of judgment that matches your beauty."

She smiled, and choked down the amused and flattered giggle that tried to burst forth. "Thank you."

Just then Barrister said loudly, "Ladies and gentlemen, Miss Patience Bolade!"

She shrugged and strode away, her long hair flying behind her. Zginski returned to the kitchen. He pushed past Vander and Leonardo, who stood in the swinging kitchen door, and emerged at the back of the dining room just as the applause died down.

Patience stood in front of a shiny black parlor grand piano and bowed. Then she settled gracefully on the bench. Someone let out an appreciative whistle.

"Stop, you'll make me blush," she said. Everyone chuckled.

She adjusted the microphone, slipped off her shoes, and placed her bare feet on the pedals. Then she began to play.

It was a familiar song: "Eight Days a Week," by the Beatles. But her version was a slow, dirgelike meditation, and she sang it as a lover begging hopelessly for her beloved to return. At first there was some restlessness, but by the chorus even that had settled down, and everyone stayed riveted to her. A few people even had tears in their eyes.

She felt their energy filling her with its power.

Behind the bar, Fauvette watched with renewed awe. The air thrummed with the combined life force as it made its way to Patience, blending and swirling so that by the time she drew it in, it was one single homogenous stream. Fauvette discreetly reached in front of one of the men at the bar, aching to sense the tingle she'd briefly gotten from Barrister. She expected it to feel like water from a spout coursing over her fingers. But evidently the force could not be physically blocked, because she encountered nothing but air.

The man reached for his drink and brushed her hand. He jumped, his concentration broken, and glared at her. "I'm not done with this one, sweetheart. Don't get greedy." He lifted his drink to his mouth, but spilled some because his attention was already back on Patience.

Prudence sat alone, at a table near the kitchen doors. It was the only one available for a single diner, and its location should have been insulting. It was perfect, though, because with the room lights dimmed, the shadows hid her from view. The little blond waitress who attended her barely looked at her, which annoyed Prudence no end even though she had no intention of ordering anything beyond the two-drink minimum. She made a mental note that if the opportunity arose, she would repay this unforgivable rudeness.

Now, though, like everyone else, she watched her sister at the piano, swaying with the music and trilling in that annoying voice of hers. Even after a century, Patience *had* to find a way to be the center of attention. Her singing voice was as pitiful as ever, full of breathy gasps and shortened phrases when she couldn't hold the notes. And her piano playing sounded like hippos stamping down the keys. Even her dumpy, pudgy body was the same, and she still displayed it as if she, not Prudence, were the pretty one. Not even her mother's constant scolding had ever been able to break Patience's self-absorption.

Prudence rested her chin on her laced fingers. She wasn't disappointed: it was as she'd expected, and secretly hoped. Her sister had not changed at all. This singing in public was just the latest gauntlet cast to the ground. It was as if they were still teenagers, competing over everything. Only this time, Prudence intended to win.

Then she noticed something strange in the air.

Zginski nodded that Leonardo should join him. They stood together in the dark at the back of the dining room, watching the show over the heads of the seated audience. Zginski tried to tell if Patience was indeed drawing energy from the crowd, but except for the unusual silence, attributable to her musicianship as easily as to supernatural means, he saw nothing. Was it possible Fauvette sensed something he couldn't? Or had he been right, that no matter how attractive she might be, Patience was seriously deluded?

Leonardo sensed nothing either, and was truthfully bored by this type of music. His attention drifted around the room, idly searching for a woman to replace Clora when her usefulness ended. He might stay within his own race this time: since his lynching he'd felt the undeniable weight of his color more vividly than ever. But would it be more loyal to his race to take on a black victim, or to slowly degrade and kill another white girl? It was a harder question than he usually pondered.

Suddenly he froze. He nudged Zginski and hissed, "Hey, man, look over there. See that woman by the kitchen door?"

"Yes."

"*That's her.* Patience's sister."

Zginski followed his nod. He was struck at once by the beauty of her profile. She had a cameo quality, long-necked and fragile, that he seldom encountered in this modern world. Even her clothes seemed drawn from the past, although their style was contemporary enough that they drew no overt attention. Like the rest she was glued to Patience's every move and note. He watched carefully to see if Patience had spotted her, but she seemed unaware of anything other than her piano.

There was an empty chair at Prudence's table.

"Stay here," Zginski told Leonardo, and started toward the woman. But he quickly stepped back into the darkness when the main door opened and Byron Cocker entered.

Cocker pushed to the front of those waiting for seats. He spotted Barrister at a table beside the stage, the other chairs filled with notables and their girlfriends. He saw no sign of Zginski, even though the Mustang was parked in the back. But there was little Fauvette behind the bar. She emptied an ashtray, then refilled a bowl with pretzels. She looked small, and fragile, and Cocker couldn't wait to get his hands on her and make her scream.

Yet Patience drew his eye even when he was determined to ignore her. She gave him the creeps even in a crowded room. She played softly, humming along with the music, and even though he didn't know the tune and only cared for country music, he found himself listening intently. It was just like before, and even though he wasn't drunk this time, just as irresistible.

🐾 Prudence watched the shimmering energy in the room twist itself, tornadolike, and funnel down into her sister. It was like nothing she'd ever seen before, and it took four more songs before she comprehended what it truly was. When she did, she felt the old jealous fury rise again. So *this* was what she was up to. Here was Prudence, a century into existence as a being who needed to drink the blood of humans to survive, and Patience had long since dispensed with that. This new feeding process was clean, involuntary, and most of all discreet. There were no bodies to hide, no wasting maladies to explain, and no blood-stains on the upholstery.

She clenched her fists in rage. This would not stand.

The little blond waitress, whose name tag read SAMMY JO, slammed Prudence's second drink down, spilling a third of it on the table, and snatched away the untouched first one before Prudence could say anything.

🎵 Patience finished her next to last song, an original called "The Tides of Time," and basked in the applause. "Thank you so much. I appreciate everyone coming out tonight, and I hope to see you all again soon. How about a big hand for Gerry Barrister for arranging all this?"

After the ovation she continued. "So once again, thank you. And here's one for the road." She dove into a gender-reversed version of a recent hit by the group America, now called "*Mister* Golden Hair." It should've been inane, and blatant, and ridiculous, but she sang it with such tenderness that those in the audience would never hear the original again without wistfully recalling this night. When it finished she stood, bowed, and accepted the adulation.

Eager patrons swarmed Patience at the piano. Because it was nearly closing time, Barrister rushed to switch on the lights, not wanting to run afoul of the liquor board just as the bar was taking off. "Thanks everyone," he said into the microphone. "Drive safely, come back often, and tell all your friends!"

Patience shook hands with her new fans, careful not to hold any of them long enough to draw attention to her cold skin. Many of them asked if she had any records for sale; a couple pressed business cards into her palm, offering representation or career advice.

A gap formed in the crowd for a moment, and she spotted Prudence still at her table. She nearly shrieked in surprise. She cried, *"Prudence!"*

When the lights first came up, Prudence had spotted Byron Cocker standing near the front door, his huge form immobile as the crowd around him filed out. He was the one person in the room not staring at her sister; instead he watched the young girl behind the bar, and that alone seemed odd. Then the sound of her name made her blink back to the moment.

"Prudence!" Patience yelled again over the heads of the well-wishers. Many turned to see who she meant. Prudence grabbed her purse and looked for the nearest exit. The kitchen door swung open again as the busboys emerged, and she rushed through it. She was not ready for a confrontation, not here on Patience's turf.

"No!" Patience yelled, and tried to push through the well-wishers. "Prudence, wait, please!" But her sister vanished.

Patience was about to pursue when she, too, spotted Byron Cocker. What did *he* want here? That night at her house should have scared him off for good. Was he more courageous than she thought? Then she realized he was watching Fauvette, and that puzzled her anew. How did *they* know each other?

A hand closed around her arm, and Barrister's freshly Listerined breath swamped her. "Goddam, honey, that was something!" he cried right in her ear. He snatched up the business cards on the piano. "You better tell me if somebody tries to take you away from me, because I'm not having that. No, sirree, not this boy! You are a Ringside exclusive!"

Patience resumed accepting congratulations, taking the last bits of energy that the crowd couldn't wait to send her way. She kept one eye on the kitchen door, in case Prudence returned.

When the lights came up Zginski stayed very still and watched Byron Cocker. The man's presence surprised and worried him, but he seemed most interested in Fauvette, of all people. How did he know about her? *What* did he know about her? Was something happening of which he, Zginski, was unaware?

Then Patience cried out a name, and the blond woman Leonardo said was her sister rushed into the kitchen. On impulse, Zginski followed. She was gone by the time he got through the swinging doors, but Vander nodded toward the back exit. He reached it in time to see the Thunderbird pull out onto Madison and drive slowly away, so slowly that Zginski confirmed the woman in question was behind the wheel.

He stood watching for a long moment. This set off all his internal alarms. One additional vampire, even one who insisted on performing in public, could be tolerated. But now there were two, and they were sisters. Nothing caused trouble like family. And trouble drew attention, which was the last thing he wanted.

Suddenly he paused and sniffed the air. He caught the unmistakable tang of fresh human blood.

He stepped out of the building, closed the door, and closed his eyes. It came from the Dumpster.

He climbed up to peer inside. The little blond waitress, Sammy Jo, lay atop the garbage. Her head was twisted hard to one side, and blood still seeped from the fresh fang holes on her neck. Her eyes were open but saw nothing. She'd been killed quickly for spite, and not for real feeding.

Zginski clenched his fists so hard they bent the metal lip. He quickly hopped down, opened the Mustang's trunk, and placed the girl's body inside. He would dispose of it far away from the bar, and hopefully no one would connect the crime with the location. Barmaids were always getting killed, after all.

By the time he returned the crowd was mostly gone, and he glimpsed Byron Cocker as the door closed after him. Patience sat on the piano bench looking bemused as Gerry waxed rhapsodic about her future. Fauvette hovered behind her, wringing her hands like an acolyte waiting for a blessing.

"You could make records, honey!" Barrister cried, practically shouting in her face. "I could be your manager. I know about that stuff, you know. I was a wrestler for a long time. You could be the biggest thing to come out of Memphis since Elvis or barbecue!"

"That's a little more than I reckoned for, Gerry," Patience said. "How about we give this a few weeks before we start planning to take over the world?" She smiled when she saw Zginski. "Well, hello. How did *you* like the show?"

"It was unique," Zginski said.

"That's it!" Gerry cried. "You hit it right on the head, Mr. Z. 'The Unique Patience Bolade!' That's what we'll call you!"

"That doesn't tell me if you *liked* it or not," Patience said to Zginski.

He was in no mood to flirt, but at the same time, her smile was hard to resist. "I found your playing quite skillful. Reminiscent of Lucy Anderson, who I once saw with the Philharmonic Society in London. And your singing was also delightful. The songs were not to my taste, but I suspect they were not composed with someone like me in mind."

"That's a mighty safe bet," Patience said. She stood and kissed Gerry on the cheek. "I'm pretty beat, boss. If it's okay, I'm going to head on out." Then she turned to Zginski. "See me home?"

Before he could answer a scowling Fauvette said, "He's *my* ride, I'm afraid."

Zginski scowled back. He did not have the patience to indulge the girl. "I believe your final words on the subject were, 'I'll plan to find my own way home.' I shall hold you to that."

Fauvette glared at him, and he felt an unaccustomed twinge of regret at the fury and hurt in her eyes. Where were these weak sympathies coming from? She said, "No, my final words were that I wished I never met you. That's still true."

"Hey, whoa, you two," Barrister said, stepping between them. "Let's not blow the evening now. Fauvette, I'll give you a ride home, or get you a cab, whichever you'd like."

"I'll keep you company," Leonardo said.

"Thank you, boy," Barrister said. "Mr. Z., you make sure Patience gets where she's going in one piece."

"That is my intent." He offered his arm to Patience.

She placed her hand lightly on it as she stood. "I need to collect some things from my dressing room first."

"Of course." They went to the door leading to the hall. Barrister, still chuckling, took the till from the bar and went to his office.

Fauvette sat down on Patience's piano bench, feeling suddenly more alone than ever before in her life. If tears were possible, she would've burst out crying. Instead she just stared down at her hands, dropped limply in her lap. Leonardo put a hand on her shoulder. There was nothing to say, at least not here.

"Hey, anybody seen Sammy Jo?" one of the bus-boys asked. "She's supposed to help with cleaning up."

CHAPTER 24

Cocker had parked the Impala so that he could see the Ringside's front and back doors. The show had left him unaccountably drained again, but tonight he was cold sober, and he'd picked up a thermos full of fresh coffee on his way to town. A little weariness wasn't about to stop him.

Patience left with Zginski in the Mustang shortly after midnight, leaving her own black LTD behind. Then nothing happened for a long time. Finally at about one-thirty in the morning, a cab stopped outside the door. The black driver got out and knocked on the bar's front door. "Somebody called a cab," he said loudly. Fauvette emerged a moment later dressed in her civilian clothes, followed by another black boy, younger than the cabbie. They drove off into the night.

Cocker followed along the mostly deserted streets. It was tricky, since there was so little traffic, but if the cabbie noticed he did not react. They entered the Projects, the low-income area of Memphis where the city's high crime rate was nurtured. At the first red light Cocker took his .45 automatic from the glove compartment and placed it within easy reach on the seat.

Finally the cab stopped. Fauvette and the black boy got out in front of a run-down apartment building. A pair of black teenagers sat on the steps, but they actually scooted aside as she and her friend passed. Cocker watched them enter the building, and then saw a light come on inside a ground-floor apartment.

He wrote down the address. Tonight wasn't the night: too many people had seen him at the bar, and the punks on the steps now eyeballed him with turf-defending belligerence. But that was okay; when it came, his revenge would be entirely out of the blue.

He smiled and headed for home.

Zginski parked on the street outside Patience's house. Except for directions, Patience had said nothing, and Zginski was content with the silence. He was confused, and needed the time to ponder out the reason.

She said, "You can park in the drive, you know."

"This is satisfactory," he said. Her presence did not make him tense or suspicious, and it had been almost a century since he'd been with someone like that.

And then there was the other woman, Prudence. Although he had barely glimpsed her at the Ringside, the image stayed with him, growing stronger with each passing moment. She was like porcelain, hard-edged and delicate, while Patience made him think of velvet and soft pillows.

And Prudence had also killed a waitress in the club that would soon be his. The quick, pointless kill was out of character for any of the others, so by default he knew it was her. It must be dealt with, and quickly.

Patience smiled and shook her head. "I have to say, this car surprises me. You don't seem like the type to draw attention, and it's awfully flashy."

"I have had the same thought."

"But you did it anyway."

He nodded.

She put her hand on his thigh. "So. Would you like to come in?"

He shook his head. "I do not believe that would be in my best interest, or yours, tonight. Other tasks require my attention."

She laughed. "Lord, how you do talk. I haven't heard that kind of language since my old fiancé. Is it because of Fauvette?"

That took him by surprise. "Fauvette?"

"You know. How she feels about you."

"I assure you, I have made no claim on Fauvette, or her on me."

"I can't speak for you, but from the way she talks it's pretty clear she's got it bad."

"Perhaps she was speaking of Mark. He was—"

Patience shook her head. "Uh-uh. It's you. Whatever was there for Mark is as long gone as he is. And she turned bright green tonight when we left together. Didn't you notice?"

"I was blinded by your beauty."

She laughed. "Good save there, Mr. Z. Isn't that what they call you?"

"Some do."

She scooted across the seat and pressed herself to him. He felt the swell of her breasts against his arm. She ran one fingernail lightly along his jawline and into his beard. "How about a taste?" she whispered. "Just to see if you like it. Fauvette will never know."

In the light from the dashboard her skin glowed, and the dark circles of her eyes seemed to draw him in. He felt his body stirring as her influence, delicate and restrained, enveloped him. He responded with a similar wave, and watched her gasp in response.

"Oh, my," she sighed.

"Indeed," he agreed, barely audible.

Their lips were close now. Since neither breathed, they felt no movement of air, but the tension was just as palpable.

She brazenly ran her hand over his chest. "I could make you very glad you came inside," she said, a little catch in her voice.

"And I could insure you had no regrets about

your invitation," he said. Then he withdrew his own influence, and blocked hers. Firmly he added, "But tonight is not the night."

She sat back slowly, adjusted her dress, and managed a wry half smile. "I suppose if anyone does, we have time."

"An ocean of it."

She opened the passenger door. "I won't ask you to walk me up; I can manage. But thank you for the ride."

"My pleasure," he said.

"And I don't think this is over."

"There is no need for it to be."

He watched her sashay up to the porch and go inside, then drove slowly away. The memory of her touch stayed with him longer than it should have, but even more vivid was the profile of Prudence he'd glimpsed earlier in the light of the Ringside's kitchen doorway.

Leonardo stood in Fauvette's bedroom staring at the huge image of a handsome, dark-haired young man taped to the wall. The enormous rows of white, even teeth reminded him of a skull. "Who is this guy?" he asked.

"Donny Osmond. He's a singer."

"Man, I hope nobody ever turns him into a vampire." He sat on the edge of her bed. "So how's Rudy's one-victim-at-a-time thing working for you?"

"Fine," Fauvette said as she undressed.

Leonardo had seen her naked many times, and it felt no more erotic than undressing in front of a sibling. "The hardest thing was training myself to stop just when the blood really started to flow." She let a huge T-shirt drop over her, falling to her knees.

"Training," Leonardo said ironically. "That's what it feels like he's doing sometimes, ain't it? Training us. But are we his partners or his guard dogs?"

She sat on the bed beside him. "You sure seem to like it. You two are best buds now."

"What does *that* mean?"

"You couldn't stand him six weeks ago. Now you follow him around like he's got a ring in your nose." She paused. "Sorry, that was thoughtless."

"Yeah. Why are you so pissy tonight?"

She drew her knees to her chest and wrapped her arms around them. "Am I?"

"Yeah, and since you ain't got monthlies to blame, there must be something else."

"I've been trying to learn to do what Patience does."

"Sing and play the piano?"

"No, draw energy from people without . . . you know . . . hurting them."

"Why?"

She closed her eyes. "Because I'm tired of death, Leo. Toddy, Olive, maybe Mark . . . I'm tired of it."

"Looked at yourself in the mirror lately? You dead, too."

She smacked him on the arm. "Why are *you* being so mean?"

"I don't know." He sighed, and lay back on the bed. The plaster ceiling above him sported a huge water stain. "Maybe because I was lynched a couple of nights ago."

It took a moment for the words to register. Fauvette's eyes opened wide. "What?"

He told her the story. "I still don't know why I went along with it. I think it was mainly to see how far they'd go. I could've gotten away at any point, but I didn't."

"What if they'd set you on fire or something?"

"Then I would've done something. I think."

"You *think*?"

He shrugged. "Fuck, Fauvette, I don't know. Between you and me, I'll tell you a secret. It wasn't entirely bad. I mean, yeah, being strung up by those dumb crackers was a pisser, but once I was there, I got to thinking about how it would feel to be really dead, and . . ." He trailed off into silence. Before Zginski came along, he never would've spoken these thoughts aloud. Hell, he never would've *thought* them. Had a few days' sunlight changed him that much?

Fauvette lay down beside him and caressed his cheek. "Do you think that we may have finally outlived our time? That this world has changed to the point there's no place for people like us?"

"Not as long as the sun still goes down every day and brings back the dark."

"Even though we know now that we were never tied to the dark?"

"Personally, I like the shadows." In an exaggerated minstrel voice he said, "If I don't smile, I'm invisible."

She grinned despite herself.

He said, "So if you learn to get by without killing people, will that make it all better?"

"It'll make me more like most of the people I pass on the street."

"Except you don't get older and you don't have a heartbeat."

"Well, one thing at a time."

He kissed her on the forehead, they hugged, and Leonardo left. Fauvette looked at herself in the bathroom mirror, wondering if death did lurk in her eyes. Certainly it could put in an appearance when she was feeding, but was it always there?

There seemed to be no death in Patience, though. Her eyes sparkled with life, and humor, and kindness. Surely if she could shed it, Fauvette could do the same.

CHAPTER 25

Zginski parked outside the decrepit old house, amazed at the utter coincidence. He and Leonardo had stopped here to ask directions on the day he bought Tzigane, the same day he met Patience Bolade. He must have glimpsed Prudence then, hidden by the harsh summer shadows. Neither he nor Leonardo had spotted her for a vampire, no doubt due to their own sun-weakened state.

He went to the garage and peered inside. The same big LTD he'd seen driving away from the Ringside sat inside. He put one hand flat on the hood, and found it still warm.

He opened the Mustang's trunk and hoisted the dead Sammy Jo onto his shoulders. He carried her onto the porch and rang the doorbell. Many minutes went by before he sensed movement within.

Finally a single lamp came on inside, a key turned laboriously in the lock, and the door swung open.

She wore an old-fashioned robe and nightgown, in a style Zginski recognized from the previous century. Its neckline revealed smooth shoulders and the hint of a firm bosom. A strand of blond hair fell down her forehead, and she seemed cool and confident. She also looked barely older than Fauvette.

Zginski dropped Sammy Jo to the porch. She landed with a loud thud.

Prudence looked at the girl, then up at him. She said in her thick, genteel Southern accent, "I thank you for the gift, sir, but I believe that girl is dead."

"Indeed. As a result of your actions."

One of Sammy Jo's hands had fallen across the door's threshold. Prudence scooted it back outside with her foot.

"You left a corpse with the clear marks of our kind where it could be easily found," Zginski continued. "That trash receptacle is used frequently, and discovery was almost guaranteed."

Prudence's expression, like her voice, remained bland. "I simply threw away my garbage. The girl was unbearably rude to me, something I cannot abide. It seemed fitting that after failing to serve me inside the establishment, she then provided refreshment outside."

Zginski was annoyed. Her lilting, honey-heavy drawl indicated she thought herself superior to him. "There were others of our kind inside, including me. Your action jeopardized us all."

"The only one *I* was aware of was my sister, the evening's entertainment."

"Even if that is true, your conduct does not speak well of your discretion or intelligence."

Her eyes flashed angrily. "Sir, I will not stand here and be insulted on my own property. Good evening to you."

She tried to close the door, but he blocked it easily, pushed her back inside, and locked it behind him. "I will leave when I am certain there is no further danger. Your best course is to convince me."

She glared at him. "Who are you, sir?" she demanded.

"I am Baron Rudolfo Vladimir Zginski."

Her lips curled up slightly as her anger turned to amusement. "My heavens, that's a mouthful. What do your friends call you?"

He did not answer, but tried to sense if anyone else lurked in the house. The paintings and furniture spoke of both antiquity and wealth, although the money could have run out long ago. Still, at one time these were the best things money could buy, and they'd been maintained so that most of their value remained.

"We are quite alone, I assure you," she said.

"Then let me get to the point. You must prove to me that your continued existence poses no danger. If you do not, your existence will end. That is the simple truth of it."

She smiled, her fangs prominent. "Sir, I always presume upon the *kindness* of strangers, not their malevolence."

"That is foolish." He looked around the foyer. "How long have you been here?"

"Since I was born," she said and turned on the chandelier. The light was dim and burnished.

"Does this estate have a name?"

"You mean like Dark Willows over yonder? No, the Crabtrees in their prime were far wealthier than we Bolades. Nor did we share their taste for ostentation. We simply called this place home."

He spotted the portrait of Patience over the mantel. "Your sister is a most unusual creature."

For an instant Prudence's anger flashed like lightning in her blue eyes. Then her calm returned. "She always has been so. When we were children, she would do anything to be the center of attention. From what I saw tonight, the centuries have not altered that."

"You sound envious."

Prudence touched his arm and met his gaze steadily, with no malice. "Do you truly wish to hear about my sister, Baron Zginski? Or would you rather hear about me? I have not had a handsome gentleman caller in ages, let alone one with the manners to present his arrogance in such a charming way."

Zginski felt a twinge of something very like nervousness; first Patience's blatant interest, and now her sister's. He was entirely comfortable being the pursuer, much less so being pursued. It was how the original Tzigane had gotten past his defenses. "I wish to know as much as possible about you both."

She fingered the sleeve of his jacket. "So you can decide which of us merits your, shall we say, amorous interest? There's no need for beings like ourselves to play coy, now is there?"

It took all his effort to maintain his normal cool. "You do not seem to appreciate the danger you are in."

She laughed, loud and musical. "Any danger you present is easily negated."

"Indeed?" he said, now fully alert to attack. "And how would you negate it?"

"In the time-honored tradition of men and women," she said, and with no warning stepped close and kissed him.

Before he could react it was over. He stayed perfectly still, expecting an attempt to exert her vampiric influence as well. But nothing happened.

She understood his thoughts. "Sir, I would not try to make you feel anything against your will. I hope you will extend the same courtesy to me."

He saw her anew, her angular, lean beauty the opposite of her comfortably curved sister. He had no real preference in physical types, but certainly could not fault Prudence as a beauty. Both Bolade sisters posed challenges, but only Prudence, with her antique etiquette and mixture of demureness and aggression, seemed to understand him. "Do you feel," he said, "that you have in fact removed me as a danger with a single kiss?"

"I am certain of it," she said.

He smiled. Then he grabbed her and pulled her against him. He kissed her with the unrestrained fury of a being unconcerned with damaging his partner, an aspect he had last released on that night in the warehouse with Fauvette. Then he had been the undisputed master, reducing her to a state of almost unbearable desire to protect her from the intimate pain she would inevitably feel.

Here, though, it was a clash of equals. Their bodies surged with power, and their mouths struck together so hungrily their fangs clacked off each other. The gnawing kiss went on for minutes and when they broke apart, they each gasped even though neither could be out of breath.

"My goodness," Prudence said. One side of her mouth was torn. "I stand corrected."

He grabbed her by the neckline of her gown. "I will open myself to you," he hissed. "Will you do the same?"

She nodded. "It has been quite some time for me, though," she said breathlessly. "Will you be gentle?"

"No."

She smiled, the rip in her flesh adding a slightly demonic quality to her face. "Then neither will I." She flung herself at him again as he tore open the front of her nightgown.

An hour later they stood naked in the moonlight outside the wrought-iron fence that protected the small family plot. One tombstone bore Patience's name, the other Prudence's. Their mortal deaths were only one day apart.

Prudence turned to face him, her extraordinary form on display. Her breasts were pert and perfect, the tiny nipples upturned; her waist was narrow, and her hips wide and smooth. The soft hair between her thighs glistened. She nodded at a particular tombstone. "That is the grave of the man who had both Patience and me. He was also my first and, until this night, only lover."

The waist-high marble pedestal sported a bas-relief of a thin-faced man with side whiskers. COLONEL VINCENT DRAKE, the marker proclaimed, 1830–1862.

Zginski's body bore the marks of her enthusiasm. "What sort of man was he?"

"He was a handsome, dashing officer in the Confederate Army," she said, her arm linked through Zginski's. "His hair was so blond it often appeared white, and his voice was so seductive he could talk his way out of, or into, anything. His family pressured him to wed Patience, and he dutifully proposed, but he was truly in love with me."

The man's date of death was the same as Patience's. "How did he die?"

"Patience killed him. He was her first victim after she became what she is. I insisted he be buried in the family plot, since by all rights he would've been part of the family, one way or another."

He turned her to face him. Her body was bone-white in the moonlight. "And you worry," he said as he raised her chin, "that I might promise my hand to her and then dally with you, as he did?"

"Oh, I don't worry any such thing. I simply insist that you respect this line of demarcation. I make no claim on you at all, sir, except that now that you have had me, you make no attempt to also have biblical knowledge of my sister. That seems, all things considered, a fairly reasonable request."

"Do you want my word of honor?" he said.

"That is satisfactory."

"Then I want something as well."

"Which is?"

With a growl of desire and domination, he carried her over the fence and took her again, from behind, atop the grave of her departed lover. He put one hand on the back of her neck, forcing her face down into the dirt.

Later, still unclothed, they stood together on the widow's walk overlooking the forest and, beyond that, the soybean fields. The black lightless hulk of Dark Willows was visible in the distance. Heat lightning shimmered across the now-cloudy sky. "That is how I knew she was back," Prudence said. "When a new vampire appears in an area, an unnatural drought may result."

"That is superstition," Zginski said.

"So, dear sir, are we. And you cannot deny the result."

"Then why was there no drought when *I* appeared?"

She shrugged, almost with delight. "I don't know, kind sir. Perhaps like people, we are all different as well, with various talents and effects on the world."

He said nothing. She walked to the railing and leaned out, gazing up at the sky. "Do you ever wish," she said wistfully, "we truly *could* turn into bats and flit through the night?"

He stood with his back against the roof. "I have no desire to do so."

"Can't you imagine the freedom, though? On the earth we're limited to two dimensions. To travel in the third, even in the most basic way, we need ungainly things like stairs and airplanes." She raised her arms. "I used to try. I would stand on this very spot, naked as I am now, and try to change my form. I willed myself to sprout wings, and grow small, and then I would leap into the night."

"And?"

She laughed. "And, I ended up flat on the front yard, bare-assed and staring up at the moon."

"It is a logical impossibility for one creature to change into another, especially one that is so much smaller."

She crossed to him and snuggled against his chest. "It's a logical impossibility to live on after death by drinking human blood."

"No, that is a *mystery.* Clearly it is not an impossibility." He brushed her hair with his fingers. "I should go."

"Why? If you're hungry, I can summon someone. I have compounds that will put them fast asleep so that they never know what happened.

They will awaken weak and confused, but the truth would never occur to them."

"I appreciate the offer, but I have other business to attend to as well." He kissed her. "But I would like to visit you again."

"Is that a fact?"

"Yes . . . ma'am."

She laughed and pressed herself to him. She drew his tongue into her mouth and raked it with her fangs.

The Impala didn't have a spotlight like his old sheriff's cruiser, so Cocker had to make do with a flashlight. It played across the back end of Bruce's beat-up Chevy Nova, parked down a tractor path far enough to be hidden from the road unless you were specifically looking for it.

Cocker switched off the light and sighed. He knew exactly why the car was here; the shadowy form of Dark Willows rose above the trees, black against the sky. Bruce was in there somewhere tomcatting around with that nubile, white-trash Crabtree girl, who probably knew just how to make a boy feel like a man. He felt a mixture of parental disapproval and pure masculine jealousy, but reminded himself that he had a date with that little waitress in Memphis before too long.

He turned the car around and headed back toward town. As he neared the driveway leading to old Mama Prudence's place, a car pulled out onto the highway and passed him in the other lane. He slammed on his brakes, unable to believe what he just saw.

The Mustang. That goddamned Zginski was leaving Mama Prudence's at three o'clock in the morning. What the hell was *that* about?

He considered following Zginski, maybe even trying to catch him and force the confrontation here in McHale County. But that would mean never getting ahold of the doe-eyed Fauvette, and he'd already invested too much time and energy in that scheme to back out now.

He took a deep breath, then drove slowly and within the speed limit back home. He parked behind his own car, went inside, and lay down on the couch. He wanted to know what time Bruce got home, and he left his coiled belt on the end table to help provide the proper greeting.

🜚 Zginski drove quietly back to Memphis, without even turning on the radio. The competing voices in his head provided plenty of stimulation.

One chastised him for leaving, accusing him of being a weakling and a coward. That voice had the shrill tone of his father, a man who hadn't crossed his mind in a century.

Another berated him for lowering his guard and deigning to have intimate relations with one woman while secretly coveting her sister. This one sounded like the priest he'd known as a young man, who made it his business to turn all the male youth of his parish away from licentious women.

Everyone knew, of course, that he actually wanted to turn them *toward* his own bedchamber.

But the oddest one, and the one that surprised him most, scolded him for ignoring and casting aside Fauvette. If any of their kind was truly capable of love, she was, and she deserved better treatment. And this voice sounded like his own.

CHAPTER 26

At the same moment Zginski knocked on Prudence Bolade's door, Bruce Cocker finished his beer, climbed from his car, and urinated on a tree. He was not drunk, but the combination of several joints at home and a couple of beers on the way definitely put him in a mellow, and amorous, state of mind. He crept through the woods toward Dark Willows.

His hazy brain found it easy to ignore what might still be hanging from that nearby tree. He was well on his way to convincing himself it had just been an elaborate prank, that the boy had not been killed and that they'd all have a big laugh over it later. Yeah, that was it. He wasn't about to go see for himself, because knowing for certain would do him no good at all.

He paused at the edge of the Crabtrees' yard. The house was dark, except for the light up in Clora's window. Her shadow passed across it, and his blood raced as much as the dope and alcohol allowed. He *needed* to get laid, to relieve some of the pressure and dispel the sense of doom enveloping him. He needed to touch her soft flesh, to hear her say she loved him, to lay back while she sucked him off.

As he stepped into the open yard, a voice said, "Hey, cracker."

Bruce froze. The voice cut through all the illicit substances and instantly sobered him. As he slowly turned, his eyes first spotted the figure's moon-cast shadow stretching across the damp grass toward him. He followed it to the still silhouette that stood between him and the house, as unmistakable as its voice and twice as horrifying.

"You done fucked up big time, peckerwood," Leonardo said. He fought down his amusement and made his voice rumble the way his preacher uncle used to do when he spoke about eternal damnation. "You sent me to hell the other night, and now I'm back to claim *your* soul." For effect he raised his right arm and pointed one finger; the shadow on the ground reached all the way from Leonardo to Bruce.

Bruce could not move, and could barely breathe. He'd never hallucinated from marijuana before, but maybe the dire things his father said about dope were true after all. "You ain't real," he whispered, his voice trembling as much as his body.

Leonardo laughed. He picked up a stick and bounced it off Bruce's head. "Real enough for you?"

Bruce winced, rubbed absently at his temple, and thought, *This is just the grass fucking up my head.* Maybe his stash was polluted by government pesticides. "Fuck you," he choked out.

Leonardo moved toward him. "The devil's gonna love your attitude, cracker. Might hang you up between Nathan Bedford Forrest and Adolf Hitler. Bet you'd feel right at home there, wouldn't you?"

Now Bruce could make out the boy's features. For a moment he wasn't sure; after all, they *did* all look alike, especially at night. But when the ghost smiled, there was no doubt it was the one they'd lynched.

And when he opened his mouth wide, Bruce saw the long, sharp fangs of a demon.

Bruce's heart pounded so loud he could barely think. In a small, pitiful voice he managed to get out the words, "Our Father, who art in heaven—"

"*Your* father ain't in heaven," Leonardo growled. "He ain't even a pimple on God's black ass. And neither are you. You think angels are coming down to save you? They got better things to do."

Bruce's lip trembled, and he began to cry as he continued. ". . . hallowed be thy name . . ."

Suddenly Leonardo was behind him, holding him by the throat and whispering in his ear. "You gonna like it deep down in the pit, son. Lots of folks just . . . like . . . *you.*"

It was too much. *"Get away from me!"* Bruce screamed, his voice going high like a girl's. He wrenched himself free and fled back into the woods. Leonardo laughed big and fake-demonic after him.

"Bruce!" a distant voice cried. Clora leaned out her bedroom window, waving to the departed teen. Plaintively she added, "Bruce, wait, come back, he's just joking!"

Leonardo scaled the building so fast that he reached Clora before she withdrew from the window. "Hi," he said with a smile.

"Don't you 'hi' me," Clora hissed. She wore only a long T-shirt, but she crossed her arms over her breasts to hide her visible nipples. She no longer felt the least bit amorous; the sight of the two men in her life facing off, and the ease with which Leonardo chased away the only one who could take her out in public, infuriated her. The rage was so spontaneous and unexpected that she had no chance to control it. "What the *hell* do you think you were doing down there?"

Now Leonardo got angry. "Maybe you should ask your friend down there what *he* was doing the other night when he and his vanilla-wafer pals tried to lynch me."

Her anger kept this from truly registering. "What are you talking about?"

"Bruce and Tiny and Travis and David. Those names ring a bell?"

"I don't believe you. You're just trying to cause

trouble for white folks. Why would they do that, anyway?"

"They saw me coming out your window, I reckon."

Her eyes opened wide. Her fury choked her to the point that she could only whisper. "*What?* They know I was with a . . ."

She stopped, but it was too late. The word hung in the air between them.

Leonardo held on to the window frame and leaned into the room, forcing her to back away. "A what?" he asked quietly.

Clora blushed. "You need to go, Leo. This has been fun, but it's time for it to end."

Something snapped deep inside him, a thread that had been holding him back for longer than he realized. He came through the window in what felt to him like slow motion, but to Clora it seemed as if he moved faster than thought. Suddenly she was pinned against the opposite wall, his hand around her throat.

The terror in her eyes made him feel oddly warm inside. "So now the white boys know you been spreading your legs for a nigger, is that it?"

"Please," she choked out, trying to pull his hand away. She kneed him in the groin with all her strength, but it had no effect.

"Is that how *you* see me? You telling me even the white trash is too good to fuck a colored boy?"

His use of the term infuriated her anew, and her face wrenched into an ugly mask of fury. All the humiliation she'd suffered as the little girl with ragged clothes, the one with no lunch money who had to make do with slices of government cheese, the one who got her boobs and period long before her friends and endured the assumption by everyone that she was "loose" and "easy," came out in one choked, gurgled, defiant syllable: *"Yes!"*

It was the last word she uttered.

He enveloped her in his influence so that even as she tried to scream for help, it was choked by lust that suddenly paralyzed her and made her legs buckle. His iron grip held her in place, though, and her feet kicked against the wall as she rode wave after wave of unwanted orgasm. He pulled her close and she saw his mouth open wide, displaying his long, sharp canine teeth. And suddenly everything made sense, and she came again, and she knew she was about to die.

He sank his fangs into her neck and drew her blood fully now, the way he used to do with his victims. It pulsed down his throat into his belly, sending warming tendrils throughout his body. Clora went limp almost at once.

You fucking honky bitch, he thought as her life coursed into him. *You redneck white-trash whore.* He squeezed her buttocks in one hand so hard he felt the tissue rupture.

Finally he drew the last of the blood from her body and let her fall. She landed in a pile of awkward limbs, and when he saw the odd way her torso seemed dented in places, he realized he'd inadvertently crushed her. Her eyes were open, coincidentally staring out the window as if she expected Bruce to come to her rescue.

He stood very still, his body absorbing the blood at its own pace. Beneath him, someone stirred in the house. The steps rattled as heavy, shuffling feet, no doubt belonging to Clora's drunken lout of a father, climbed toward the attic.

Leonardo looked around to insure nothing remained to incriminate him. He had been scrupulous before to make sure he left no traces behind, but this time his anger had caused him to be loud and sloppy. Clora's death throes must've reached the living room below.

That done, Leonardo leaped in utter silence out the window, far enough to clear the edge of the roof. He landed in the yard below with a muffled thump, his feet slamming onto the drought-hardened ground. In an instant he vanished into the woods.

At some point, as he drove back to Memphis with the music turned up loud, it occurred to him that he'd taken no precautions to stop Clora from rising as a vampire. But he did not turn back. On the radio, a singer described his mother's relief when his cop father survived a Chicago gang war.

CHAPTER 27

Jeb Crabtree knocked on Clora's door. His head hurt, he needed to pee again, and his knees protested at climbing so far in the middle of the night. Whatever his daughter was up to, she would pay for rousing him from his fitful sleep.

He called out, "Girl? What's all that banging about in there?" When he got no answer, he knocked louder. "You got them headphones on? I done told you about that before, you gonna end up needing a hearing aid before you're twenty-five. Now open this door."

There was still no response. He burped, tasted a mixture of beer and corn bread, and choked it back down. He pulled out his Case knife and snapped the blade into place; he wasn't going to make this climb for nothing. "I'm picking the lock, girl. You better be decent."

He slid it between the door and the jamb, then pushed the latch aside. His wife once showed him how to do that, in case Clora locked herself in the bathroom as a toddler. The door opened at once.

It took Crabtree a long moment to understand the tableaux before him. Clora lay on the floor, eyes open, her body unnaturally contorted. Her skin was even paler than normal. The T-shirt that was her only garment had gathered at her waist, exposing her hoo-ha for all to see. Wind through the open window billowed the curtain, and beyond it a hoot owl cried mournfully.

"Clora?" Crabtree said. His voice sounded unnaturally loud in the silence.

He nudged her with one foot. She did not respond.

"Oh, honey," he breathed. He knelt and gently tried to scoop her into his arms. When he did, her shattered spine and torso caused her to bend unnaturally, and he screamed in revulsion. He scooted back against the wall, his own eyes now wide and staring. He intended to scream, "No!" but the simple word dissolved into an incoherent cry of rage and loss, the kind that only a man who's seen everything of importance leave him can muster. It filled the room and blazed out the window, startling the sleeping birds into flight and making his dog howl in sympathy far below.

It only ended when his body forced him to finally take a breath again.

Then the next one came.

🦊 There was no conscious decision involved in any of his actions. As the gray dawn lightened the sky outside, he carefully picked up his daughter's broken body and carried her downstairs, murmuring to her as if she were a baby with a tummy ache. When he brought her outside the dog rushed up and began barking at the smell of death.

He carried her up the hill behind the house and into the woods along the trail leading to the Crabtree family cemetery. The wrought-iron archway was all that remained of the once-immaculate landscaping. Beyond it were a dozen rows of tombstones, most too worn to be read, all overgrown with weeds and vines. Except one.

That one was still white and shiny, its name and dates plain. He placed Clora on the ground beside her mother's grave, carefully arranging the T-shirt to protect her modesty. The dog continued to yap at the corpse.

Crabtree put his hand on his wife's tombstone. "Your baby's coming to see you, honey," he said to the marble. "She shouldn't be, but then again, you shouldn't have been taken away from her, either. Reckon God's to blame for everything."

He knelt and kissed Clora's already-cold cheek. "I'll be right back, honey." Then he kicked the dog as hard as he could, sending him yelping off into the underbrush.

In a few minutes he returned with a shovel. The sun was fully up by now, though it hadn't yet cleared the treetops. Insects buzzed in the air as he dug into the hard, dry ground beside his wife. The difficulty did not register. His wife had died in a hospital, and a professional dug her grave with a backhoe, but there would be no hospital for Clora.

By the time he finished he was barely able to stand. Drenched in sweat and shaking from adrenaline, he climbed from the irregular hole and again picked up his shattered daughter. Humming "I'm a Little Teapot," the song she most loved as a baby, he carried her into the hole and tenderly placed her on the ground. Belatedly he closed her eyes, having to chase away the gnats already swarming to them.

It took a fraction of the time to fill the grave. He shaped the fresh mound with the shovel, making it as neat as he could. Clora deserved that.

He leaned on the shovel and looked over his handiwork. The dog skulked up behind him and lay down at his feet.

He stretched and yawned. There was no time to rest yet. One more task remained, something only the father of a murdered child could appreciate. He knew who was behind this, knew where to find him, and knew what must be done. He grabbed the appropriate tool, let the dog jump into the truck's passenger seat, and climbed behind the wheel.

❧ A short time later he knocked on the door. He kept up a steady rhythm, and eventually he heard a voice say, "All right, just a minute, hold on."

The door opened and Bruce Cocker stood there, eyes red from sleep and probably other things. He was shirtless, his tan torso gleaming with sweat in the heat, and his hair was a tousled mess. It was easy to see what Clora liked about him: even this way he was a handsome young man, and with a shower and some fresh clothes he must've been irresistible.

"You looking for my dad?" Bruce said through a yawn. His head pounded like John Bonham at a sound check. "He's not here right now."

Crabtree's voice was soft and steady. "No, you little shit. I'm here for you."

He slammed the two barrels of the shotgun into Bruce's mouth so hard they dislodged most of his front teeth. He pushed him back into the nearest wall. Gagging, Bruce's hands grabbed for the barrel.

"You killed my daughter," Crabtree said, and pulled both triggers.

❧ Later, Jeb Crabtree seemed to awaken from a dream. He found himself on his porch, the sun pounding down on him, his dog asleep beside him.

He looked at the shotgun propped against one of the columns, then down at his own blood-spattered shirt and arms. When he touched his face, he felt dried blood beneath the stubble.

He stood and looked around. *Oh,* he thought calmly, *now I remember. Bruce Cocker killed my Clora. I buried her, then I killed him.*

There was one other thing to finish. It took barely a moment to reload the gun, and then another to complete his final task. His last sensation was surprise at the gun barrel's flavor, and the realization that he now shared this final taste with the boy who killed his girl. The noise sent the dog scurrying under the porch, but he emerged shortly and began wolfing down the chunks of meat and bone scattered around the yard.

In the Bolade house, Prudence sat up at the sound of the shotgun blast, followed by the dog's urgent barking. It wasn't an unusual sound for the area, since someone was always hunting something regardless of what season it might be. But this sound carried a finality that got her attention.

She rose from the bed and padded to the open window. She squinted out into the late-morning sun and tried to get a sense of what had happened. She faintly smelled blood, but could not identify its source.

She felt the corner of her lip. The rip in her flesh had healed, leaving no trace of the passion that tore it. Baron Rudolfo Vladimir Zginski had awakened the desire she'd denied for over a century, and had shown her a mastery that she was all too eager to experience again. Certainly he had controlled her, but with the common goal of mutual satisfaction. And no doubt she had had a similar effect on him, given the way he'd driven himself into her.

She cinched her ruffled robe tight around her waist and blew a touseled strand of blond hair out of her eyes. Duty, she reminded herself, before pleasure. Patience would never return to the Bolade home now, not even after seeing Prudence at the bar. So the confrontation and score-settling would have to take place in the city.

She didn't mind, though. It gave her a reason to dress up.

Byron Cocker got out of the beat-up tow truck and waved to the driver. "Appreciate the lift, Mr. Privitt."

"No worries, Byron," Herm Privitt said. His face looked distended from the massive chaw of tobacco tucked into his lip. "See you around."

Cocker fluttered the front of his shirt against his sweaty chest. He'd returned the Impala and caught a ride home with Privitt, and now it was time to deal with Bruce. He'd either slept right through the boy's return or—more likely—the little pissant had snuck in through a window or the back door. Either way, it was time to explain why the son of Byron Cocker shouldn't be dipping his wick in a

Crabtree honey pot. He was coming up on his senior year, and Cocker would be making damn sure the worthless shit kept up his grades and got into Union University in Jackson. It had been Vicki Lynn's fondest wish.

He stopped as he was about to put his key in the front door. The hairs on the back of his neck stood up the way they always did in the presence of a serious offense. He looked around but saw nothing out of the ordinary; the neighbors' houses were all quiet and still, the men gone to work and the women watching their stories on TV. There was no traffic at all.

He looked down at the door. The knob was intact and showed no sign of being jimmied. None of the front windows were broken. Yet experience had taught him this feeling was never wrong. A crime had been committed here.

He tried the knob. The door was unlocked. He had a gun in his car, but chose not to retrieve it. He mentally counted to three, then threw the door open and charged through with a bellow he'd learned as a novice wrestler.

He nearly tripped over his son's headless corpse.

CHAPTER 28

Zginski looked out at the Mississippi River shimmering in the heat and said, "Do you remember this place?"

Fauvette peeked over the top of her sunglasses and said drily, "I think so."

They stood in the riverfront park where he had taken her the morning he demonstrated that sunlight would not, in fact, reduce her to dust. The night before he had knocked her unconscious and kidnapped her; she had never been so scared, either as a mortal or a vampire, as on that morning when he held her before the window and drew back the curtain.

The moment of revelation had been transcendent, and the sunrise walk afterward only slightly less so. Joggers had passed them, and in the distance a chain of barges drifted downstream surrounded by hovering seagulls. Other birds sang in the trees along with cicadas and stubborn crickets not yet ready for sleep. Buildings had shimmered in the sunrise; it hurt her eyes, but she had not looked away. It had been the most exhilarating and terrifying moment of her existence so far.

Seeing her dressed like any other teenager now, Zginski recalled the way she looked that morning. When he found her she was covered with dirt, filth, and grime. His victim at the time, a thick-headed beauty named Lee Ann, had bathed and dressed her so that she looked more like the child she had been at her death. Now, even though her physical form was unchanged, she radiated the weariness of a sad, mature woman. He felt another of those annoying twinges of conscience at the certainty he was a source of at least some of that sadness.

He hoped his smile was mockery-free. "And how go your feeding lessons?"

"Not so good," she sighed. "Patience doesn't really know how she does it, so that makes it hard for her to teach it. I can almost feel it during her shows, like the air is trembling, but I can't make it happen for myself." She shrugged. "I tried. It didn't work. End of story."

"It would seem to be a unique skill."

"So you believe it now?"

"I believe *you* believe it. Or rather, that you did."

She cocked her head at him. His tone was

gentle, but his words implied the same old arrogance. The last time he'd been truly gentle with her was the night after they'd survived the attack at the warehouse, when he implied a future that had not come to pass. "Why did I think you'd say anything different? You already have all the answers, don't you? Except you keep them to yourself."

Inside, he winced at her venom. "Are you angry with me, Fauvette?"

"Would it matter?" Before he could reply she continued. "You are really something, you know that? Do you even remember that night in the warehouse? That was *important* to me. I let my guard down with you."

People turned toward them at the sound of Fauvette's raised voice, and continued to stare due to their apparent age difference. Zginski said quietly, "And I believe I fulfilled my part of our agreement. You experienced pleasure with a minimum of pain and discomfort."

"Jesus, listen to yourself. I thought . . ." She bit off the rest of the sentence.

"What?" he prompted.

"I thought you felt something for me."

He knew what he should say, knew that it was true. But he resolutely kept silent. He had felt the same for Tzigane, and that had ended badly indeed.

Fauvette continued. "And what about Patience? She practically drools every time you walk in the room. Are you going to use her and throw her away like you did me?"

"I have not thrown you away, Fauvette."

"No, you keep me around for the next time I might be useful to you. Like when you need to find out whether or not Patience is a danger. What do you use Leonardo for, I wonder? And what . . ." Her fury caused the words to jam in her throat. Finally she said tightly, "And what exactly *did* happen to Mark?"

Zginski fought down the emotions struggling for expression. "Mr. Luminesca left," he said in his normal cold tone. "Of his own free will. I neither requested nor compelled him to do so, and was unaware of it until after he had departed. I have no explanation for his conduct, and bear no responsibility for it."

Fauvette felt as if her chest would burst from the rage building in it. "And why, exactly, should I believe you? You've told us all how expendable we are many times."

"I have never been dishonest with you, Fauvette."

"No, but I *am* expendable, ain't I? *Aren't* I?" she corrected.

"I am sorry you feel that way."

"I could say the same to you."

She waited until a young couple, holding hands and basking in each other's presence, sauntered out of hearing. Then she said more calmly, "Look, would it be a huge inconvenience for you to stay the hell away from me for a while? Whenever I see you my heart breaks just a little bit more, and I'm afraid it'll fall apart for good before too long."

They stood in silence for a long moment, not looking at each other. A child on a bicycle rode past, swerving at the last minute to miss them. Finally Zginski said, "If that is what you wish. But I do insist that you inform me if anything happens that I might need to look into."

"You insist?"

"I do."

"Well, we all know how well you can do that." She walked away into the pedestrian traffic and quickly vanished. Everyone who passed her saw only an upset teenage girl who probably should've been in school.

Was this emotional discomfort a result of the blood bonding he'd shared with Fauvette? Had he absorbed some of her weakness while she drew on his strength? Or was he belatedly coming to terms with his own greatest failure, his inability to see Tzigane—the woman, not the car—for what she truly was?

Like Fauvette she had appeared fragile, in need of his protection and kindness. The other peasants traveling with her, sullen Russians relocating to Ireland, treated her like a dangerous outcast. In his presence her dark eyes grew wet with tears at the slightest reproach. And she knew how to make a man feel powerful, using her moans and cries to bind him to her as surely as chains or locks.

Only it had all been an act that proved fatal for him and then for her. Was it even possible for Fauvette to be that devious *and* that deadly?

Suddenly a voice said, "You one of them mimes

or something?" A black man with a little girl in his arms looked quizzically at him. He realized that he'd remained absolutely still in the middle of the sidewalk, staring into space as he reminisced.

"Can you do that thing where you're stuck in a box?" the man added.

He ignored this, walked away, and sat on a bench beneath a large maple tree. A squirrel approached him in jerky, furtive movements, seeking the handouts it usually received. It stopped several feet away, no doubt puzzled by what it sensed from him. Then it scurried up the nearest tree.

Everything runs away, he thought bitterly. It was a feeling he could not recall experiencing before, and he had no idea what to do about it now.

🦂 Prudence kept watch through the grimy front window of the River City Pawnshop, located across the four-lane boulevard from the Ringside. Behind her, the store's lone clerk sat on a bar stool behind the counter and stared at the floor, eyes glazed and openmouthed. His erection bulged visibly at the front of his tan polyester slacks. He was not dead, but neither was he conscious; Prudence had simply turned his mind to its own sexual fantasies, and he would stay that way until she released him. He certainly didn't put up any resistance.

Her own mind was weak and fuzzy from the sun; it was difficult to exert her powers during the day. She had arrived at the Ringside before it opened, then spotted the clerk unlocking the barred door that protected the pawnshop entrance. She reached him before he could flip the sign to OPEN and made him lock up behind them.

A few people had come to the door, expressed their vulgar outrage that it was closed, and then stormed away. Had any of them peered inside, they would have taken Prudence for one of the mannequins. Vampires could remain still longer and with more consistency than any living being. Prudence saw no reason to pace or otherwise expend energy, so she simply stood in the darkened shop and watched.

At last a big black car pulled into the Ringside's lot and parked in the limited shade. Patience emerged, stretched, and spent a moment looking at Prudence's old Thunderbird, left in the spot farthest from the building. She could not possibly recognize it, since Prudence had bought it a century after her sister left home. As Patience removed her guitar from the LTD's trunk another woman joined her.

Prudence squinted through the glare. This newcomer was the same young woman she'd seen behind the Ringside's bar. Prudence focused all her attention on them, and was able to read their lips as long as they faced her direction.

"Wow," Patience said when she saw Fauvette's expression. "You look pissed off."

"I am," Fauvette agreed.

"What happened?"

She raised her chin proudly. "I told Rudy Zginski to kiss my ass and go to hell."

Patience's eyebrows rose. "Really?"

She nodded. "I told him I didn't want to see him anymore, or talk to him, or fuck him." She punctuated this with a little nod of certainty.

It didn't fool Patience. "Is that true?"

"That I said it?"

"That you *meant* it. Especially about that last one."

"Hell, yes, I meant it. I have enough to worry about without sex getting in the way. Maybe I'm an eternal virgin for a reason."

"So the Catholics can worship you?" Patience said teasingly. "And hey, didn't you say the first time with Zginski was also the only time it wasn't agony?"

Fauvette scowled. "Yeah, but I'd damn well rather be celibate than fucked by someone who would kill me in an instant if it was convenient for him."

Patience smiled and shook her head. "He's not like that, really. He just wants you to think so."

"You don't know him like I do."

"Maybe not in the same ways. But I know him."

Fauvette was tired of this whole subject. "Can we drop this? I have to get changed for work." She nodded at the Thunderbird. "Whose car is that?"

"Probably broke down and the driver went to get help," Patience said.

"He better," Fauvette said as they went around

the building to the kitchen entrance, "'cause Gerry will for sure have it towed if it's still around when he gets here."

🎜 Across the street, Prudence released her hold on the pawnshop's owner, who climaxed inside his trousers and collapsed to the floor. He lay there shaking, disoriented and confused, then began to cry at the vivid memory of making love to his dead wife.

She shielded her eyes as she went outside and dashed across the street through the midday traffic, eliciting only one horn honk of protest. She found the back kitchen door unlocked and opened it enough to peek inside. A cold blast of air-conditioning blew over her. She saw no one, but heard muffled female voices. She slipped inside and followed the sound to a door marked WOMEN. She stood close to listen.

Fauvette quickly undressed, her uniform on a stall door hook. She said to Patience, "I guess instead of chasing him off, I should try to be more like him. He definitely gets what he wants."

Patience leaned over the sink and checked her eyeliner in the mirror. She watched Fauvette's reflection; stripped down to her underwear, her physical youth was even more apparent. Fourteen years old forever, with the pert breasts and wide hips of maturity as well as the baby fat and touch of unformed softness still left from childhood. Patience often regretted being doomed to immortality with twenty extra pounds on her frame, but had long since realized that, for a vampire, appearance was entirely beside the point. Looking a certain way was useful only as camouflage. "Honey, do you *want* to be like that?"

"No," Fauvette said wearily as she stepped into her skirt. "I *want* to be like you. I want to be able to move through the world without leaving a trail of death and destruction." She pulled up the zipper and turned the skirt into place.

"I'm sorry, honey, I wish I could tell you more. I don't *know* how I do it. I don't even know how I became what I am, really." She turned away from the mirror. "Maybe you and I aren't even the same thing. I mean, maybe we just superficially *look* alike, but we're actually completely different."

Fauvette buttoned up her blouse. "You have fangs. You could drink blood if you wanted to. Just like me."

"That's true," Patience agreed sadly.

Fauvette fluffed her hair from her blouse's collar. "Did you know Gerry actually wants me to start going without a bra? 'Nipples sell more drinks,' he says. Can you believe that?"

"From what I know about men, yes. Are you going to do it?"

"I might. Not tonight, though." She went to the mirror and applied some lipstick. "Tonight I'd like to hang on to just a little bit of dignity."

When she finished, Patience went to her and wrapped her in her arms. "I'm *really* sorry, Fauvette. It seems like I've been nothing but a source of disappointment to you. It might be better if I'd never come along."

As always, Patience's soft embrace reminded Fauvette of her long-dead mother. She closed her eyes and said softly, "Just don't leave yet. I don't care about the whole energy thing anymore, I just . . . please stay, okay? You're my only friend."

Patience stroked her hair. "I'm not going anywhere, little girl. I promise."

At the words "little girl," Fauvette felt the hot sting in the corners of her eyes from tears she could not actually produce.

Outside the door, Prudence smiled and had to bite her knuckle to keep from laughing with delight. Fate had conspired to give her the perfect way to get back at her sister, to start this campaign of retribution with a nuclear strike.

Fauvette reluctantly pulled away from Patience. "I'm sorry, I just got a little carried away. It's been a difficult morning."

"No need to apologize. I'm here if you need me."

"Thanks." She kissed Patience on the cheek.

"Well, I need to go see about this piano I have to use. If last night is any indication, it's been spending its time in a whorehouse run by deaf people. I have to see if I can fix it up a little."

She left, and in a few moments Fauvette heard her playing in the dining room. She smiled and applied eye shadow, then bent down to retrieve her hairbrush. When she stood back up, a blond woman was reflected in the mirror.

She turned, startled. How had she not sensed this woman's approach? "Wow, I didn't even hear you come in. Are you a new waitress? Gerry should be here pretty soo—"

Prudence grabbed Fauvette by the throat and pushed her back against the wall. She crushed the girl's neck, feeling the bones snap against her palm. The spinal cord was also severed, leaving Fauvette immobile, her body hanging limp in Prudence's grasp. Her eyes opened wide and her mouth worked to try to speak, but she could make no sound.

Prudence smiled. "I should probably tell you this is nothing personal, but that's really not true. It's *very* personal. Just not to you."

She drove her other hand, fingers first, into Fauvette's belly, piercing the skin and grabbing a handful of intestines.

Fauvette was grateful for the numbness below her neck, although the wet sounds of the woman's efforts were almost as bad. Whatever the woman did would be repaired after a night's vampiric rest, but that did nothing to make the disembowelment any less terrifying.

"You should never get emotionally involved with someone like my sister," Prudence said as she pulled a string of intestines out and tossed them aside. They landed with a wet smack on the tile. Then she reached up into Fauvette's body cavity for her heart.

Fauvette realized what was happening, what the woman intended to do, and tried with all her strength to scream. Patience would rush to her if only she knew. A single cry, a lone shriek of terror, would summon rescue.

She made no sound at all.

"Only one person can get close to Patience, honey," Prudence said as her fingers dug for the organ. "And that's me." Then she smiled. "A-ha. There you are."

Prudence tore Fauvette's heart free of her body.

Fauvette had time to see her own heart in the woman's grasp. Then Prudence opened her mouth wide, bared her fangs, and sank them into the organ. She tore out a bite-size chunk and spat it into the sink.

Fauvette's vision suddenly receded, and she sensed her hair crumbling and the skin of her face growing tight and parchmentlike. Over fifty years had passed since her biological death, and all of it was catching up to her now that her heart had been destroyed. The last thing she saw, the last moment of consciousness she had before she finally, truly *died*, was the woman's arrogant sneer.

CHAPTER 29

Patience had turned out the bright house lights in the Ringside dining room and noodled at the piano in the semidarkness. It really did sound like a whorehouse instrument; she remembered playing one very similar when she had actually worked briefly as a whore. It was during that time she learned to love both music and sex, although music eventually won out as a priority. However, since meeting Rudy Zginski, she wondered if she needed to reevaluate.

Something indefinable changed in the empty room's atmosphere. It now felt icy and dangerous. She looked up and gasped. *"Prudence!"*

Her sister was a silhouette in the kitchen door, still but unmistakable. "Hello, dear Patience. It's been a long time. My, how you haven't changed."

Patience stood, instantly on her guard. She looked around the room to make sure they were alone. "I saw you here last night," she said, hoping she sounded casual. "You ran off before we could speak."

"What on earth would the two of us have to talk about?" Prudence said with mocking frivolity. "Everything we needed to say should've been said a hundred years ago. Saying it now would just make a mockery of a good man's death."

"A good man?" Patience snapped. "Vincent? What kind of man proposes to one sister and then seduces the other?"

"A man who needed more than his fiancé could give him," Prudence shot back.

Patience clenched her fists. "What do you want?"

"Why, to settle accounts. Even the score. Balance the ledgers. Choose the metaphor you like."

"Can't we put the past behind us?"

"The past is what we *are*, dear sister. The past, when our hearts beat and our blood raced. Everything since then is just one long, breath-holding *moment*."

Patience moved through the empty tables toward Prudence, who was still a sharp black outline against the harsh kitchen light. "So what do you want me to do? Go away again? *Stay* away?"

"Good heavens, no. I want you to stay right here, close to the bosom of your family. I want us to play our games again, like we did before. But as it stands now, you are ahead by one, and it's time for me to even the score."

She held up something shriveled and black that crumbled even as she displayed it.

"What is that?" Patience whispered.

"Something you once had, and don't anymore. You made it so easy, Patience, just like with Vincent. You opened yourself up wide to let someone in, which gave me plenty of room to reach in myself and yank them out."

Patience felt a jolt of fear. "What are you talking about?"

"You'll find out. And then we'll be even, and we can begin again. Like the song says, we can play our games of blood. See you soon, big sister." She backed into the kitchen and the doors swung shut behind her.

Patience rushed to follow, fast enough to hear the back door slam as Prudence fled. When she passed the women's restroom, though, she froze. Something lay on the floor and blocked the door open.

She stood over it, staring. She switched on the hall light. It took a moment for the withered, musty corpse on the floor to register on her. Only the incongruous little skirt and tattered remains of the white blouse identified it.

She should have screamed, or wailed, or smashed something. She should have chased after Prudence, who was no doubt nearby, gloating and listening for the cries of rage.

Instead she gently picked up Fauvette's withered corpse and carried it downstairs into the cellar. One leg broke off at the knee when she bumped into the rail.

🜊 When Zginski reached the Ringside just after sunset, he immediately sensed something wrong. One clue was obvious: the place should've been packed, but the parking lot was empty and the CLOSED sign still hung on the front door.

He drove around back and parked in his usual spot. The kitchen door was unlocked. When he opened it he immediately smelled blood, but it took him a moment to identify the peculiar tang to the odor. It was not, he realized, living human blood or the animal scent carried by some of the raw meat. It was unmistakably *vampire* blood.

He closed the door silently behind him. The odor seemed to come from the women's lavatory across the narrow hall, so he carefully peered inside.

Something lay in the middle of the floor. It looked like a chunk of animal tissue, perhaps a string of sausage, which had somehow crumbled to dust. He touched one intact section, and it collapsed into black ashlike powder. A similar, smaller lump lay in the sink.

He felt a pit of feeling open inside his own chest. But he resolutely refused to let the thought form. It *must* be something else.

He went through the empty kitchen to Barrister's office. None of the appliances were turned on to prepare for the evening. He pushed the swinging doors open, and saw that the chairs were still atop tables in the darkened dining room.

He knocked on the office door and said, "Barrister? It is Zginski." Without waiting for a reply, he opened it.

Barrister sat behind his desk, head down on his folded arms.

"Barrister?" he repeated, but got no response; the man was under a vampiric spell. "I did it," a voice said behind him.

He turned. Patience stood there, dressed for work, but with a smear of blackened blood across her pale cleavage. Her expression lacked its normal wry amusement. "First I had him call everyone and tell them not to come in. Then I put him to sleep for a while."

"Why?" Zginski demanded.

Patience's voice was quiet and even. "Because Fauvette is dead, Rudy. Really dead."

Zginski's world tilted around him, but he did not let it show. "Are you certain?"

"Yes." Her voice cracked as she added, "She's in the basement where no one can disturb her. I knew you'd want to tell her good-bye."

He followed her down the stairs. The withered thing that had once been Fauvette was laid out on an old wooden door placed atop two beer kegs. A ring of fine dust already outlined the body, and more fell as it slowly crumbled to bits.

Zginski felt as if gravity had tripled beneath

him. The three steps to the corpse were the hardest he'd ever taken. The adorable face he'd first seen drinking blood in the back of a pickup truck now consisted of cords of blackened flesh stretched tight over a skull so small it was heartbreaking. The teeth, including her slightly curved fangs, were white and plain through gaps as the cheeks flaked away. Eyes that had gleamed with sadness, desire, hope, and a love he could never acknowledge, were now orbless pits.

Patience remained respectfully at the bottom of the stairs. There was nothing to be done, and Zginski no doubt knew that.

He touched, as lightly as possible, Fauvette's nearest hand. The skin felt like dry tissue paper that crackled under even the feather-light pressure, and black ash puffed out through a multitude of tiny splits.

Zginski withdrew his fingers and stood silently for a long moment. He asked calmly, "Who did this?"

"My sister," Patience said. "She did it to hurt me."

"And why would this hurt you?"

"Somehow she knew I loved Fauvette like a sister more than I ever loved Prudence."

He turned to her. His voice and demeanor stayed the same, but something terrifying burned in his eyes. "So you drew her into this blood feud between the two of you?"

"Not on *purpose,* Rudy. I never even told Prudence I was back. I have no idea how she found out."

"But you knew she was capable of this."

Patience nodded.

Zginski's backhand knocked her into the concrete wall so hard it cracked, rupturing a pipe above her. Water cascaded down on them. Stunned, she tried to move away, but her shoes slipped in the water and Zginski caught her by the hair. He pulled her to her feet and hissed, "I will not *allow* this. You have come into my world and brought destruction. This will not happen again."

Holding her by the hair, he picked up a discarded wooden chair and smashed it to pieces against the wet floor. He took one of the legs, now jagged and sharp, and raised it over his head.

"No!" Patience screamed and struggled to escape. The rising water was now ankle-deep, and the empty kegs began to float. He slammed her face-first into the wall and pressed her there until she stopped struggling.

"You deserve a slower death for the danger you have brought," he snarled. "But expediency has granted you mercy."

He drove the makeshift stake through her back. The jagged point erupted from her chest and buried itself in the wall, pinning her there. She stiffened as long-delayed death immediately seized her. By the time Zginski stepped away, her skin was already withering and turning gray. The water sluicing down on her quickly sheared the collapsing flesh from her skeleton.

Zginski again stood still for a long moment, watching the water dissolve Patience into sludge. A scraping sound made him turn as the kegs supporting Fauvette began to float, and the door fell to one side. Her corpse slid toward the water.

With no thought he rushed over and caught it. The water had the same effect as it did on Patience, and the body fell apart, sifting through his fingers as it dissolved. He clutched at her clothes, the only things that remained. But they were mere empty garments.

The next moment he was driving down Madison, with no memory of leaving the Ringside and getting into his car. But he knew exactly where he was going.

Byron Cocker pounded on the door of the Bolade mansion until Prudence opened it. He started to speak, then did a double take at the beautiful young woman before him. At last he said, "I need to see Mama Prudence."

She laughed at his discomfort. She wore a low-cut gown and her hair was brushed loose and shiny around her shoulders. "Why, Sheriff, don't you recognize me?"

He was too distraught for games. "I don't know who the hell you are but I *need* to see Mama Prudence! *Now!*"

She stepped back at this hostility. "Byron Cocker,

you will behave like you've been to town before or I will send you on your way. What is it you want to see me about?"

His eyes, red and blurred from crying, finally saw the truth. "Mama Prudence?" he said pitifully. "Is that really you?"

"Given your attitude, you may call me 'Miss Bolade,'" she sniffed. "Now state your business."

With a wailing cry he fell to his knees, his great weight making the floor tremble. Something crashed and broke in another room. He bawled, *"My boy is dead!"*

She stepped away from him as he blubbered, his red face a contrast to the white scar tissue. "And what is that to me, sir? I certainly didn't kill him."

"But you can bring him *back*! You're a witch-woman, everybody knows it! My God, look at what you've done to *yourself*!" He gestured at her as if she had somehow missed the fact that she was now young and beautiful.

She laughed coldly. "I'm not a *witch*, Sheriff. I know a few Gypsy tricks and scams, but that's all. It's enough to keep you simple rednecks at arm's length, and that's what I need."

He stared in confusion, mucus running from his nose. Then he crawled on his knees to her and wrapped his huge arms around her waist. "I don't *care* what you are, just please, bring back my boy! He's all I have!"

"And you will join him soon enough," a new voice said.

Cocker and Prudence both turned. Zginski stood in the still-open doorway. In one hand he clutched a long, jaggedly sharp piece of wood.

"Well, this is a surprise," Prudence said. "Byron Cocker, this is—"

"We've met," Zginski and Cocker said simultaneously.

Prudence laughed in delight. "How marvelous." She took in his bedraggled appearance. "Why, Mr. Zginski, you're soaking wet."

Zginski held up the broken chair leg stained with Patience's blood. "I drove this through the body of your sister. Now I intend to do the same with you."

Prudence's eyes opened wide, and all the amusement left her face. "You mean . . . Patience is *dead*?"

"As you are about to be."

She shoved Cocker away so hard that he slid across the floor into a side table, dislodging the vases arranged there. Their crash echoed in the foyer. "I don't believe you!" Prudence hissed.

"Your belief does not concern me," Zginski snarled. "Your presence has brought danger and destruction to me, and I will end it. And you."

"*No!*" Cocker yelled and threw himself at Zginski. His bulk and the element of surprise gave him the momentary advantage. Mama Prudence was his only hope for bringing back his son, and this foreigner, who'd stolen his car out from under him, would not stop him now. He grabbed Zginski's neck, lifted the smaller man off the floor, and squeezed with all his might.

Zginski's uppercut hit Cocker's jaw so hard the rewired mandible shattered like a clay pot. The man's head snapped back, the bones and muscles in his neck snapping like tent lines in a hurricane. He dropped to the floor, blinked twice, and died.

Zginski pointed at Prudence. "Now you."

She hid her fear and gave him her sweetest, most demure smile. "Rudy, please. We're two of a kind. Remember last night? That was freedom, Rudy, a meeting of equals. You can't pretend you ever got that with my sister, or that silly little Fauvette."

At the name, Zginski roared his fury and threw the stake, not at her heart, but at her head. It struck below her nose, in the soft cleft above her lips, and stuck out the back of her skull.

The impact made her stumble back into the staircase. She screamed, but the stake distorted the sound into something ghastly. She tried to pull it out, but before she could Zginski snatched her by the wrist, put his other hand against her torso, and ripped her arm from her body.

She pushed him away and careened toward the parlor. He kicked her in the small of the back and sent her crashing across a padded chair into a low coffee table.

She landed facedown and tried to rise one-armed. He planted one foot between her shoulder blades to hold her in place. She made another sound, like a wounded elephant crossed with a shattered boiler.

"You should *never*," he said icily, "have drawn so much attention." Then he crushed her upper chest against the floor, smashing her heart beneath the sole of his platform shoe.

He stepped back and watched yet again as another vampire withered away, this time into a powdery pile of bone fragments and dust.

The fire as the Bolade mansion burned to the ground could be seen for miles, the smoke rising straight and black into the still afternoon sky. And Leonardo, from his vantage point in the forest beside the Crabtree family cemetery, was tempted to investigate. But he would not abandon the fresh unmarked grave. Already he'd chased away two coyotes and a wild pig attracted by the scent of corruption seeping through the dry soil. He would keep watch until the next dawn, to see if Clora Crabtree might rise from her death to join him.

CHAPTER 30

At the moment Rudy Zginski ground Prudence Bolade's heart underfoot, he was solely focused on one thing: vengeance. This purpose was so single-minded that somewhere between Memphis and McHale County, he inadvertently severed his connection to Alisa Cassidy.

She sat at her desk finishing yet another potential translation of a line from the *Festa Maggotta*. As always this translation, even though it accurately deciphered the individual words, might not be correct if it didn't make sense when read along with the rest of the passage. And sometimes even coherent passages might be wrong if they failed to mesh with what had gone before. It was one more reason that the book, despite existing for centuries, had never been rendered fully readable.

Had old Sir Francis Colby understood the academic aggravation he was creating when he bequeathed it?

The pain struck deep inside with the force of a knife carving clumsily through her midsection. Her scream of surprise and agony was choked by its sheer intensity, and her back arched against her chair. Her hands clawed at the air, and her feet kicked against the desk. She couldn't get breath to even gasp.

Sometime later she awoke on the floor beside her desk. It was now dark outside. Papers and books lay scattered around her, dislodged by her mad thrashing. The pain was still there, but both duller and more widespread. She managed to sit up, tears running down her face.

This can mean only one thing, she thought. *Rudy is dead. Destroyed. He'd never do this to me deliberately.*

She used the desk for support as she stood, one hand uselessly cradling her belly. She took several deep breaths and wiped the tears from her eyes. She had made plans for her death based on Rudy's presence. Now that he was gone, she'd have to change everything.

She looked up as the front door opened and Zginski entered.

She could think of nothing to say. Then she noticed his dishevelment, including unmistakable dark red stains.

She tried to speak. Her throat was so raw she managed only a croak.

Zginski looked up and seemed surprised to find himself there. His eyes opened wide as he realized what he'd done to her, and immediately he enveloped her in a huge surge of power.

In its way, the total cessation of the agony was as bad as the pain itself. Alisa cried out and would have fallen again, but instead managed to land back in her office chair.

She sat gasping, her body alive with sensations that had nothing to do with the torture she'd been experiencing. She began to cry again, and it took several minutes to get herself under control. She blew her nose using a page of scribbled notes, then noticed Zginski had not moved. "Rudy?"

He said nothing. His shoulders sagged, and his long hair hung in loose strands around his face. She'd never seen him any way other than in total control, and this really frightened her. She used the wall for support as she went to him.

She touched his arm. "Rudy, what's wrong?" Then she looked at the red stain on her hand. "Rudy, is that *blood*?"

He looked as if he'd been told the worst news in the world. "I apologize for neglecting you," he said flatly, staring at the floor.

The blood from killing Patience soaked his sleeve and most of his shirt. "Sweet Jesus, what did you *do*?"

He pushed the hair from his eyes and tucked it behind his ears. "I did . . . what was necessary."

She backed away from him, her bloody hand out like Lady Macbeth. "*Necessary?* You told me you didn't have to kill people to feed, that a little blood from me was enough!"

"No, you misunderstand. Most of those I killed were fellow revenants."

"*Most?*"

He finally raised his eyes and looked at her. "I did kill one man. Byron Cocker."

"*You killed Byron Cocker?*" Alisa gasped. "My God, you *are* crazy. You are truly insane."

He should have taken offense, but he had no reserves of outrage left in him. He said calmly, "I assure you, each decision was made quite rationally, and there is no way to trace the events back to me. That, in fact, was the point."

She backed into the wall and dislodged a picture of her with Chad. The glass shattered when the frame struck the floor. "Stay away from me, Rudy. I'd rather have the pain than this."

He swallowed hard. The terror in her eyes, where previously he'd seen only kindness, desire, and understanding, made him feel somehow weak. She was the second person to demand his absence that day. "Alisa, I assure you, it was nothing that could be avoided. Had I not acted, the danger would have only grown. Fauvette . . ." The name choked him and he could not continue.

"Who?" she asked.

Of course she didn't know. He never mentioned the others to her. "A friend."

"A vampire?"

He nodded. "She was . . ." And something wrenched in his heart, a surge of emotion he neither expected nor knew how to handle. "She was beautiful, and kind, and now she is dead."

He sat on the foyer's tile floor, his legs too weak to hold him. He stared down at a spot where light reflected from one bit of texture. The room was silent except for the air conditioner and the occasional traffic.

At last Alisa said in wonder, "Oh, my God, Rudy. You *loved* her. Like a human being."

Zginski continued to gaze at the floor. "Yes."

Alisa took a tentative step toward him. "And you never told her."

"No."

She laughed at the absurdity. "You son of a bitch. You come off like some icy death machine, and you were in love all the time."

He looked up. "I never lied about my feelings for you, Alisa."

"I know you didn't. You don't lie, you just paraphrase to your own advantage."

"No, I will lie if it suits me. But I have not lied to you."

She knelt and touched his cold face. Once she'd known a German shepherd who was vicious beyond belief until a car struck him and broke his leg. Zginski's numb acquiescence reminded her of that dog's blank, cowed expression. "I know you haven't, Rudy. It must hurt you a lot if it's left you like this. Is there anything I can do?"

"There is nothing to be done. She is dead. The ones responsible for her death are dead. All evidence has been destroyed. It is over."

She paused, weighing the benefits of silence against Zginski's visible anguish. Her plan was logically idiotic, and had been developed for something else entirely, a contingency against her own cowardice. But now there was a chance to turn it to a selfless use that, if she were lucky enough to face St. Peter, might count in her favor. Helping the damned was surely as meritorious as feeding the poor.

Carefully, making sure each word was clear, she said, "I *might* be able to help you."

"Help me?"

Even more deliberately she said, "Yes. You might still be able to save her. Fauvette."

"Her heart is destroyed. No vampire can survive that. Her body has irretrievably decomposed." The thought of it made him wince again. "If she could be saved, I would have done so. There was no way."

"No way that *you* know."

Some of the haze cleared, and with a hint of the old arrogance he demanded, "What are you saying? Speak plainly."

She stood and offered her hand. "Come with me."

When he touched her, she felt a surge of the old desire for him, and sucked in a sharp breath. He got to his feet and gestured for her to precede him. He followed her into the kitchen. As she washed the blood from her hands she said, "I finished translating the section of the *Festa Maggotta* that deals with vampires. A lot are things you already told me. In fact, because that spoke well of its accuracy, I believed the parts you didn't confirm."

She dried her hands, opened a cabinet door, and removed a plastic half-gallon pitcher. A dark liquid sloshed in it as she placed it on the counter. "And one of the things I believed," she finished, "was the recipe for *this*."

"What is it?"

She smiled wryly. "You won't believe me."

"You have never lied to me, either."

"This is a time travel potion for vampires."

He was silent for a moment, then said, "That is absurd."

"Of course it is. Time travel is an impossibility in the H. G. Wells sense. But this doesn't work the way you think. It rewinds your inner existence, like a tape recording. So you essentially go back in your own consciousness, and yet keep all the memories of what has already happened. It gets rid of that whole being-in-two-places-at-once problem, because it all happens inside your head."

Zginski leaned down and sniffed at the spout. The liquid smelled foul. "What does it contain?"

"Black tea, hemlock, datura, belladonna, and something called ricin. Along with some other things."

He lifted the olive-green top. The substance was deep burgundy, like the color of a bruise. It even left a yellowish skim around the edge. "How far back is one able to go?"

"If I've translated it right, twenty-four hours.

You drink it, and suddenly it's yesterday, yet you remember everything that's going to happen tomorrow." She paused. "Would that give you time to save . . . what was her name?"

"Fauvette."

"Yeah, Fauvette. Beautiful name."

His eyes narrowed as his normal skepticism arose. He replaced the pitcher's top and said, "And exactly *why* would someone develop this?"

"It's to give a new vampire a second chance. If you simply can't abide your undead condition, you drink this and change the circumstances that turned you into a vampire."

"Then it takes you back to a mortal existence."

"That was its purpose, yeah."

"I have been a vampire far longer than twenty-four hours."

She shrugged. "I don't know what to say. It might work, it might not. The ingredients are all toxic to humans, but I don't think it can kill *you*; you're already dead, after all. And ultimately, it's the only chance you have, isn't it?"

"And why have *you* created this concoction?"

She laughed. "Why do you think?"

It took a moment, but he realized. "You believed that as your death neared, your conviction would waver."

"That's a very wordy way to say it."

He smiled. "You worried that you might . . . 'chicken up'?"

"Chicken *out*," she corrected with a giggle. "Yeah."

Despite himself, he was intrigued. "But what proof do you have that it works?"

"None. I just thought you might like to know about it."

Again he gazed at the pitcher, wondering if this ridiculous claim could be true. Fauvette's face, unbidden, sprang to his memory with a vividness only timeless beings like vampires possessed. A fresh wave of fury and, worst of all, *guilt* swelled in him. He could not believe he had judged things so badly that it resulted in Fauvette's destruction.

"It is possible," he mused, "that this concoction was simply *presented* as what you say. In reality it might be a means to destroy a new vampire, or compel one to destroy itself. I have encountered substances like that before."

"That's true. I guess the question is, how important is this Fauvette person to you? Is she worth that big a risk?"

The liquid's surface stilled until it reflected a steady image of the ceiling light fixture. "What is the prescribed dosage?" he said at last.

"All of it. As fast as possible. In one swallow, if you can."

He picked up the pitcher and raised it to his mouth. At the last moment he paused and lowered it. "You would not betray me at this moment, would you, Alisa?"

At one time this paranoia would have angered her, but now he seemed almost pathetic in his suspicion. "There's only one way to find out. One choice, one chance. But just in case . . ." She kissed him on the cheek. "Thank you for making me forget the pain."

He nodded. He touched the plastic spout to his lips. The fumes enveloped his face, stinging his eyes and making his flesh crawl. And in the brightly lit kitchen of a fancy Germantown home, a centuries-old revenant drank an elixir to send him back through time.

CHAPTER 31

At first nothing happened.

Zginski drank the pitcher's contents in one long swallow. It was the first time he'd consumed anything other than blood since he'd been turned, and everything about it felt wrong.

The taste was awful, like some industrial solvent obscenely mixed with an excess of citrus. It smelled like the surplus drippings of some offal collection tank. It slid down his gullet in slime-coated lumps and congealed in his belly like some sort of gelatin. He leaned against the counter as physical nausea swept over him. The whole ghastly contents threatened to leap back up his throat and splatter on the polished Formica.

"Rudy?" Alisa asked. Her voice seemed very far away. *Something* was happening to him.

It was stranger than he could've imagined. His body grew warm, then hot, radiating a sensation as if he were about to burst into flames. He heard sizzling as the caustic chemicals chewed into his flesh, and his vision grew blurry and indistinct. He attempted to place the pitcher back on the counter, but misjudged his strength and crushed it instead, cracking the countertop beneath it. *It is destroying me,* he thought. He turned to Alisa, determined to make her pay for her treachery.

Suddenly everything went blank.

Not black, *blank*. Black was a sensation of color, and now there was nothing at all. He tried to move, shout, run. He tried to think. He felt himself drifting even as he stayed immobile, and the contradiction terrified him.

A roaring grew in intensity until his ears throbbed with the pain. He tried to cover them, but could not get his hands to move. He felt a rush of disorientation as he realized he had no physical form at all, just a consciousness stripped free of the corporeal world and sent into the void.

Then he recognized where he was. He *knew* this place.

It was the same nowhere, the same nothingness that Sir Francis Colby consigned him to in 1915 by driving a golden blade into his heart. He was back in it, and this time there would be no rejuvenation.

The realization triggered a rush of panic. Alisa had destroyed him as a final act before her own death. Women were treacherous, and he'd been a fool to ignore the danger. And now, like Fauvette, it was too late.

He cursed the universe for allowing this. He cursed Alisa for tricking him, and he cursed himself for falling for it. And he cursed Fauvette for being so beautiful and kind and alluring and perfect that he would risk his own existence in a pointless, doomed attempt to save hers.

The void swallowed him, burrowed into him, consumed him, and made itself part of him. He tried to scream. But he needed a mouth for that.

CHAPTER 32

Then, like a train ending its downhill run by slamming into a mountainside, he was suddenly back in his body and aware of his surroundings. He opened his eyes.

He stood on the porch outside Prudence Bolade's door. It was night, and the trees and grass hummed with insects. The dead waitress Sammy Jo was draped across his shoulders. His legs wobbled from the unexpected weight, and he almost collapsed. He leaned against the door frame and waited for the dizziness to subside.

The reality of the moment overwhelmed him. *It worked,* he told himself. *I am where I was last night, before Fauvette's death.* He recalled making certain Sammy Jo's corpse was destroyed in the fire, so if it was here, intact, there could be no other explanation. He had indeed rewound his own life and traveled *back in time.*

But now what? He could rush back to Memphis and protect Fauvette, but that would be awkward and uncertain. No, since he was here, the most efficient thing would be to eliminate the threat before it could strike. That would also spare him any uncomfortable explanations.

He silently put down the body and stood very still, listening. Nothing moved within. He had rung the doorbell before; had he done so yet?

He waited many long minutes. No lights appeared, and no one opened the door.

He turned the knob firmly until it stopped, then wrenched it so that the lock's mechanism failed. In the silence the metallic breaking noise sounded like a cannon. He pushed the door open and peered into the darkened house.

Prudence slept in an upstairs bedroom; she'd shown it to him, or rather *would* show it to him had the night followed its original course. They had coupled on the ancient bed, their exertions sending clouds of dust into the air.

He ascended the steps in silence, opened the bedroom door, and found her lying still and immobile on the bed, a corpse for all intents and purposes. The mattress and bedclothes were permanently impressed with her form.

He shook his head. A vampire resting at night when she was most powerful was a sad mockery of her prior life. She held on to it the same way she clung to the grudge against Patience. She was so beautiful, like a china doll, with her hair softly arranged on the silk pillow. The lace at her bosom gave her a gentle, angelic countenance. Her lips, full and bowed, begged for a final kiss, like a storybook heroine awakened by Prince Charming.

Instead he drove his fist through her chest, out her back, and halfway through the ancient down mattress. Her heart was destroyed.

He did not stay to watch her body crumble. He searched the house from attic to cellar, using up time originally spent on sex to check for anything that might prove valuable to him. He found nothing; there were many antiques and pieces of artwork, but nothing that would aid the existence of a being like himself. Then he repeated the burning of her house. The Bolade homestead, like its undead occupant, had outlived its time.

He reached the end of the driveway only moments later than he had done in the original timeline, but it was enough. Another car approached on the dark highway, and instead of passing it slowed and stopped, blocking his way. The door opened, and Byron Cocker got out. He stood in Zginski's headlights, one big fist clenched around a baseball bat.

Zginski emerged from his own vehicle. "This is an ill-advised course of action," he said.

Cocker pointed with the bat. "Looks like something's on fire back yonder, and here I see you driving away. I think that merits a little looking into."

"You are no longer an officer of the law."

Cocker smiled. He was so ecstatic at this coincidence that he could barely keep from laughing aloud. He smacked the bat into his palm. "Son, this bat is all the law I need. You and me, we're gonna settle things right now."

"What is the basis of this enmity?" Zginski demanded. When he saw the confused frown crease Cocker's face, he rephrased it as, "Why are you determined to do me harm?"

Cocker pointed the bat at the Mustang. "That should be *my* car. I deserve it, for what sheriffing in this miserable county cost me. And then *you* pop up, not even an American, and swipe it right out from under me. That just plain ain't right."

This had not happened in the previous reality, and Zginski was unsure how to proceed. Should he destroy the threat or try to avoid it?

"Got nothing to say?" Cocker taunted. "Why don't you try begging me not to kick your ass? That'll make it even sweeter."

Zginski said nothing. Instead he simply got back in his car, put it in gear, and floored the gas pedal. Cocker barely jumped aside as the Mustang careened down into the ditch to avoid the Impala and bottomed out before bouncing back onto the road. Then it roared off toward Memphis.

"*Get back here, you son of a bitch!*" Cocker screamed as he flung the bat after Zginski. It clattered uselessly on the road.

"You're not doing this to me," Cocker seethed. He jumped back into the Impala, squealed tires in a U-turn, and left long black streaks before the rubber finally caught the road.

Zginski had a head start, and a faster car. Cocker knew this yet continued to chase him, the gas pedal slammed to the floor. He flew down the straightaways and took the curves on two wheels as the taillights ahead of him grew smaller and fainter.

"No," he snarled at the universe, "this *ain't fair*!"

The Impala left the pavement on the next curve at nearly a hundred miles an hour and hit an oak tree. The momentum split the car in half so that the tree trunk ended up in the center of the dashboard. Cocker was ejected through the windshield, smashed into the bank of a culvert, and rolled down into it. He was dead on impact.

Unaware of the crash, Zginski slowed down to the normal speed limit when he was certain he'd lost Cocker. He drove back to Memphis and, instead of going straight to Alisa's as he'd done before, detoured to drive slowly past Fauvette's apartment. He saw nothing, and the sunrise kept him from sensing anything. But just knowing she was in there comforted him more than he expected.

When he finally reached Alisa's house, he carefully washed the soot and Prudence's blood from his hands, and changed into a clean shirt before going in search of Alisa. She was asleep on the daybed in her study, the blanket pulled up to her chin despite the heat. The cancer's bite was growing stronger, and she had little time left. He sat down on the floor beside her and touched her hand.

Instantly he knew she was dead.

He remained beside her for a long time. The sun rose until it no longer shone directly in the windows. At last he stood and gently tugged the blanket over her face. He turned to her desk, intending to gather her notes on the *Festa Maggotta*.

It was empty. Everything was gone: photocopies, notepads, all her pages and pages of translations. He checked the drawers, the filing cabinet, everywhere. Then he noticed the fireplace.

It was late summer, so a fire shouldn't be necessary. But the ashes were fresh, and voluminous. And he found an unburned scrap of paper that had come from her notebook.

She had burned everything.

He sat in her desk chair, stunned and confused. In the day's original timeline, Zginski's fury caused him to lose touch with her, and her pain returned full force. But in this new reality, he had been careful to maintain the link so that she would not suffer. Yet this time he had been so preoccupied he hadn't felt her die.

He looked at the body on the sofa. Had she died of natural causes, or had she killed herself? If the latter, surely she must've left a suicide note.

He searched the house from bedroom to garage, and found no trace of any of her work. The time-travel elixir was gone as well, because in this reality, she'd never concocted it; the pitcher she'd used remained dusty and untouched in the cabinet. He sat and stared at her dead face for a long time before it occurred to him to check his own resting place in the cellar.

A neat envelope lay on his bed. He opened it and found a note that read:

> *I've decided to end this now. What I've discovered in the book convinced me to destroy my notes and translations. Some knowledge is too dangerous for man's eyes. And I can't take the chance of seeing you again. Thank you for all you've done.*

He put the note back on the bed. Apparently the universe would have its pound of flesh, whether undead or otherwise. He had saved Fauvette from Prudence, at the cost of arriving too late to save Alisa from herself. If that was the barter, then he could accept it.

There was nothing to be done except remove the few traces of his presence and arrange for the body to be found. He had taken care of everything else.

It was past ten when he left Alisa's. Fauvette would be arriving at the Ringside to prepare for the lunch crowd, and he wished to see her. He considered very briefly relating the truth about what had happened, and telling her that he loved her, but decided that moment could wait. Blurting it out like some adolescent would just make him look foolish. The right occasion would present itself. Their kind always had plenty of time.

He parked his car in the back and entered through the kitchen door. Patience tinkered away on the piano in the dining room, but otherwise the building was empty. He stopped outside the ladies' room, recalling the other time and its ghastly surprises. This time he knocked softly and said, "Fauvette? Are you in there?"

The door was yanked open and she peered out. Her blouse was half-buttoned. "What?" she said coldly.

"May I speak to you?"

"Words are coming outta your mouth, so you must be speaking."

He tried to push the door open, but she blocked it. "I have to get ready for work, Rudy. We can talk later."

She had never been lovelier than at that moment. Her long brown hair, big eyes, and soft face were hardened by her anger. Her dishabille added a touch of sexiness that surprised and pleased him. Even though he would always bear the memory of holding her corpse as it fell apart in his arms, the relief he felt at seeing her, at knowing she'd avoided that awful fate, was stronger than any other emotion he could recall. He wanted to laugh from joy.

"I understand, and I will not keep you," he said. "I wish to simply say one thing."

"What's that?"

He might've said he loved her. But he never got the chance.

CHAPTER 33

Someone grabbed Zginski violently from behind and threw him out the back door. He soared over the asphalt and bounced off the side of the green Dumpster. As he got to his feet he saw Prudence Bolade's Thunderbird parked haphazardly beside the building, the driver's door still open. A haze of smoke drifted from the interior.

That is not possible, he told himself.

"You all right, mister?" a child's voice said. He turned to see three preteen black children on bicycles staring at him.

"I am fine," he said. "Now run along."

They continued to stare. He was about to do something to frighten them away when, from inside the building, Fauvette screamed.

Zginski stopped just inside the door. Prudence

Bolade indeed awaited him, but it was a far different Prudence than the one he remembered. She was burned along one side of her body, the skin blackened and leathery, while the rest of her countenance had aged so that she resembled a child's dried-apple doll. Her nightdress was also burned in places, and one foot had charred so badly it resembled a hoof. There was a hole in her garment torn by his fist, but he saw no evidence of the gaping wound that should've been beneath it.

She clutched a blackened, cracked table leg in one hand, the jagged point still smoldering. And that point was jabbed into the chest of Fauvette, who stood with her back pressed to the wall, eyes wide and terrified, straining on her tiptoes to keep the stake, already imbedded in her flesh, from piercing her heart. Blood ran down her legs and pooled at her feet.

When she saw Zginski she cried, "Rudy!"

"Oh, yes, *Rudy*," Prudence growled, her voice dry and brittle. "You tried to destroy me, and you *did* burn down my house. That was my ancestral home, you know that? It had stood for over a *century*!"

Zginski said nothing. The door slammed shut behind him, leaving them in the dim hall. Prudence was a mere arm's length away, but he doubted he could move fast enough to dispatch her before she drove the stake home.

Fauvette will not die again, he insisted to himself. *I will not let her die again.*

Fauvette watched little tendrils of smoke rise

from the stake. The tip needed only a slight upward shove to find its mark. "What's she talking about? Who *is* she?"

"She's my sister," Patience said. She came down the hall from the opposite direction. "Let her go, Prudence."

"Patience," Prudence said, drawing the last syllable out as a snakelike hiss. If she worried about being trapped between two other vampires, it didn't show.

"Please, let me down," Fauvette whimpered. "I don't know you, I haven't done anything to you."

Prudence ignored Fauvette. "The game is still on, dear sister," she breathed raggedly. "Your little friend here is our newest play-pretty."

"She's just some waitress, Prudence," Patience said with faux annoyance.

"Ah, but you're lying," she drawled. "You haven't asked what happened to me, or how I got here, or how I found you. Your first concern was for this adorable little *tick*. And that means she matters to you an awful lot." She turned her remaining eye toward Zginski. "And to you as well. I'd have thought you had better taste."

"What do you want?" Patience said.

"I want to see the look on your face when she crumbles to dust. And I want you, Mr. Baron Zginski, to try to rescue her, so I can see the look on your face when you fail."

"Oh, God," Fauvette whimpered. She could not physically rise on her toes any higher, and the stake was working its way toward its target. The tiny hallway had become the arena for her life, and she could do nothing to save herself.

"Can you wait me out, dear?" Prudence sneered at her sister. "How much of that vaunted patience do you possess?"

Zginski's mind raced to comprehend all the forces at work. He was *certain* the blow he delivered should have destroyed Prudence; for it to fail, she would have needed a source of blood and power greater than any he could conceive. Certainly greater, he knew, than anything in the house, which he had thoroughly searched.

"I will take her place," he said. Even he was a bit surprised by his words. He nodded at Patience. "I have used you both against the other. And I love neither of you."

Prudence's damaged face hid her reaction, but her eyes flickered to Patience and back to Zginski.

"Just like Vincent," Patience added. "I'll even help you kill him if you want."

Zginski wasn't completely sure this was a bluff, and for a moment he thought Prudence would accept the trade. Then she smiled. "Ah, he's not like Vincent. Vincent *loved* me. He just *diddled* with you."

Zginski clenched his own teeth in rage. And then, as if a light appeared in the darkness, he understood what needed to happen. It should have been obvious all along.

He said with all the contempt he could muster, "Prudence, do you realize how utterly pathetic you are?"

Prudence blinked in surprise.

Patience warned, "Rudy, please—"

Zginski continued. "You exist only because your *sister* does. You are no more independent of her than is her shadow. Your every decision, your every emotion, is merely a reaction to her behavior. You have no true reality of your own."

Prudence said through clenched teeth, "That's not true. *She* told you that."

"No," Patience said slowly as she comprehended his meaning, "I didn't."

"Guys, I don't think this is helping!" Fauvette said. Prudence twisted the stake again and Fauvette froze, eyes scrunched shut.

Zginski saw it then: the slight tremble in the air, momentary but definite, just as he'd glimpsed it the night of Patience's concert. It showed the energy flowing not just from one sister to the other, but *between* them. Thanks to Prudence's hatred, they were now connected at a fundamental level of existence.

He looked at Patience and raised an eyebrow. Prudence might not sense the energy, but Patience could not avoid it. The next decision would be hers.

Patience smiled with the secret certainty of someone stepping off a cliff. She nodded, a century of weariness in the gesture. Then she spread her arms wide as if anticipating an embrace.

They were so close in the little hallway that it only took one step to put him within reach of her, and another to drive his fist through her body just as he'd done to Prudence. Her only sound was a slight whimper.

Fauvette opened her eyes and screamed in horror.

The injuries that should have proved fatal before, finally did. Without a sound Prudence collapsed, and the stake clattered to the floor. The suddenly freed Fauvette landed on top of Prudence and got to her knees in time to see Zginski withdraw his arm from the round hole he'd made through Patience. She collapsed as well, and within moments both sisters were withered corpses.

"Oh, my God!" Fauvette cried, and crawled to Patience. She tried to lift her head into her lap, but the skull came loose in her hands. She screamed again as it cracked in half, dislodging the dark, crumbling remains inside.

Zginski stood absolutely still. His arm from fingertip to elbow was once more red with Patience's blood.

Fauvette wailed at his feet. "You *bastard!*" she screamed, and threw herself viciously at him.

Zginski caught her wrists. "Behave," he snapped, and enveloped her in his influence.

Her eyes opened wide as the unbidden lust took her over, and she gasped. She choked out, "How dare you . . . make me want you . . . after what you did?" But there was no denying the effect, which made her press herself to him and slowly writhe, desperate for him.

She had not seen Patience assent to her own death, he realized. Her eyes had been closed in anticipation of the stake. "Please," he said, "allow me an explanation."

She was too aroused to notice his uncharacteristic tone. "No," she moaned, her rage still evident. "I'll fuck you right now because you make me want to. But I'll never give you *anything* else willingly."

He released her wrists and took her face in his hands. Even as she ran her own hands over his chest and arms, he saw a new strength in her, a certainty that she could resist something that had always overpowered her before. She might be susceptible to his power, but she was no longer a slave to his influence.

"Fauvette," he whispered, and kissed her. She moaned and returned the kiss hungrily, but with a hollowness he could not avoid sensing. She raised one leg and wrapped it around his thigh, pulling him close to her.

"Fuck me, Rudy," she sighed. "Or let me go."

Tell her, something in him cried. *Tell her what you did for her.* But to do so would be to ignore all the skills, experiences, and intuitions that had preserved his existence. The last time he ignored them, Francis Colby sent him to limbo for sixty years. He could not risk that level of agony again, even if his silence brought him a whole different agony.

He released her, turned, and walked out the door.

The Bolade sisters were now mere dust and piles of clothing, with only a few bone fragments among them. Fauvette, her legs shaky, stepped over them and screamed after Zginski, "I don't *ever* want to see you again, do you hear me? *Never!* You come near me, and I swear I'll find a way to kill you. I *swear* it!"

The boys on their bicycles remained where they'd been, still watching. Zginski got into his car, started the engine, and turned up the radio. A man sang about whiskey, a levee, and pie. He drove away into the summer heat with no destination.

CHAPTER 34

Night fell on Dark Willows. Leonardo had turned around at the Memphis city limit sign and driven back, his conscience chewing at him the whole way. He was ashamed of himself for losing his cool, and appalled that he hadn't taken even the most basic precautions to either hide the cause of Clora's death or insure she did not rise as a vampire. Now it was too late, and all he could do to make amends was greet her when she rose and give her the basics of what he knew of their nature. *If* she rose. He wasn't even sure it would happen.

He arrived just before dawn, but spent the day resting in the dirt beneath the floor of one of the old slave buildings. The irony both amused and annoyed him.

When he rose, he immediately smelled smoke. Dark Willows was undisturbed, but smoldering tendrils still rose from the remains of the Bolade mansion, drifting above the trees into the twilight sky. He snuck close and saw a lone fire truck parked in the drive, with two men in distinctive gear seated in lawn chairs. Letters on the side of the truck identified it as the APPLEVILLE VOLUNTEER FIRE DEPARTMENT. They ate pizza from a common box and watched the ruins to insure the fire was truly out. He was able to catch some of their conversation, but they seemed to be talking only about baseball.

On his way back through the woods he came across the Crabtree family plot, and its fresh burial, just at sunset. It was no trick to figure out who occupied this new grave. He stretched out on the ground and put his ear against the dirt. Something moved below.

He sat down cross-legged beside the mound. Darkness fell, and the moon rose. An owl watched silently, and an opossum crawled through the leaves but gave him a wide berth. The Crabtrees' dog appeared, but stayed at a respectful distance. Leonardo looked for a stick to throw at it.

Then the dirt began to move. Something struggled beneath it, dislodging clods from the top and sending them rolling down the sides of the mound.

The owl hooted in alarm and decamped for a safer perch. The opossum scurried away. For yards around, insects and tree frogs fell silent. Only the dog's low growling broke the quiet.

Leo stood and backed away to get a better view.

A bone-white hand suddenly shot up into the air. A second followed, pushing the dirt aside. Between them rose the wriggling form he'd been expecting.

Clora Crabtree emerged into the moonlight and stood on wobbly legs. She wore only the T-shirt in which she died, now torn and covered with dirt. Her bones and musculature were still damaged from his inadvertent crushing, and she had a hard time maintaining her balance. Her tangled hair draped over her face.

The dog began to yelp in alarm, but it did not flee.

Leonardo did not move. He was both horrified and fascinated by what he'd wrought. She pulled her feet free of the grave and spun around, confused and disoriented. She made a sound like a wet rock scraping on concrete.

"Clora," he said quietly.

Her head cocked as if she heard him distantly, like some voice carried on the wind. She stumbled awkwardly from the mound, fell in a heap, and thrashed there for a moment. Then she stood and tottered off toward the house.

The dog rushed forward, still barking. She paid it no mind.

"Clora," he said louder. "Look at me."

She turned toward him and croaked a wet gurgling sound. He vividly remembered the intensity the thirst that beset him on his own first night, and knew she could easily run amok. The two firemen nearby wouldn't stand a chance.

"I need you to listen to me. Please."

She got close enough to touch him. He brushed the hair from her face, exposing her eyes. When he did, he knew the cause was lost: what he saw there was the empty, feral gaze of a creature operating entirely on instinct. Clora, the sweet sad princess in her tower, had not returned from the grave.

She looked him over, evaluating him the way a snake would a mouse. Then she walked away as if he didn't exist; he had nothing she needed. The dog stayed at her heels, rushing forward and then leaping back.

"Clora!" he cried after her. "Clora, please, stop!"

She ignored his words and his presence as he followed her to Dark Willows. She used the side of the house for support as she staggered along it to the front.

Leonardo stayed a few steps behind. He should've expected this. She wasn't the most sophisticated girl, and no doubt the experience of being resurrected in a crushed and imperfect body had wrecked her sanity. But he had hoped that she would at least recognize him, and that he could make some sort of peace with her.

Now, he knew, there could be none. She was a mindless revenant drawn to the nearest source of familiar, familial blood: her father.

She went around the corner to the front yard. He leaned against the wall and rubbed his temples. He'd have to finish what he started, b some reason the thought repulsed him. He'd killed plenty of human beings, including her; but he'd never destroyed another of his own kind.

He smiled at the irony. *His own kind.* I guess now he knew what that meant.

He followed her, intending to make the end fast and neat. The sight that greeted him stopped him in his tracks.

Clora hunched over her father's corpse. Crabtree's head was missing, splattered across the porch, and the family dog busily licked at the dried chunks of brain matter. A raccoon crouched at the far end of the porch, awaiting its turn.

Clora stuck one hand into the stump of his neck, withdrew it, and licked the gummy blood from her fingertips.

Leonardo swallowed hard. He had seen many repulsive things, but this moved immediately to the head of the list. A big reason was his certainty that it was all his fault.

She looked up at him and snarled a warning.

"Shit," he said, and did what had to be done.

CHAPTER 35

A month later, Leonardo stood beside Zginski in the front yard of Dark Willows. The house had not been touched since that night; Leonardo had dismembered Jeb and Clora Crabtree and dumped the pieces in the Hatchie River. The county sheriff, at Zginski's instigation, classified it as abandoned, and the register of deeds notarized the sale. Rudolfo Vladimir Zginski once again had a home.

"So you got it," Leonardo said.

"Yes," Zginski replied.

"Your victim left you all her money, and you used that to buy the Crabtree place from the bank."

"Yes." He studied the dilapidated structure, wondering if repairs were best started from the ground up, or the roof down.

Leonardo was silent for a moment. "Can I ask you something? And if you say 'you just did,' I'll get really pissed off. You got Fauvette draining Gerry Barrister so you can take over his club when he finally croaks, right?"

Zginski said, "Yes."

"Did you sic me on Clora for the same reason, so you could get this house?"

Again Zginski said, "Yes."

Leonardo sighed, and shook his head. "Well, fuck me."

"It served both our purposes. You learned the value of a long-term victim, and I was able to acquire a home suitable for my needs."

"You yanked my fucking chain," Leonardo corrected.

"I did what was necessary to get what I wanted."

"That's cold-blooded, man, you know that? Really. And I was starting to like you."

"I neither sought nor desired your approval or affection."

Leonardo laughed. "No, you sure didn't. Just like you never did with Fauvette, either."

Zginski was in no mood to discuss that topic. Since the day at the Ringside Fauvette had not spoken to him or even really looked at him. There was a hardness to her now, a brittle rage that had replaced the ineffable kindness she used to possess. Still, he felt an odd relief each time he saw her, as if just knowing she still existed was enough, for now.

"Leonardo," he mused, "do you recall the day we mingled our blood at that old warehouse?"

"Yeah, yeah, I know, you saved our lives, we owe you, blah-blah-fucking-blah."

"That is not my meaning. Since that day, have you felt any change in your thinking?"

"What?"

Zginski shook his head. "It is no matter."

"You know what, Mr. Z.? I don't think I want to hang out with you anymore. You may be the fucking James Brown of vampires, but as a friend you're a jerk. Maybe someday you'll figure that out."

He went to the pickup, started it, and drove away. Zginski put his hands in his pockets and climbed the steps to his new home just as the first rain began to fall since Patience Bolade arrived in Memphis.

Fauvette stood in the rain beside the Bolade family plot. With neither umbrella nor coat she was soaked to the skin, but in her case that meant nothing. Behind her, all that remained of the house was a stone foundation and a pair of unbroken chimneys rising like rib bones from the muddy ruins. It had rained for a week, causing flash floods and ruining what few crops had survived the drought. The air smelled of life restored, but was nearing the rancid quality of damp things about to rot.

Water beaded on her eyelashes, standing in for the tears she could no longer create. The bodies of the Bolade sisters had crumbled to dust, but these stone markers remained, and they would do for her purposes. After all, mourning was for the ones left behind.

Suddenly, she looked around. She sensed someone approaching, a vaguely menacing yet familiar presence. The urge to flee hit her so hard she froze, unable to pick a direction.

Then Zginski emerged from the trees clad in a black raincoat and protected by a smiley-face umbrella. She sighed as disgust and hatred dissolved the fear. His platform-booted feet methodically squished in the mud as he joined her, his umbrella blocking the rain over them both.

"Are you following me?" she asked flatly as she looked up at him. "Because if you are, that's really pathetic."

"I have acquired property on the other side of this forest," he said by way of explanation.

"Lucky you. And you just happened to be watching this graveyard, I suppose."

"I have a sense of your nearness."

She thought of her own momentary premonition, and wondered if she might be able to improve it so she'd have more warning when he approached. Probably about as well as she'd learned Patience's energy trick, she thought bitterly. Yet she *had* felt him before she saw him.

"I have things I wish to tell you," he continued.

"I got no interest in hearing them."

"I would like you to nonetheless."

"Then make me. You can make me want to fuck you, so making me listen ought to be a snap."

He said nothing. Only the pattering on his umbrella and the distant highway noise broke the silence.

Finally she said, "If you're just going to stare at me, then take a picture, it'll last longer."

He smiled. Then he plunged the golden crucifix dagger, the one that Sir Francis Colby used to send him to limbo six decades earlier, into her heart.

Zginski tossed the umbrella aside and held her close to him as she stiffened and withered. The light in her eyes faded to milky obliviousness, then blackened to nothingness. Her body shrank within her clothes, her arms and legs growing stick-thin. He felt her rib cage and the individual bones of her spine through her tank top. An intense rotting smell filled the immediate area, but quickly faded as Fauvette passed rapidly through decomposition.

He was careful to leave the dagger in place, just as Colby had done. He lowered the now-fragile corpse to the muddy ground.

Quickly, he wrapped her in a plastic drop cloth he'd brought just for this. He scanned the area for any onlookers. Then he scooped up Fauvette's feather-light remains and strode down the hill, toward the forest and the trail to Dark Willows.

Two cinder-block walls blocked off the cellar's corner, creating a space roughly the size of a walk-in closet. It had been filled with empty Ma-son jars and stacks of pornographic magazines before Zginski cleaned it out. The room had a lone overhead light, but he did not need it.

He unwrapped Fauvette's remains and placed her on the bare earthen floor. Then he removed her modern clothes, careful not to dislodge the crucifix dagger. The garments would be burned in the fireplace upstairs, erasing all evidence of her contemporary identity. Should anyone discover her, they would find only an unidentifiable corpse, clearly left here long before Zginski bought the house.

He leaned over and looked into her face. The flesh had turned withered and leathery over her cheekbones. Her eye sockets were mere pits. The dehydrated tendons had pulled open her jaw and revealed her fangs. The rest of her body was similarly desiccated, but otherwise intact, just as he had been all those years in Colby's storage.

He punched the point of one fang through the tip of his index finger. A single drop of blood beaded there, and he let it drop into the gaping mouth.

There was no visible change. But something intangible shifted in the room, and he swore he heard, faint and at the back of his mind, Fauvette's scream as the blood pulled her from limbo back into the helpless, immobilized corpse.

After a moment he said, "I know you can hear me. My blood will bind you to your physical self, and I will return periodically to repeat the process."

The dead features did not move, but the faint voice seemed to cry, *"No . . . no. . . ."* Was he imagining that?

"I gave you the chance to listen to me. You refused. Now you have no choice."

"Bastard . . . no!"

"It may take decades," he continued. "Or centuries. Eventually, though, my blood will overcome your hatred for me. *Then* I will allow you to again walk the earth."

He stayed on his knees beside her until he realized he was expecting a reaction which, of course, could never come. He rose to leave, but stopped in the doorway. The scream was still there, like the indistinct voices conjured by the whirring of a fan.

He returned to the corpse on the floor. Already he sensed vermin stirring in the soil, disturbed by the rising groundwater and drawn to the new feast above them. He was unconcerned; whatever they devoured, his blood would restore. "Once I told you that for men time is a river, with a beginning and end, while for our kind it is an ocean with an infinity of shores. You are adrift in it only as long as your will resists mine. So *you* will decide when your exile ends."

He ran his finger along the dry, brittle lips. He was uncertain if she could feel physical pain in this form; if so, the sense of her ongoing decomposition should add urgency to her acquiescence.

He closed the heavy wooden door and locked the three padlocks he'd installed. Then he put an roofing over the door to hide it. It now blended in with the rest of the detritus-ridden cellar, and gave no sign of the small room.

Standing in the darkness, he allowed himself a smile. He had an era to make his own, and a future waiting for his domination.

As he climbed the stairs, the voice in his mind grew fainter but conversely more distinct. He paused at the cellar door, shook his head, and finally decided the voice *must* be his imagination. She could not defy him so strongly.

"*Never,*" the voice seemed to say. "*Never!*"

TOR

Award-winning authors
Compelling stories

Please join us at the website
below for more information
about this author and other great
Tor selections, and to sign up for
our monthly newsletter!

www.tor-forge.com